# *Bluebonnet* BELLE

**Center Point Large Print**

This Large Print Book carries the
Seal of Approval of N.A.V.H.

# *Bluebonnet* BELLE

## LORI COPELAND

CENTER POINT PUBLISHING
THORNDIKE, MAINE

This Center Point Large Print edition
is published in the year 2007 by arrangement with
Harlequin Books SA.

The text of this Large Print edition is unabridged. In other
aspects, this book may vary from the original edition.
Printed in the United States of America.
Set in 16-point Times New Roman type.

ISBN-10: 1-60285-065-8
ISBN-13: 978-1-60285-065-1

Library of Congress Cataloging-in-Publication Data

Copeland, Lori.
    Bluebonnet Belle / Lori Copeland.--Center Point large print ed.
        p. cm.
    ISBN-13: 978-1-60285-065-1 (lib. bdg. : alk. paper)
    1. Texas--History--1846-1950--Fiction. 2. Large type books. I. Title.

PS3553.O6336B57 2007
813'.54--dc22

2007032530

Dear Reader,

Thanks for picking up a copy of *Bluebonnet Belle*. My heroines are usually strong-minded women who come to believe that God has called them in a unique and exciting way. Often inspirational fiction is misunderstood. My purpose as an author is to engage the reader in an uplifting, fun story that shows life in abundance . . . the way life is meant to be lived, and my prayer is to never be preachy.

My hope is that when you read my books, you'll laugh a lot, for real. And also that you'll be blessed, and maybe see that your life, whatever its problems, is much the same as mine and others.

On the home front, I'm busy these days writing, working in my yard, playing with my smaller grandchildren and traveling in our motor home.

Speaking of grandchildren, my daughter-in-law and I took Audrey, six, and Gage, eight, to the circus this week. During intermission, Audrey and Gage wanted to ride the elephants—or Gage did until he spotted the giant boa constrictor. For a small fortune you could have your picture taken holding the snake. My grandson's eyes lit up and he said, "Forget the elephant. I'm going to face my *worst* nightmare!" And he proceeded to have his photo taken with the boa draped around his neck. A passerby asked: "What did that cost you?" I told him the monetary value but reminded him, "In memories? Priceless." Audrey stuck with the elephant and eyed the snake as though it remained her worst nightmare.

That's my wish for you this fall. Forget your elephants, face your worst nightmares and live life abundantly . . . as life was designed to be lived.

In His name,

*L*

To my lovely high-spirited granddaughter, Audrey Lauren, who will be every bit as feisty, charming, ornery, and give some lucky man a merry chase before she enters the ranks of matrimony.

# Bluebonnet
# BELLE

I praise you because I am fearfully and wonderfully made; your works are wonderful, I know that full well.

—*Psalms* 139:14

## *Prologue*

Show me a man who suffers the monthly miseries, and I'll show you a man bent on finding relief.

Women should show the same gumption when it comes to female complaints. And since April Truitt believed so strongly in her philosophy, she'd made up her mind to do something about it.

Anxiously fingering the printed envelope, she glanced around the general store. It was busy this morning. Faith Lawson was buying fruit jars to put up the remainder of her vegetable garden. Lilly Mason was counting out eggs, the amount to be credited to her account. Lilly had dark circles under her eyes this morning. Poor Lilly suffered unnecessarily.

If only the women of Dignity would listen to Lydia Pinkham, their woes would be over!

*Mail the letter, April! Mail it!*

Edging the envelope closer to the mail slot, April eyed Ellen Winters, the town postmistress. The silver-haired, robust sixty-year-old was busy sorting mail, glancing up occasionally with a smile.

"Nice morning, isn't it?"

"Beautiful."

"I'm always happy to see the heat of August give way to September."

Nodding, April took a deep breath, shoving the letter into the slot. The missive disappeared into the empty receptacle with a soft *whoosh*.

Elly glanced up. "Sending off for another catalog, dear?"

Pretending she hadn't heard her, April hurried out the front door, closing it firmly behind her. Exhaling a deep breath, she started down the walk at a fast pace.

Of course, once Elly saw who the letter was addressed to she would blab it all over town that Riley Ogden's granddaughter was in cahoots with Lydia Pinkham. But April would deny it as long as she could. Grandpa's heart was wearing out, and she didn't want to upset him. She knew the townsfolk believed she was impulsive and didn't think things through properly, but she liked to describe herself as spontaneous, impromptu—blazing a trail of new, exciting discoveries!

She believed in Lydia's vegetable compound. Though no one outside the family knew the exact formula, it was said to contain unicorn root, life root, black cohosh, pleurisy root and fenugreek seed mashed up. The compound was touted to be the best thing that had ever happened to women, curing everything imaginable.

And she intended to help Lydia spread the good news about the wonder tonic. She wanted to encourage women to help themselves with their personal problems. She remembered her mother's distress and tragic death because she'd listened to unsympathetic doctors.

Grandpa, along with most of the doctors, thought

Mrs. Pinkham was a quack, but wasn't that just like a man? *Men* didn't suffer female problems, so they didn't see what all the fuss was about. It was much easier to dismiss the subject with a shrewd wink and send the woman on her way.

Women had been getting short shrift for too long by men who had no understanding of their physical problems, showing little sympathy for complaints about backaches, nervousness and lack of energy. If a woman was happy, peppy and full of fun, a man would take her places, but if she was cross, lifeless and always tired out, well, he just wasn't interested.

Doctors were too quick to offer surgery as a remedy for women's functional disorders, invasive procedures that were inadequate, ill-advised, often too late, and usually creating even larger problems for the patient. Medical men thought that by removing the source, the problem would be alleviated.

When faced with irate women, physicians argued they were doing everything possible to find better, more acceptable alternatives, but April had her doubts. She was certain there had to be a better way to treat medical issues of mood problems, heart palpitations and hot flashes in the year of 1876. Some claimed that Lydia E. Pinkham's Vegetable Compound provided relief for thousands!

April longed to inform Mrs. Pinkham in person about her decision, but Lynn, Texas, was nearly nineteen hundred miles from Houston, so a letter offering her assistance was more sensible.

It was done. Now all she had to do was wait to hear from Mrs. Pinkham.

Crossing the street, April nodded good-morning to John and Harriet Clausen, who were crossing from the opposite side. John tipped his hat pleasantly.

"Morning, Miss Truitt."

April smiled. "Mr. Clausen. Mrs. Clausen."

"How's your grandfather?"

"Very good, Mr. Clausen. Thank you."

"Give him our best."

"I will."

Wagon teams lined the streets of Dignity, Texas, this hot August morning. Truckmen loaded the long wagons, which were balanced on one axle and pulled by two horses harnessed in tandem. The carters wore long, loose frocks of heavy cloth or leather that were gathered on a string at the neck and fell to the calf, an outfit that dated back to the 1600s.

The men unloaded hogsheads of molasses, flour and brown sugar from the wagons they'd driven from Houston. They would haul back produce grown by the local farmers and wooden goods carved by artisans.

In the distance, sunlight glinted off sparkling blue waters in the port. The mercantile and livery were doing a thriving business this morning. The mouth-watering smells of cinnamon and apples drifted from Menson's Bakery. Many a Dignity housewife would abandon her hot kitchen and buy one of Addy Menson's apple pies for supper.

Striding past Ludwig's Pharmacy, April paused long

enough to tap on the front window. Beulah Ludwig glanced up, smiling when she saw April peering in at her.

Grinning, April mouthed, *"I did it."*

Shaking her head, her friend made a face that clearly expressed her disapproval.

Dismissing the look with a cheerful wave of hand, April walked on. She didn't care what anyone thought. When April Truitt believed in something as important to womankind, as exciting as Lydia E. Pinkham's Vegetable Compound, then she had to support it.

Period.

She was committed.

Feeling surprisingly confident about the decision, she hurried toward Ogden's Mortuary, sitting on the corner of Main and Fallow Streets. The funeral parlor had become her home when Delane Truitt, her mother, died seven years ago. Riley Ogden had taken his granddaughter in and raised her with stern, but loving, care.

At times he was prone to throw up his hands in despair, stating, "You, young lady, have too much of your father in you!"

But April didn't take offense. She knew he thought the world of his son-in-law, Jack Truitt, and had grieved as hard as his daughter when Jack died in a train derailment at the age of thirty.

Someday April would marry Henry Long. Grandpa was finicky when it came to April's suitors, however, which made telling him a difficult, and as yet unresolved problem.

Maybe Henry didn't make her feel heady and breathless—not like that arrogant Gray Fuller did—but he was considered a good catch and they shared the same spiritual convictions—and the same philosophies about the Pinkham compound.

Right now, April planned to do what she could to improve women's lot in modern society.

And the first step was to tell every woman she could about Mrs. Pinkham's elixir.

Now. If only Mrs. Pinkham would accept her invitation and come to Texas and sell her marvelous product. April breathed a heartfelt prayer, then turned to go home.


## Chapter One

*Dignity, Texas*
*August 1876*

"Ladies, ladies! Please! May I have your attention! There's no need to shove! There's plenty to go around for all!"

As Lydia Pinkham shouted to gain order, April stood behind a long table piled high with bottles of Lydia E. Pinkham's Vegetable Compound, eager to sell to those brave enough to try the revolutionary new cure-all for female complaints.

"Sickness is as unnecessary as crime," Lydia

declared as the women pressed closer, trying to get a better look at the small brown bottles. "And if I may be so bold, no woman should be condemned to suffer when there is a curative readily available!"

Eyes widening, the women drew back as if a snake had bitten them.

"Ladies, ladies! Don't be alarmed. The Pinkham Compound is a special formula of nature's own elements," Lydia explained.

Having accepted April's offer, Mrs. Pinkham and her entourage had arrived late yesterday afternoon. The women of Dignity were about to be catapulted into the modern age. Lydia was clearly skilled in marketing. Offering her product directly to women seemed to be a shrewd sales tactic.

Ladies were hesitant to talk about such things, but the group who'd come today to hear Mrs. Pinkham's theories on women's health issues seemed eager to learn what the product would do. April was excited by the response and delighted to be part of the Pinkham team.

Lydia brewed her compound on a stove in the cellar of her home. The rows of brown bottles lined up on the table in front of April had labels detailing all the ailments the tonic could cure.

Lydia was usually too busy making the compound and writing advertising copy to conduct a rally herself, but she'd decided to take the campaign on the road to the Houston area.

April considered today a plus. Since Grandpa was

unaware of her involvement, she was relieved when the small Pinkham entourage—Lydia; two of her sons, Dan and Will; Henry Trampas Long and April herself—had left Dignity to conduct sales in a small town closer to Houston.

So far, Dignity residents chose to overlook her involvement with Mrs. Pinkham in order to keep word of her activities from an aging Riley. The town mortician and cofounder was narrow-minded on the subject of Pinkham's Compound.

"The perfect woman," Lydia continued, "should experience no pain, but that individual would be rare indeed."

Lydia Pinkham's sad but compelling eyes met the gaze of every woman in attendance as she walked the length of the table, holding aloft a bottle of her vegetable compound high for all to see. Tall placards held by Dan and Will displayed copies of advertisements that had run in newspapers in Houston. The headlines decried the major complaints of women of the day. I Am Not Well Enough to Work, one stated, followed by the photo of a contrite woman standing before an angry husband who had no dinner waiting on the table and no clean shirts in the wardrobe. In the descriptive, Lydia E. Pinkham offered her "sympathy and aid," but reminded readers that there was a ready remedy. Lydia E. Pinkham's Vegetable Compound would, the ad stated, "restore to vigorous health the lives of those previously sorely distressed."

Another claim boldly stated Operations Avoided;

another, I'm Simply All Worn-out, followed by the picture of a woman who had collapsed from fatigue.

Yet another touted Social Tragedy—Women Who Brave Death for Social Honors, detailing how one very socially prominent woman suddenly leaped from her chair with a scream of agony, then fell insensible to the floor. The doctor told the victim's husband that she was suffering from an acute case of nervous prostration, and hinted that an operation would be necessary.

Fortunately, a friend suggested Lydia E. Pinkham's Vegetable Compound.

Surgery was avoided.

The din was growing louder, and Lydia raised her voice to be heard above it. April shifted from one foot to the other, wishing she'd worn more comfortable shoes.

The pandemonium only verified how badly women needed the Pinkham cure.

More than once during the brief time she'd been working for Lydia, April had wanted to sink right into the ground when pandemonium broke out. Sometimes containers were knocked over and broken as women clamored for a little brown bottle that would change their lives. Selling to customers who pushed, shoved and made it impossible to conduct business in an orderly fashion unnerved April.

But she believed in what Mrs. Pinkham was doing, so she wouldn't think of giving up her job. She not only took pride in her work, but was earning her own money for the first time in her life. It gave her a sense of purpose and fulfillment.

As Lydia continued to lecture, Will Pinkham passed out the "Guide for Women" leaflets to ladies who were not as convinced as Mrs. Pinkham that their ailments should be openly discussed in a public forum, even among other females.

The babble was getting louder, and a couple of the attendees were red-faced.

Lydia continued, "I wish every woman who feels dissatisfied with her lot would realize that she is sick, and take steps to cure herself. Lydia E. Pinkham's Vegetable Compound will make you cheerful, happy, eager to meet your husband's wishes. Ladies! Once more you will realize the joys of your home! You will have found your true vocation—to be a devoted wife and loving mother!"

"It's hard to believe that a compound could do all that!" a tall, raw-boned woman called from the back of the crowd.

Lydia, thin lips pursed, her face pale except for the two coins of high color on her cheekbones, leveled a look at the individual who would dare to question her claims. "Have you tried the product, dear lady?"

The woman shrank back. "Not yet."

April readied copies of the four-page "Helps for Women" pamphlet that Lydia and her sons had printed to encourage sales.

Glancing up, April took an involuntary step backward when three women in the crowd voiced their skepticism about the claims, declaring them nonsense.

"It just doesn't seem proper to talk about female complaints so boldly in the newspaper for everyone to read," a deep voice interjected.

April mentally groaned when she saw Gray Fuller join the crowd. Having stationed himself conspicuously to her right, he stood, arms folded, a scowl on his handsome features as he listened to the sales pitch.

Dr. Fuller had made quite a stir when he'd moved to Dignity a month ago. Speculation ran rampant about him, and about why he'd chosen a small coastal town to establish a practice.

Then there were his looks.

No kind, comfortable country doctor, this man. Tall and lean, he wore his "city clothes" like one of those men in the catalog in Pearl Mason's mercantile. Even Beulah said that the rich, dark brown hair that the young doctor wore just a shade too long was outrageously attractive. From what she'd heard, every single woman in a twenty-mile radius was making a fool of herself over Dr. Gray Fuller.

*What is he doing here?* April thought resentfully, squirming at the expectation that he might recognize her as the woman he'd seen at a distance at the mortuary. He and Grandpa had struck up an instant friendship, and for the past week visited nightly on the mortuary side porch. She purposely steered clear of them during the doctor's nocturnal visits, preferring to keep a safe distance between her and any doctor. But still, he could have gotten enough of a look at her to associate her with Riley. . . .

Slouching behind the table covered with bottles of compound, April prayed he wouldn't recognize her.

Standing back from the crowd, Gray listened with growing skepticism as Lydia Pinkham make her sales pitch.

The majority of the women present this morning were older, he observed.

His eyes narrowed as he studied the young woman with honey-brown hair crouched down behind the table stacked with bottles of elixir. Her captivating eyes were the color of bluebonnets growing wild along the roadside, he decided. Studying her for a moment, he tried to place her.

He'd seen her before.

But where? She looked a lot like the elusive woman he'd seen in the shadows when he visited Riley at the mortuary.

Since coming to Dignity a month earlier, Gray had seen a sea of new faces. But this one . . . yes, he was sure he'd noticed her somewhere before.

Focusing on the speaker, he listened to Pinkham's outrageous claims. He was relieved that druggists were reluctant to display the Pinkham posters or sell the compound. He was told many women refused to read the pamphlets because the explicit language embarrassed them.

It was a good thing. Women in pain, who had seen

family members and friends debilitated by health problems, were vulnerable. Open to all kinds of shysters who promised relief.

It was ridiculous how someone could cook up a batch of weeds on the stove, bottle it and peddle it as a "cure." More often than not such concoctions worked against normal bodily function.

Still, snake-oil salesmen were often successful. Public trust in the medical profession had dropped so low that women were beginning to abandon doctors in favor of charlatans such as Lydia who promised a non-surgical option.

He regarded Mrs. Pinkham and her kind as overzealous, pure and simple. She, and others like her, was a great part of the reason he'd decided to practice in a rural area rather than Houston.

If he could convince people to trust well-schooled physicians, then he could save lives. That wasn't always possible, but he was dedicated to eliminating needless death.

Gray suspected that Mrs. Pinkham's effort to sell her medicine was not born of a need to help the sick. The Pinkhams were victims of the financial panic of September 1873. After the banking house of Jay Cooke failed, credit had frozen, factories shut down, businesses folded and wage workers had faced a winter of starvation. Isaac Pinkham, Lydia's husband, was one of the thousands who'd seen their speculative ventures fold. When the banking industry fell on hard times, Cooke's had foreclosed and threatened to arrest those unable to pay their overdue bills.

Isaac Pinkham had collapsed under the threat of losing everything he'd spent his life accumulating. When the bank's attorney, who turned out to be a distant relative of the Pinkhams, arrived to serve notice of foreclosure, the family had persuaded him to spare Isaac the embarrassment of arrest and jail because of his illness.

Isaac had not improved; Dan, one of the sons, had lost his grocery store and went into bankruptcy; son Will had given up his plans to attend Harvard and was working as a wool-puller.

Charlie, another Pinkham son, was working as a conductor on the horse cars, along with helping the family endeavor. Daughter Aroline, who had just graduated from high school, helped support the family by teaching.

The Pinkhams had given up their grand house in Glenmere and moved to a smaller home on Western Avenue in Lynn, and recently, with what little resources they possessed, begun their vegetable compound effort. Marketing the elixir was now a family venture. Everyone contributed to the enterprise. Dan and Will provided the brains and sinew. Lydia made the medicine. Charles and Aroline turned over their wages to help pay for herbs. And together, Will and Lydia had worked up advertising copy and put out relevant pamphlets. Even Isaac contributed. Sitting in his rocker, he folded and bundled the pamphlets for Dan to hand out.

Gray was told that at first Lydia had made the compound for friends. Before long women were coming from far away to purchase it. Now the family had expanded the manufacture of the elixir, and Gray was worried. Pinkham's business was growing. More and more women were forsaking a visit to the doctor in favor of self-medicating with the Pinkham compound.

The newspapers were full of ads for remedies like Wright's Indian Vegetable Pills, Oman's Boneset Pills, Vegetine and Hale's Honey of Horehound and Tar.

Natural remedies had gained wide popularity, and Gray wasn't sure how the growing tide could be stemmed.

Today, looking around at the crowd, he felt his worries were well founded.

"Just try the compound for thirty days—"

"Excuse me," Gray called out above the growing din, interrupting Mrs. Pinkham's sales pitch. "Ladies . . ."

The sound level lessened enough for him to be heard.

"If you believe in potions, you're placing your health in untrained hands! Your faith is better placed in educated physicians—"

*He's just like all the others,* April thought, irritated.

A voice from the back interrupted. "My doctor says I have to 'put up with pain' because it's 'woman's lot,'" she parroted. "Is that fair? Aren't we deserving of more concern?"

*That's what Mama should have done,* April thought. Put up with the heavy bleeding until she could find something like Lydia's tonic. The memory of her mother's surgery and ensuing death fed April's anger at the situation in which many women found themselves.

"Of course you are," Gray stated. "But you must be patient! We're looking for remedies. . . ."

"He's as blind as all the others," April murmured, her hands balling into tight fists. This arrogant man was going to be a thorn in her side, she could see that.

"My doctor prefers to talk to my husband, as if I didn't have enough sense to know what he's speaking about!"

"And it was one of those 'educated physicians' who let my mother die," April blurted.

When Gray's gaze swung to her, she wished she'd kept her temper in better control. Ordinarily she avoided drawing attention to herself, but today she couldn't help it. He was a rude, boorish . . . *man!* She met his gaze, lifting her chin in defiance.

"I say we take responsibility for our own bodies," a tall, heavyset woman declared. "I'm buying two bottles right now."

The crowd shifted restlessly, and April watched the onslaught coming toward her with growing alarm. She braced herself, her gaze darting about for a quick escape if things got out of hand. Boxes of compound were stacked to her right, two bramble bushes grew to

28

her left. Mentally groaning, she feverishly searched for an out. She'd have to make a break for the middle, and run straight at . . . him.

She was sure Gray Fuller would recognize her now. Grandpa might look like a genial old Santa Claus without the beard, but when he was riled he didn't have that jolly old person's mild temperament.

Far from it. The rotund octogenarian had a razor-sharp wit and a tongue to match.

April was jolted back to the present as the crowd bore down on her, attempting to squeeze between the table holding the vegetable compound and boxes of the product.

Aware that she wasn't going to be able to get out of their way quickly enough, she braced herself for the attack.

A robust matron hit her sideways, knocking her into the heavily laden table. Stumbling, her hand flailing for support, April braced again as she was slammed from the other side. When yet another hard bump came from the rear, she fell against the table, knocking bottles of compound over in a domino effect.

Reaching out, she tried to save the batch of tonic from ruin, but the table legs collapsed, and it and the bottles tumbled to the ground with a thunderous crash of splitting boards and breaking glass.

The women kept coming, undaunted.

April was pushed forward onto the splintered table and broken bottles whose sticky contents were draining onto the earth below. She hit the ground with a thump.

Attempting to get up, she was knocked aside, whacking her head on a piece of wood. Pain shot through her temple and everything went blurry as she fell back, clasping her palm to her eye.

Silence fell over the crowd as all heads turned to her wilted figure.

"Oh, my!" a shrill voice exclaimed. "She's fainted!"

April hadn't, but she certainly wished she had. Not only had she humiliated herself, she was going to have a whale of a headache.

Moaning, she stirred ever so slightly at the feel of a cool hand on her cheek. She kept her eyes tightly closed, wishing everyone would leave her alone so she could just crawl away, unnoticed.

"Is she injured?"

"Oh, my, my." A hand gently fanned her face. "Someone bring me a dipper of water!"

"Stand back!" another woman cried. "This man says he's a doctor!"

April froze when she heard *his* voice. Drat. Now she'd really done it. Of course Dr. Fuller would offer his services!

"Someone get this table out of the way." Gray Fuller waded through the crowd, issuing orders. "One of you ladies loosen her collar. Please, the rest of you stand back and give her some air."

April felt the pressure of four manly fingers rest against her neck for a brief moment. A pleasant woodsy scent drifted down to her, and she wondered why *he* smelled so good when other men smelled like . . . like . . . well, men.

Embarrassed, she groaned in frustration at the situation she'd gotten herself into. Most of the women she knew would give their eyeteeth to draw the handsome doctor's attention. She might feel the same if the circumstances were different. She'd hoped to be introduced to him at church, or a social function, not while lying on the ground surrounded by broken glass and brown, sticky goo.

Pressing his head to her chest, he pretended to listen for a heartbeat as he whispered, "You're going to have to groan louder. They didn't hear you."

April's left eye flew open, then quickly closed. "Wh . . . what?"

Lifting his head, he grinned.

Cracking her eye open once more, April looked up into a pair of startling dark green eyes set off by lashes so thick any woman would envy them.

His smile, focused directly on her, was decidedly wicked. The firm set of his jaw drew her. She had never seen that look on Henry's face.

She mentally cringed. If they were handing out awards for good looks, Dr. Fuller would take the prize. His practiced masculine gaze ran over her lightly. She shivered, even though the day was blazing hot.

She felt a warm wave of breath in her ear as he repeated, "You'll have to groan louder. They can't hear you."

Embarrassed that he had seen through her ruse, she mumbled through closed lips, "Are you sure?"

"Trust me."

Of course. Trust him. The first thing he was sure to do would be tell Grandpa that she was helping the controversial Lydia Pinkham sell her medicinal elixir. And when Riley heard that, along with what had happened here today, he'd have a fit of apoplexy.

"Moan!" Fuller ordered quietly.

Complying, April rendered a loud, mournful wail.

"Stand back," he demanded, rising to clear a path through the crowd. The women obediently stepped aside, murmuring approvingly among themselves about the man's quick action.

"Is she all right, Doctor?"

"She appears to be coming around."

The women oohed and aahed, their eyes anxiously trained on the young woman lying on the ground like a rag doll.

Assisting April to her feet, Gray led her to a nearby bench. She pretended to still be dazed, and if the truth were known, the good doctor did set her head spinning.

Although uneasy at the sudden physical intimacy, she kept up her pretense, wavering convincingly for the women who watched with open concern.

With the excitement over, the crowd began to break up. Most refused to leave without purchasing a bottle of Lydia E. Pinkham's Vegetable Compound.

Henry Long rushed to April's side, concern on his babyish features. "April, are you ill, darling?"

Patting Henry's hand consolingly, she assured him she wasn't, only a bit shaken up.

Lydia stepped over to ask if April had sustained any serious injuries. When told she hadn't, she made her way back into the crowd, where Will and Dan were selling the compound as fast as they could dole it out.

When the area finally cleared, Dr. Fuller attempted to conduct a brief examination. "You've got a bump." He touched her forehead. "Should make a nice bruise."

"Wonderful," she muttered, drawing a deep breath to clear her head. Something else to explain to Grandpa.

"Are you experiencing any pain?"

"No, and you've done quite enough, thank you." April felt like a fool! Not only had she drawn undue attention to herself by speaking up like that, she'd created a scene that was sure to get back to Grandpa and all of Dignity before she did. Still, it wasn't that unpleasant being administered to by Dr. Fuller. The feel of his gentle hand on her forehead lingered, and she reached to finger the spot.

"Ouch!" It had felt much better when the doctor touched the bump.

Gray's brows lifted. "I'm trying to place you. Haven't we met, Miss . . ."

"I have a common-looking face," she said, standing up hurriedly. He'd been at the house several times, but she'd managed to evade him. His very demeanor frightened her—and doctors plain scared her. Still, he might have spotted her lurking in the porch shadows. . . .

Regaining her bearings, she straightened her dress, smoothed her flyaway hair, remembered to thank him, and took off in the opposite direction at a hurried pace.

"If you have any blurring of vision, be sure and see a doctor . . . miss?"

She dismissed him with an absent wave. "I'm fine, really."

He would remember where he'd seen her, and tell Grandpa. She might as well brace herself for the explosion.

Gray stared after her, watching the sway of her slender hips as she hurried along. He searched his mind, trying to recall meeting her. How could he possibly have encountered such a beautiful woman and not remember?

One thing was certain: the incident today would not be forgotten. It would take some doing to forget this woman.

If he ever saw her again, he'd remember.

## Chapter Two

Francesca DuBois didn't understand the word *no*.

"Have you not missed me, *chéri?* It has been too long." The ebony-haired beauty seated across the desk smiled provocatively.

"It's difficult for me to get away. I'm the only doctor in town. A lot of people need me."

"But, my darling, I need you, too." She frowned. "Are you aware of how difficult it is to explain your continued absence to my friends?"

"You knew when I took this practice I would be in Dallas less frequently." He tossed a folder on his desk, annoyed that she was here. He'd made it clear that when the time was right—and if he changed his mind and decided to honor the engagement—he would send for her. True to form, Francesca had jumped the gun, and here she sat, looking as though she was here to stay.

Her eyes roamed the small office. "Honestly, Gray. Why would you want to bury yourself in a backward town like Destiny?"

"Dignity."

As usual, she ignored the correction. Had he noticed this irritating trait before?

"Even more appalling. You had a glowing Dallas practice, more patients than you could handle. Now—" she swept a gloved hand at the Spartan quarters "—this."

At first she had argued about his decision, but when

it became clear he was going to make the move, she'd stopped. Gray knew she thought the forced separation would strengthen their shaky relationship. But just the opposite had occurred.

Gray had realized his calling. Dallas had its share of progressive doctors, and few people who needed, or wanted, them. The rural communities still depended on midwives and herbalists to serve their medical needs—people with no training, who gained what little knowledge they had through information passed down from a grandmother or an aunt.

No, Gray wasn't needed in Dallas. But he was needed in the countryside. Francesca couldn't understand that; couldn't or wouldn't understand it. Her father wasn't much better.

Though he was indebted to Louis DuBois for financing his medical internship, he didn't agree with the older doctor's focus on medicine merely as a means to make money. Somewhere along the way, Louis had forgotten medicine was a service to humanity.

When Gray announced his intentions to take over Joe McFarland's practice in Dignity, Louis hadn't argued with him. Instead, he'd figured it wouldn't take long for Gray to admit his mistake and return to Dallas, where he would then be taken into one of DuBois' three clinics as a full partner—a stance Francesca also embraced.

Uncomfortable under the resulting pressure, Gray

had broken their tenuous engagement. Only Francesca had ignored that fact. She'd refused to return the ring or to accept Gray's declaration that the relationship was over. Now here she was in Dignity, sitting in his office and acting as though he should be thrilled to see her.

Louis' offer was tempting. Only a fool would refuse it. But Gray had dedicated his skill to treating the ill rather than catering to the privileged.

Now that he had been in Dignity for a little over a month, his convictions were even stronger. He wanted to set down roots in the small town and develop a busy practice. Exactly how he was going to convince this woman that his life was here now, in Dignity— without her—he wasn't sure.

Admittedly she was a beauty, and entrenched in Dallas society. Would she be willing to give up the social whirl and move to Dignity? He doubted it.

She extended an entreating hand. "Why won't you listen to reason? Move back to Dallas. That is where you belong."

"I believe Dignity is where God wants me to be."

"God?" She shook her head. "You always had a streak of religious idealism. I find it hard to believe God cares where you practice medicine."

Gray shrugged. "You're entitled to your opinion."

She slapped a hand on his desk. "I do not understand why you feel you must live in this bumpkin town. What is there in Destiny?"

"It's Dignity. And it's people. They need a doctor."

"There are sick people in Dallas, as well. People who pay for a doctor's service with things other than chickens, produce from the garden and baked offerings from their kitchen."

"They give what they have. I find it sufficient."

Sighing, she sat back in the chair, drumming her fingers on the desktop. "Will you just listen? Give up this crazy idea and move back to Dallas. Papa will set you up in a practice with Jake Brockman, Lyle Lawyer and Frank Smith. We can be married in a month."

Drawing a deep breath, Gray pulled back the curtains to look out on the street. Dignity wasn't Dallas, and that was what attracted him. He liked the town's sleepy lifestyle. He liked its people: good, hardworking, God-fearing farmers, their children and wives, town merchants and neighboring families who came from miles around to seek his medical advice. Gray Fuller's knowledge, not Brockman, Lawyer, Smith and Fuller's advice, as Francesca would have it.

The area itself drew him; the small community sat near the upper corner of the port. Rail service of both the Houston and Texas Central and Texas and Pacific lines made travel practical. Hired carriages were available to take one anywhere in the city quickly. But out here in Dignity he enjoyed windswept land, trees shaped by gulf breezes, rolling surf . . . No, he would not abandon his dream. Not for her, not for any woman.

Families strolled around the common on a cool evening, or brought picnics on Sunday afternoons.

Dignity was interesting, compelling, and more to his taste than the Dallas Francesca loved.

It was a sense of peace that had drawn him when he first visited here six months earlier. The doctor in him demanded it, the man in him wanted it.

"Papa was asking about you before I left. He worries that you're being a fool. He asked if you had come to your senses—"

Gray cut her off. "How is Louis?"

"Oh, *chéri*," she complained, "someone has stolen your mind in this town! You are surely not thinking clearly!"

He suddenly lost his patience. Francesca was a beautiful, charming, but spoiled young woman who'd been raised in the lap of luxury, a woman who used her position as leverage to get whatever she wanted. Position her father had earned for her.

Louis DuBois had come to the United States from France shortly before Francesca was born. Starting with little more than ingenuity, he'd built a successful group of medical clinics in Dallas. Francesca was his only child, and he wasn't subtle about his desire for his daughter to marry Gray.

At first Gray had toyed with the idea; what sane man wouldn't be intrigued by the offer? Then sanity had returned and he'd decided marriage to Francesca was too high a price to pay for what a life of bondage it would in essence be.

He watched as she rose from her chair and sauntered to the mirror. She appeared to be studying her reflection, but he was aware of the intensity of her deep blue eyes.

"Papa is not a patient man," she mused. "I fear he will soon tire of asking you, Gray, and bring someone else into the clinic."

Gray heard the veiled threat in her voice. Submit or else. His independent streak refused to compromise.

"You could return to Dallas and never have to work long hours again. There will be three other men to see to your patients when you have better things to do. Papa will furnish everything we would ever want or need."

She turned ever so slightly to allow him a better view of what he was refusing. "This would be the perfect time." Her voice took on a husky timbre, as she mistook his silence for conformity. "The old Tealson mansion is up for sale—I've always wanted that house. It has been left to molder a bit, but it's such a beautiful place. I will decorate it, make it the showplace it should be. We will throw the biggest, most elaborate Christmas parties the city has ever seen! It will be so . . ."

As she droned on about the possibilities, Gray's mind turned to Dignity, and Lydia Pinkham's show a few days earlier. The nerve of that woman, claiming her elixir could cure everything from cramps to kidney ailments. And women were listening to the exaggerated claims!

His irritation eased when he thought about the spunky young woman who'd pretended to faint.

Surely if she was the girl he had seen at the mortuary, she would have said so. He smiled. She'd felt rather at home in his arms—

"Gray? Gray?"

Francesca's strident tone drew him back.

"Sorry. You were saying?"

"You're not listening to me. You do miss me, don't you?"

"Of course, Francesca, but my work keeps me busy and I get distracted."

"If you would only return to Dallas, your life would be so much easier. There is no need—"

"Francesca, we've talked this to death."

"You are entirely too practical, Gray Fuller. But I can wait. For you I will wait."

"Francesca . . ."

"Oh, I remember that silly declaration, when you said the wedding was off, but you didn't mean it." She came closer and kissed him lightly. "I forgive you, darling. You are coming to Dallas on the twelfth? You know Papa is entertaining some very prominent doctors, and he'll expect you to be there."

Though Gray would begrudge the time, he would be there. He'd have the next installment on his debt to Louis by then. Though DuBois had assured him many times that repayment wasn't necessary, Gray was determined to owe him nothing but gratitude before the next year was finished.

"Gray!" she wailed. "You promised!"

"Of course I'll be there, Francesca." He jammed his

arms into his jacket. "I'll instruct all my patients that they are under no circumstance to become indisposed on the twelfth." Suddenly he needed fresh air.

"Oh, wait! I have something for you." She picked up a small hatbox and carefully opened it. "You're going to adore this."

Gray stared at what he had to assume was a hat, though he'd never call it that himself.

Holding it up for inspection, she grinned. "Isn't it just the most extraordinary thing?"

Extraordinary? Every bit of that.

"Very nice. You'll look lovely in it."

"Me? Oh, you silly goose! It's not for me, it's for you."

Gray's heart sank. Surely she didn't expect him to wear . . . *that.*

"It's marvelous, isn't it?" She turned the hat around.

"What is it, exactly?"

"A pillbox hat. It's the latest thing in bicycling attire. You're to wear it with tight-fitting knee britches, a very tight, military kind of jacket, and when you're cycling down the street, you carry a bugle to warn pedestrians of your approach. I ordered it from France."

"I don't bicycle."

"No?" She frowned. "Well, you should. It's the most amazing sport. Daddy bought me one. . . . Of course, I've purchased britches and a jacket for you also, so we can dress alike when we cycle."

"I don't have a bicycle."

42

Her eyes sparked devilishly. "You do now!"

She smiled as she turned the hat round and round. "Here. Try it on."

Feeling stupid, he let her settle the navy-blue pillbox atop his head. This was what marriage to Francesca would be like. Manipulated, controlled . . . Between her and her father, he wouldn't stand a chance of being his own man. He felt even more certain that God's plans for him didn't include this woman and a Dallas practice.

Gray stood before her wearing the ridiculous hat, wondering how much he could be expected to tolerate for money's sake. If Louis called in his loan early he would have to cease practice; he couldn't afford to do it. He had to keep peace with Louis' daughter until the loan was paid in full. But he would not marry her. He rode horses, not bicycles.

Francesca ignored his protest, clapping her hands with delight. Catching a glimpse of his reflection in the surface of his glass-fronted bookcase, Gray grimaced. The hat made him look like an organ-grinder's monkey. All he needed was a tin cup.

"Francesca, I don't wear hats." Feelings be hanged; he wouldn't be caught dead in it.

"Nonsense." Standing on tiptoe, she kissed the end of his nose. "You look splendid, darling. Absolutely splendid."

He looked like a fool. A splendid one.

"I have to go. I have patients to see."

"You work much, much, much too hard, Gray." She

tried to wind her arms around his neck. He promptly removed them.

Relinquishing her hold, she sighed. "When will I see you again? I will be waiting," she promised. She blew him a kiss as he left the room.

As he walked through the lobby of the hotel, he carried the pillbox hat hidden beneath his jacket.

Eyeing the trash receptacle, he pushed temptation aside and walked out the front door. Francesca had an elephant's memory. She recalled every article of clothing she'd ever purchased for him.

For now, at least, he was stuck with the thing.

## Chapter Three

"How much?"

April told her customer the price, folding brown wrapping paper around a bottle of Lydia E. Pinkham's Vegetable Compound. "And thank you. You'll be feeling better in no time."

The past week had been a bonanza. Sales were up, and women were beginning to return for second bottles.

April was starting to relax. Apparently Gray Fuller hadn't recognized her. At least she assumed he hadn't. Grandpa hadn't blown up, and he would if he knew what she'd been up to.

It was enough that Riley wouldn't approve of her involvement with Henry. Learning about her involvement with Lydia Pinkham would do him in.

April worried about his health, but his lectures bothered her, as well. He was stubborn and easily worked into a tizzy when she did something that went against the grain. It was best to just keep to herself things that would cause Grandpa fits.

"Miss?"

April returned to the business at hand. "I'm sorry. How many bottles?"

"Five. I wouldn't start a day without a dose of the elixir."

"Wonderful." April smiled, counting out the woman's change.

By the time the rally was over, April's feet hurt, her back ached and she was thinking about taking a sip of Lydia's elixir herself. Not a big one, just enough to revive her sagging energy.

"Well, we've had a good day," Mrs. Pinkham commented as she sank into a chair beside April's table. It was nearing dark now, and the last happy customer had left the meeting hall with a bottle of vegetable compound.

"We made eighteen dollars today," April told her.

"Eighteen? That's wonderful."

April put the money into an envelope and handed it to Mrs. Pinkham, then began placing the remaining bottles of compound into a box. Dan would carry it to the carriage later. She glanced up, smiling when she saw another of Lydia's sons, Will, busily gathering up pamphlets the crowd had left behind.

Rubbing the bridge of her nose, Lydia closed her

eyes wearily. "Wouldn't it be wonderful if we could place a bottle of compound in every woman's hand?"

"The way sales are picking up, that might not be so implausible."

"Oh, my dear." She chuckled. "It's a very large world, and there are so many, many women who are trying to cope with female problems. . . . If they only knew there were alternatives." She smiled at April. "I appreciate all you're doing, dear. You've been a big help. Very dedicated."

April hesitated, then decided to tell the truth. "I believe in the healing powers of the compound, Mrs. Pinkham, but I also see this as my ministry."

Her brow furrowed. "Ministry?"

"Yes. I believe God has called me to help women, and he brought us together for that purpose. We're doing more than selling a compound. We're providing God-given health to the women of Dignity."

"My," Lydia said faintly. "I am indeed indebted to you for your service. Thank you."

"Don't thank me, Mrs. Pinkham. Thank the good Lord for taking pity on us women." April grinned. "And you and your family for making the long journey from Massachusetts."

"Ready to go, Mother?" Will called.

"Coming, dear." Getting up, Lydia smoothed back a stray hair. A tall, striking woman, she was imposing enough to compel people to accept her claims. "We'll not have a meeting tomorrow, dear. Dan is traveling to Austin to look into new market opportunities."

April tried to conceal her relief. She'd spent three weeks hiding, evading Dr. Fuller. He wasn't coming to the house as often, yet she had to be on guard every moment for fear something or someone would alert him to the fact that she was Riley's granddaughter. Very soon the Pinkhams would move on and her covert activities would cease. Every rally she attended left her anxious and full of guilt. If it wasn't for the community's concern for their kindly old undertaker, Riley would already know what his granddaughter was doing.

Lydia hesitated a moment at the door. "Is Henry coming for you?"

"Yes, he'll be here any moment now." Consulting her pendant watch, she noted the time. Henry was always prompt. If today's meeting hadn't ended early, he would be waiting now.

"I'm glad he's working with us. He'll be going with Daniel tomorrow. They have sound ideas for getting the compound into stores all over Texas." Lydia shared a tired smile. "Well, there's advertising copy for the newspaper to write yet tonight. Good night."

"Good night."

Henry was going to Austin with Dan again? Why hadn't he told her? April wondered. That made the third trip in as many weeks, trips he'd failed to mention.

Checking her appearance by feel, April carefully rearranged her hat on curls that had taken her a full hour to fashion. She hoped she looked pleasing to

47

Henry today. She'd worn the princess-style dress he favored, recalling how he swore its bluebonnet belle color exactly matched her eyes. The dress was outrageously overpriced, but Grandpa was good about letting her purchase whatever she wanted from the mail-order catalogs.

Turning slowly, she glanced down, perusing the cut of the dress. The jacket was fashioned atop a full overskirt. The buirasse bodice was tight and molded to the hips—an effect, if the look in Henry's eyes was any indication, he appreciated.

Tugging at the close-fitting waist, she wished she could wear the style without a long, tight corset. It was a good thing her job required her to stand, for the skirt of the dress was so tight, she couldn't have hoped to sit with any semblance of grace.

Straightening the stiff sleeves, she absently reached for her reticule and turned toward the front door of the small meeting hall to see if Henry had arrived.

He had not, but it was still early. She'd told him seven o'clock, and it was barely six forty-five. Yet, she hoped he would hurry. They had so little time together anymore. His involvement with the compound kept him working long hours, sometimes late into the night.

Henry Trampas Long. Yet another secret she was keeping from Grandpa. One that would most certainly give him fits if he ever learned of it. Grandpa didn't see Henry as she did. Handsome, with flaxen hair and bright blue eyes that seemed to see right through her,

Henry was admittedly more a "woman's man" than a "man's man."

Although they'd just begun working together, she'd known Henry all her life. They'd been schoolmates during their growing-up years.

Henry was a natural-born charmer. He got the nickname "Sweet Talker" after he'd persuaded the teacher to end classes a week early one summer. Miss West, clearly enchanted with her handsome pupil, who was a mere two years younger than she, had fallen for his concocted story about spring fever being counterproductive to learning.

As they grew up, April and Henry had had their spats, but after they left school she began to view him differently—less as a former schoolmate and more as a potential suitor.

At first April wasn't sure how she felt about the gradual change in their relationship, but then she realized how exciting it was to be courted by a man like Henry. Not only did they know one another well, but also he could charm the petals and thorns off a rose.

Grandpa, of course, still saw Henry as the fool who'd turned over outhouses and played pranks on unsuspecting Dignity residents. It was easy for him to consider Henry's occasional appearances at the front door as innocuous.

But April didn't consider anything about Henry innocuous. Their relationship was growing closer every day. In fact, he'd been dropping hints recently that led her to believe he was about to propose any day now. If it wasn't for his precarious health, she would tell her grandfather about Henry. She didn't like keeping things from him, but she didn't dare say anything until Henry actually proposed. April prayed the good Lord understood the situation, and while he wouldn't approve of deceit, he would understand the sensitive issue.

Hearing Henry's runabout buggy turn the corner, she stepped to the doorway, watching him masterfully bring the bay to a halt in front of the building. Smiling, he climbed down, his wry grin half hidden beneath his flaxen mustache.

April's heart swelled as she watched him approach. He was indeed a fine figure of a man, resplendent in a navy-blue, double-breasted cutaway coat over a matching vest, with slim trousers in a subtle check pattern. A jaunty tie was just visible beneath the collar of his snow-white shirt.

His hair, thick and full, was tamed somewhat by pomade, his mustache meticulously trimmed. He carried a flat-crowned hat in his left hand, and his gaze was pinned directly on her.

"My bluebonnet belle," he murmured, reaching for her hand as he approached.

"Henry," she whispered, embarrassed that he would utter such an endearment in public, though delighted he would be so daring.

Concern filled his face. "Have I kept you waiting?"

"No, we finished early. You're right on time."

Assisting her into the conveyance, Henry climbed

aboard, and, with a smile in her direction, gently slapped the reins against the horse's rump.

"I hear we had a very good day," he commented as the buggy rolled along.

"A very good day. No problems, and we sold a number of bottles." Turning in the seat, she looked at him. "Henry, Lydia said you were going to Austin."

Glancing sideways, he smiled. "Didn't I mention it to you?"

"No . . . no, you didn't."

"Really? I thought I had. Dan and I will be looking for new marketing possibilities." He glanced her way again. "Why?"

"Well, there's the Founders Hall event next week . . ."

The party was an annual gathering everyone looked forward to. April had purchased her dress months ago, a frivolous evening-blue silk.

Meeting her troubled gaze, he smiled. He was merely doing his job. There would be other events, his eyes suggested to her.

"I'm sorry, dearest. It was thoughtless of me not to mention the trip earlier, but I kept hoping it could be delayed until after the Founders Hall celebrations. Alas, it can't be."

She ignored the awful sense of disappointment she felt, vowing to conceal it. It would only make Henry's business commitments more difficult.

Arching his brow in concern, he said, "Forgive me, dearest?"

"Of course, Henry, it can't be helped."

"Dan and I will be going to Austin tomorrow. Had I known sooner, I'd have planned something special for us today."

"How long will you be gone?"

"I'm not sure. A few days." He reached over to clasp her hand. "Miss me?"

"You know I will."

"We'll have a very special supper when I get back."

He smiled down at her and her pulse accelerated. A "special" supper. Had the time finally come? Was he about to ask her to be his wife? Her mind whirled at the implication. Was that what she really wanted? She suddenly felt a trifle ill.

Henry halted the carriage at the side of the mortuary, where a large mulberry tree grew. April insisted on it, for Grandpa wouldn't be as likely to see them together here. His eyesight was failing dreadfully.

"I wish—"

"Don't say it," she interrupted. "I have to persuade Grandpa that I'm grown-up enough to make my own decisions." And of course, tell him that she was seeing Henry. Seriously. "He still thinks of me as a little girl."

Henry's eyes swept her slender figure. "You're a lovely young woman now."

Her cheeks colored. Henry was so bold. So much more exciting than any of the other single men in Dignity.

"He also still thinks of you as that hooligan who tied my sash to the school desk so my skirt would fall down around my ankles when I stood."

Henry's grin was irresistibly devilish. "It was one of my better pranks."

"I was mortified!"

The grin widened. "I know. But your cheeks turned pink and your eyes got so wide with surprise, I was captivated by you from that moment on." Leaning forward, he stole a kiss.

Henry was a godly man; his youthful pranks seemed uncharacteristic now. Not a foul word escaped his mouth these days except on rare occasions—which she promptly chastised him for. And Henry was always quick to beg her pardon.

She glanced nervously toward the house. "I need to go." She adored his affectionate gestures, but in private. Not here in public, where someone might catch a glimpse.

Henry settled back with a wry smile. "I'll see you when I get back from Austin."

For now she contented herself with the tightening of his hand on hers.


Dignity's apothecary was midblock between Main and Fallow Streets. The establishment had been there for over twenty years. The sign over the door was faded, the building comfortably weathered.

Inside were shelves of medicinal concoctions, bandages, alcohol for cuts and scrapes, liniment for strained muscles. One corner of the room held potions for farm animals. A long wooden counter stretched along the back, with the pharmacist's desk behind it, a step or two higher. This was Eldon Ludwig's throne from early morning to nearly twilight. From it he dispensed medicine and advice for everything from boils to congestion to broken limbs.

At the moment, Eldon's seat was vacant, and a squarely built figure dressed in a butternut-brown dress stood behind the long counter, explaining the directions on a bottle of headache powders to Judge Petimount's widow.

April browsed through the store, reading labels on funny-looking bottles while she waited for Beulah to finish with her customer.

Beulah was "Porky" to the town residents—an affectionate nickname she'd been given over the years. April didn't approve of it, finding it hateful and hurtful. Beulah never complained. She'd smile when someone tossed the name in greeting, but in her large, serious brown eyes April detected pain. She herself would never, ever call her friend the name. Beulah was Beulah. Special—and with a heart the size of Texas.

Mrs. Petimount made her purchase and left.

Wiping her hands on her apron, Beulah grinned at April. "I thought you were busy selling Lydia E. Pinkham's Vegetable Compound to the enlightened ladies of Dignity and surrounding areas."

"I'll have none of your sass, Beulah Ludwig," April bantered, resting her hands lightly on her hips. "Lydia E. Pinkham's Vegetable Compound will cure what ails ya."

Giggling, she came around the corner and grabbed April's wrists to pull her into a brief hug. "Now tell me, how is the sales job going?"

April settled herself on a worn bench near the counter, and Beulah sat beside her. Beulah had been her friend forever. The daughter of Eldon Ludwig, she spoke with the thick German accent of her parents, who had emigrated to the States before she was born. When the other children had teased her, April had defended her, then taught her to speak with a Texas accent. Instead of "you all" she quickly learned to say "y'all," which admittedly sounded a little strange with a German inflection.

There was little else April could do to protect her friend from the other children's cruel barbs. Beulah Ludwig, unfortunately, was the victim of her mother's good cooking.

In response to April's friendship, Beulah had appointed herself April's protector. In grade school, Bud Grady had taken a shine to April, but she hadn't shared his feelings. Every recess he waited for her by the swings, trying to grab her for a kiss. Once he'd managed to smear his lips across her cheek, and her stomach had rolled.

The day before summer vacation, Bud had apparently sensed that his opportunity to make any headway with April was almost past. He'd waited for her by the water pump and, when she came out, had grabbed her, nearly knocking her to the ground. She'd managed one shrill screech before Bud planted his lips on hers.

Beulah had been waiting for April beneath the big oak in front of the schoolhouse. When she saw Bud pounce, she started running. Before he could get in a second kiss, she'd grabbed him by the collar, whirled him around and tossed him facedown into the dirt.

Turning to April, she'd dusted her hands triumphantly. "There. We're even."

The two girls had been inseparable ever since.

Beulah had begun helping her father in the apothecary when she was barely old enough to see over the counter. She'd cleaned the shop at first, then gradually worked her way into sales when she was old enough to make correct change. April, meanwhile, became mistress of her grandfather's house. She helped at the funeral parlor when needed, making sure the services moved along smoothly, that overwrought family members were comforted, even filling in when a vocalist failed to arrive in time.

April's slim, delicate frame and light features were a stark contrast to Beulah's dark features and five-foot, two-hundred-pound frame. Beulah had inherited her father's stockiness, and April knew it had long ago ceased to concern her. She was happy with her lot, eating cinnamon rolls without apology, while April was still trying to find her purpose in life.

"So, how's the job?" her friend repeated.

"I wasn't sure at first how I was going to like it, but I do. I feel I'm doing something important, and I like that."

"Your grandpa find out what you're up to yet?"

April shrugged. "No. You know he wouldn't understand."

"Your mother was his daughter. He knows she didn't have to die."

"I'll grant you that if men had the same problems as women, there'd be no unnecessary surgeries without some very serious deliberation."

"Oh, hogwash! You're getting radical."

Beulah got up and dusted a shelf of medical supplies as they talked. "I do think you ought to tell your grandpa you're selling Mrs. Pinkham's compound. If he finds out what you're doing—"

Not wanting to hear any more about the subject, April abruptly switched topics. "I'm not going to the Founders Hall event."

Glancing up, Beulah frowned. "You're not?"

"No, Henry has to go to Austin on business."

"Oh." Her friend's face fell. "And you bought that lovely blue dress."

"I know, but I can use it another time. Henry's work comes first."

Resuming her dusting, Beulah muttered, "Rather thoughtless of him to plan a business trip at this time."

"It couldn't be helped, Beulah."

"Mmm, maybe."

"Are you going to the dance?" April asked.

"Of course."

"Wonderful. With anyone I know?"

"Papa. Mother is still away tending to Aunt Mary."

"Oh."

"Don't sound so disappointed. You know no man is going to ask me to a dance."

"Beulah Ludwig, you stop that!" Crossing the room, April gently took her by the shoulders and shook her. "Don't ever say that again in my presence. If the men in this town are so blind they can't see anything but a woman's dress size, then I say shame on them! Their loss!"

"Dash it all, I don't care," Beulah said as the two hugged each other. "My life is full. I don't need any man to boss me around. Not one like Henry, that's for sure."

"I know you don't like Henry, but you don't know him like I do," April whispered.

"I've known him as long as you have."

"He's so . . . charming, attentive," April argued. "Do you know what he calls me?"

"Slave?"

"No, be serious."

Eyeing her warily, Beulah said, "What?"

"Bluebonnet belle. Isn't that just the sweetest thing you've ever heard!"

"Simply ducky."

Just then the bell over the door rang, and aged, nearly deaf Mrs. Faith hobbled in.

"Good day to you, Mrs. Faith." Beulah greeted the elderly lady loudly. "What can I do for you?"

"Eh?"

*"What can I do for you?"*

Mrs. Faith leaned on her cane and waved a piece of

paper. "Got this prescription, Porky. That young doctor gave it to me and told me to bring it over here and give it to you."

"Let me see what you have," Beulah said, reading the prescription. "Yes, we can fill this for you."

"Eh?"

*"We have this!"* Beulah shouted toward her less-deaf ear.

"You sure? I wouldn't want to get the wrong thing. Doctor says it would help my gout."

"I'm sure it will. It'll only take a minute."

"Well, hurry up. It's been paining me something awful lately."

April motioned to Beulah, who excused herself from her customer, saying she'd be right back.

"Give her some of Mrs. Pinkham's Vegetable Compound."

*"What?"* Beulah demanded in a hushed whisper.

"Give Mrs. Faith some of the compound."

"Are you out of your mind? She's got the gout, not the monthlies!" Glancing at her customer, Beulah smiled. "Just take a minute, Mrs. Faith!"

"Eh?"

"Some of the compound, Beulah. Pour some in a bottle and tell her to use it in addition to the prescribed medicine."

"Never. The compound is not going to help her gout, and Papa would have a fit. Do you know the consequences of dispensing medicine without the proper authority?"

"It isn't medicine. It's just an herbal compound. But it will really perk her up. You'll see."

It was the perfect answer. April had been trying to think of a way to boost sales and get the word out about the compound, and the solution was right under her nose!

"The compound is for female problems," Beulah argued in a quiet tone, glancing at Mrs. Faith again.

"Oh, come on, do the woman a good deed and give her some of the compound."

When Mrs. Faith glowered toward them again, Beulah waved. "Be right with you, ma'am."

"You do have some, don't you? You didn't pour it out?" April had brought her friend a sizable jugful a few weeks ago, thinking she might use it.

"I have it," Beulah snapped. "I intended to throw it away, but Papa's always around when I think of it."

"Then do it." April took her arm, urging her toward the back room. Mrs. Faith looked up again, glowering.

April and Beulah waved, grinning.

"I can't tamper with Papa's prescriptions," Beulah whispered.

April made sure she kept smiling as she led her friend to the back room. "What tampering? There's nothing in the compound to hurt her. I want to see if it really does what Lydia says it will."

"I can't."

"Come on, come on, please. I need to know how good this tonic really is."

It would make her decision to help Lydia Pinkham

60

in her endeavor to improve women's health so much easier if she knew for certain the compound worked. Not to mention make her feel less guilty about keeping her activities from Grandpa.

"Then take it yourself."

"I don't have any problems—except the wicked monthlies."

"Mrs. Faith doesn't even have the wicked monthlies. She's got the gout!"

"*And* female problems, I bet. She has to. She's old as dirt. At least offer her some, and see if she agrees to take it."

Dragging a chair to the shelf, Beulah climbed up on it, balancing her bulk as she reached for a gallon jug well hidden behind a row of bottles. "If Papa ever gets wind of this he'll take a belt to me."

"Just tell him the truth. In addition to filling Mrs. Faith's prescription, you suggested a mild tonic that one of your customers makes and uses herself." April helped lower the gallon jug. "That isn't a lie."

"Well . . . we do sell and ship a lot of nettle tea to Mrs. Pinkham."

Reaching for a funnel, Beulah poured some of the compound into a small brown medicine bottle. "See what you're making me do?"

"You'll be glad you did it when you see how perky Mrs. Faith becomes."

When the bottle was full, Beulah stuck a cork in it and hurriedly shoved the jug of compound back on the shelf.

The two young women emerged from the back room, smiling. "I'll fill your prescription now, Mrs. Faith."

April browsed the small pharmacy, keeping an eye on her friend as she attended her duties.

"Here you are, Mrs. Faith," Beulah said a few moments later, as she came down the steps carrying the medicine.

"Humph. High time," Mrs. Faith grumbled. She dug in her purse for a coin. "How much, Porky?"

"Twenty-five cents."

"*Twenty-five cents!* Where's your gun? Does that young whippersnapper doctor think I'm made out of money?"

"Papa's working hard to get the prices down."

"Does he believe money grows on trees?"

"I don't think so."

Handing her the coins, Mrs. Faith turned to leave.

Shooting a warning look, April motioned to the bottle of compound Beulah was still holding. Her friend's face screwed into a stubborn mask.

April held her gaze, daring her to back down.

"Oh, Mrs. Faith?"

The old woman paused in the doorway. "What is it?"

Clearing her throat, Beulah grinned. "Would you like to try some tonic?"

She frowned. "Some what?"

"Some tonic. It will give you get up and go."

The old woman glared indignantly. "Are you saying I don't have get up and go?"

"No, of course not. You're in fine shape . . . for your age . . ."

Mrs. Faith's frown turned menacing.

April quickly stepped in. "Oh, you mean that *wonderful* tonic everyone is talking about? Do you have some?"

Beulah nodded halfheartedly. April could see she wasn't in the spirit of the sale.

"Well, *I'd* love to try some. Wouldn't you, Mrs. Faith?"

"Don't need it." She started out the door again.

"Wait!" April hurried over to take the bottle out of Beulah's grasp. Handing it to Mrs. Faith, she smiled. "Just take a couple of spoonfuls a day for the next week and see if you can tell any difference in how you feel."

"I feel fine."

"I know, but you'll feel even *better*." April confidently tucked the bottle into the small basket the woman habitually carried on her left arm.

Mrs. Faith studied the bottle. "Don't think I'm going to pay for it."

"Certainly *not*—you wouldn't think of charging her for it, would you, Beulah?"

Shaking her head, Beulah busied herself dusting the foot powders.

"Well, guess it can't hurt." The old woman eyed the two girls sternly. "Porky Ludwig, does your papa know you lollygag around, whispering and giggling, when he's not here?"

"Yes, ma'am, he does, and he's warned me about it," Beulah assured her. April held the front door open as the woman hobbled out.

When the door closed, Beulah flew into her. "I hope you know what you're doing, April Truitt!"

April laughed. "She'll be swinging from the rafters this time next week."

Returning to her dusting, Beulah fretted. "Dr. Fuller will tell Papa if he finds out I gave her Lydia Pinkham's compound."

"He won't know it's Lydia's compound."

"Dr. Fuller caters to Mrs. Faith, you know. Tells her she's beautiful. She laps it up—but then, most of the unmarried women in town and half the married women suddenly have a 'problem' now. Have you noticed?"

"That he's single?"

"That he's handsome, silly."

"I've noticed." April brushed an imaginary speck of dust off the counter.

"Now, there's a man I'd like to kidnap."

"Well, he is nice-looking, but he isn't my type."

"Meaning he doesn't agree with your opinion of Mrs. Pinkham's compound?"

"You should have seen him at the rally the other day. I don't know why he was there. Standing there in the midst of all those women, arms crossed, looking as if he couldn't believe what he was hearing. Spoke right up about how females should trust doctors. Nearly started a riot. He saw me, and

64

if looks could kill, I'd be lying in Grandpa's front parlor right now."

"Golly." Beulah's eyes widened. "Does he know who you are?"

"No. He visits on the porch with Grandpa occasionally, but it's dark and I keep well-hidden. He hasn't seen me, I'm almost certain, or he would have told Grandpa about the compound. He's a snitch."

"How do you know?"

April shrugged. "He's too good-looking to be honorable."

"Well, if the compound's everything Mrs. Pinkham claims it is, the good doctor would be out of business in a week."

April snorted. "I don't think he's threatened either by the compound or by me."

Beulah paused, her dust cloth suspended in midair. "You didn't make a scene."

"No . . . well, sort of. I fell over my table of elixir."

"Accidentally?"

"No, on purpose. The crowd was out of control, coming at me. I backed up, fell over the table, cracked my head, then pretended to be unconscious."

"And it worked?"

She blushed, recalling how Gray Fuller had seen right through her little ruse. Undoubtedly he had had a good laugh at her expense.

"You should have seen me. It was humiliating. The table collapsed, making a horrendous scene. I would've been smarter to let the crowd trample me."

Beulah laughed. "And Dr. Fuller saw you?"

"Saw me? He rushed over to help. Naturally, I pretended to faint, but he knew what I was doing."

Her friend's hand flew to her mouth. "He knew?"

"Without a doubt, but he went along with me. Actually, he was rather charming about the whole thing."

April knew his kind. All charm, certain his diploma gave him all kinds of rights—including meddling, if he could.

"I don't know, April. Eventually he'll know who you are. Maybe you should go to him and explain about your grandpa's heart, and why you don't want him to know you're working with Lydia."

"No. It's none of Dr. Fuller's business."

"After your mother's unfortunate death, your grandpa might understand why you're working to help save other women from the same fate," Beulah mused.

"Grandpa refuses to talk about Mama."

The loss of his only daughter during a routine hysterectomy seven years earlier had traumatized him. Riley had never fully recovered. When Delane's name was mentioned, he refused to discuss her.

"Any man who takes in a fourteen-year-old girl to raise—a pigheaded fourteen-year-old, I might add—can't be as close-minded as you paint him to be."

Sighing, April went to look out the pharmacy window. "I saw Mama die. And she didn't need to. If that doctor had known more, if he'd had something like Lydia's vegetable compound to at least try before surgery, my mother might still be alive. That's why I do what I do—not to torment Grandpa, but in the hope that someone else won't lose their mother or daughter to needless medical procedures."

"Then why wouldn't your grandpa encourage you to sell a product intended to help women?"

"He thinks the compound is nonsense, and it wouldn't help anyone."

"He told you this?"

"He doesn't have to. I've heard him talking. He thinks women are silly for taking it."

"Still, I think you should tell Riley what you're doing."

"You're entitled to your opinion. Just make sure you don't let it slip when Grandpa comes in to buy sundries."

"Don't worry about me," Beulah told her as April opened the door to leave.

"And you don't have to worry about me."

That was the nice thing about best friends; they didn't have to worry about each other.

## Chapter Four

Datha Gower had kept house for Riley Ogden for over five years. Since she was eleven years old she'd polished floors, hung wash, cooked and cleaned.

Ogden's Mortuary was a towering, two-story landmark with a large, wraparound front porch that caught the sun in the morning, and a roomy back porch that offered a cool breeze in the afternoon.

It took a powerful lot of work to keep it all clean.

A screened-in porch on the north side of the house allowed Mr. Ogden privacy after a long, trying day. He was known to sit for hours, drawing on his meerschaum pipe while watching the foot traffic that passed in front of the mortuary, knowing that one day, like as not, he'd be burying every last passerby. Why, he could guess within an inch how tall anyone was and what size coffin it'd take to put them away.

Riley lived with his granddaughter in six big rooms above the main parlor. The place had been tastefully decorated by Riley's deceased wife, Effie, who had favored overstuffed chairs, cherrywood and a passel of worrisome trinkets that needed dusting.

Wisteria vines trailed the length of the white porch railings shaded by large, overhanging elm trees. Datha and Flora Lee, her grandmother, lived in servants' quarters behind the main house. Flora Lee had been with the Ogden family all her life. Flora Lee's daddy, Solomon Tobias Gower, had served the Ogden family during the Civil War, refusing to leave them when the Emancipation Proclamation was effected. The Gowers thought themselves lucky to serve such a fine, upstanding family.

When Flora Lee had gotten too crippled to do much around the house, Datha took over. She'd lived with Flora Lee since her mama died in childbirth. On good days Flora Lee still came to the main house to help clean, but most days her rheumatism kept her home. Comfortably lodged in nice quarters, the two served the Ogden family with humble gratitude and tireless loyalty, counting their blessings that April and Riley were kind, caring people who were more family than employers.

In Flora Lee's youth, long before the dead were taken to funeral homes for eulogies, long before the Ogdens had turned their private home into a mortuary, Flora Lee had helped Owen Ogden, Riley's papa, to prepare friends and neighbors for burial.

Datha loved to hear stories about how her grandma had cried along with distraught wives and inconsolable mothers as they bathed and dressed their loved ones, then laid them out in the front parlor. Folks would come from miles around to view the body, offering words of comfort. Flora Lee liked to tell how she'd curl up in a corner, pulling her legs up beneath her, out of the way, but there to serve if anyone needed her.

Friends, in an effort to share the grief, brought overflowing baskets of food, arriving throughout the day to mourn the deceased. The yard would fill with buggies and neighbors standing outside visiting as the deceased lay within.

Datha hummed now as she dusted the mortuary entryway, remembering Flora Lee's stories.

Neighbors had ridiculed Owen for taking a personal interest in his household help, but anyone who'd known him would tell you that he was a good man. Gossip had never bothered Owen Ogden, God rest his soul. He'd gone about his business, serving the citizens of Dignity in their time of need, reading the Good Book and following its teachings.

Never one to judge others, he'd made it clear that he didn't intend to be judged by anyone other than himself and his Maker. When his health began to fail, Owen had turned the funeral business over to Riley, then up and died.

Just like that.

One minute he was sitting on the porch enjoying his nightly smoke, and the next he'd keeled over dead as a doornail.

But things went on like always. Riley had the same goodness in him that Owen did. Datha knew the senior Ogden only through her grandmother's memories, but Flora Lee said that when Owen passed on, Riley hadn't treated them any differently. He'd told her that this was her home and Datha's as long as they wanted it, and that's how it was going to be. Datha could hold her head high, proud as could be because she wasn't ignorant. No, sir. Mr. Riley Ogden had seen to it that she was schooled as good as or better than most folks.

Grinning, Datha realized that she had just about everything she wanted, with the exception of Jacel Evans. Jacel was a fine black man who, because of Riley Ogden's generosity, was about to go off to Boston to attend a university. Harvard, Riley called it. Real fancy school somewhere up there in Cambridge.

Jacel's family was dirt poor. The rich folks the Evans family worked for owned the sawmill, but they didn't share their good fortune with others. Certainly not with their black help.

Ellory Jordan provided meals and shelter for his servants, but that was all. If they needed more, they could just do without.

Most did without.

There was one young man determined to do more than just "make do." He'd decided to pull himself out of that rut, and one man in the community saw potential in him. Jacel Evans, youngest son of Tully Evans, was a tall, powerfully built man who did more than his share of work in the sawmill. On his dinner break he read books, while other boys his age lay in the shade and dipped cool water over their sweat-drenched bodies.

Pride nearly suffocated Datha when she thought about her man. Why, her Jacel could saw more logs than any two men put together. Work harder than a team of Kentucky mules.

And he was smart. Real smart. Thought about things most folks never thought about. Things like how it wasn't fair one man should be treated more poorly than another just because he had a different color of skin. Jacel would lie for hours, looking up at the sky, and say to her, "Datha, why is it the rich get richer and the poor get poorer?"

Or he'd ponder why some folks were born with good fortune, while for others if it wasn't for bad luck, they'd have no luck at all.

Why did some suffer with bad health and others

rarely see a sick day? Why did the good die young and the evil prosper?

Why were death and senseless tragedy deemed to be the will of a loving God?

Why did some work hard, only to go to bed at night with a hungry ache in their belly, while others made gluttons of themselves?

Why were innocent children mistreated because of someone else's rage?

All questions to which she didn't know the answers. But Jacel worried them about, turning them over and over in his mind—a fine mind hungry to learn.

Her Jacel was going to be a lawyer someday. An upstanding lawyer who wanted to undo some of the injustice he saw in the world. Once his practice was established, they were going to get married.

Datha smiled as she flicked a cloth at a spot of dust she'd missed on the foyer table. Yes, someday she was going to be Mrs. Jacel Evans. Her heart nearly burst from the joy of it. She and Jacel, holding hands, would "jump over the broom." What a fine day that would be!

Once Jacel had his law office, they could have their own place. But until then Datha planned to stay right here, taking care of Riley, April and Flora Lee for as long as they needed her. Jacel said that was only right, seeing how good the Ogdens had been to him and to her.

April would marry someday, and not far off, if Datha guessed right. April was bound to hook a man soon, pretty as she was. Chances were it'd be that Henry Trampas Long, the handsome, no-good swain she'd had a crush on lately.

Riley had never liked the young scamp, and he would be having a fit if he knew April was interested in Henry. It wasn't Datha's place to say anything, but rumor had it that April was seeing Henry more than socially.

Of course, Mr. Ogden was blind as a post when it came to April. Anytime Henry's name was mentioned, he'd change the subject, saying he had better things to talk about. Datha didn't have any trouble seeing that Miss April had a powerful crush on Henry Trampas Long, so why couldn't her grandfather?

The gossip mill predicted that Henry would be asking her to marry him soon; then he'd whisk her off to some high-falutin city, and they wouldn't see much of her after that.

Datha could either take Henry or leave him. He was too smooth for her liking, but she could see why April would be caught up by his youthful good looks. Words poured out of him like honey, words that sounded nice but didn't make a whole lot of sense.

But Datha knew her place, and she kept it. If April wanted to waste her life on the likes of Henry Long, it was hers to waste. Datha only worried for Mr. Ogden's sake. What with his heart acting up, she sure didn't want him finding out that April was selling Pinkham's Vegetable Compound with Henry Long. Law sakes, it would be like waking up a nest of snakes, and no one wanted to do that. Certainly not Datha.

Humming to herself, she dusted around a lamp.

When she heard April coming in the front door, she hurriedly stuffed the dust rag in her pocket and called out, "Supper'll be on the table in ten minutes, April girl."

"Thanks, Datha. I'll tell Grandpa."

The cloying scent of gladioli permeated the air as April passed the open parlor doors. Clarence Deeds was laid out in his best blue suit, awaiting services in the morning.

It was sure to be a big funeral.

Clarence had been town mayor, and friends and business associates from neighboring communities would turn out in droves to pay their final respects.

Proceeding to the side porch, she found Riley sitting in his rocking chair, staring off into space. He'd been sitting like that when she left the house early this morning, and she was starting to get concerned. It wasn't like him to just sit and stare at nothing.

"Grandpa?" When he didn't respond, she pushed open the screen door. "Are you all right?"

"Right enough," he said.

"Supper's ready."

Riley got slowly to his feet and followed April to the dining room table, which was set with fresh flowers and white china. Taking his place at the head, he reached for the butter, silent as a mouse.

74

Shaking out her napkin, April noticed his hand was trembling as he buttered a piece of cornbread. Perusing his pale features, she frowned. He hadn't had a spell with his heart for weeks now. Was he ill again and not telling her?

Picking up a dish of Datha's watermelon pickles, she offered it to him. "You're awfully quiet today. Don't you feel well?"

He was bad about not telling her when he felt poorly, thinking to spare her unnecessary worry. But she worried anyway. Grandpa wasn't young anymore, though the way he worked like a harvest hand around the mortuary, lifting bodies and moving heavy pine caskets, you'd never guess it.

"I feel fine, thank you." Riley's face flushed with color as he snapped open his napkin.

"You look odd. Is the heat bothering you?"

It was insufferably hot for fall. Muggy, as if a storm was waiting just off the coast. A good rain to settle the dust and cool dispositions would be appreciated.

"Nothing wrong that a little dinner won't take care of. Pass the preserves, please."

They waited in silence for Datha to bring the main course.

"Clarence looks nice. I'm sure Edith is pleased."

"Hmm," Riley muttered, taking a sip of coffee.

Datha carried in a large platter of roast beef, boiled potatoes and carrots. Dishes of cooked cabbage, brown beans, plump ears of corn, festive red beets and thick brown gravy followed.

April's distraught gaze swept the heavily laden table and she sighed. Datha cooked enough to feed an army of foot soldiers, but April had given up complaining. It didn't matter what she said. Having learned at her grandmother's side, Datha couldn't seem to cook meals for fewer than twelve people.

Now the two of them just let her cook to her heart's content, resigned to share leftovers with neighboring shut-ins.

Serving herself potatoes and meat, April smiled. "This looks delicious."

"Thank you, April girl." Smiling back, Datha returned to the kitchen.

The two of them ate in silence, until Riley suddenly cleared his throat and laid the butter knife aside.

April, knowing some kind of pronouncement was forthcoming, put down her fork.

"April Delane, I've mulled this over all afternoon."

Her pulse jumped. Grandpa never used her middle name unless he was upset with her. By the thundercloud forming on his face, he was more than upset. He was furious. . . .

Oh, no! He knew she was working with Lydia Pinkham. Someone—some blabbermouth doctor—had told him! Dr. Fuller had recognized her, after all!

Dabbing the corners of her mouth with her napkin, she steeled herself. Riley Ogden was a patient man, but when he was angry, he was just like Great-grandfather Owen. Impossible to reason with.

Managing to keep her tone light, she asked, "Is something wrong?"

"April." Riley's voice held a rare hint of authority as his faded blue eyes pinned her to the chair.

Swallowing, she feigned unusual interest in the bowl of potatoes. "Yes, Grandpa?"

"Young lady, you're old enough to do what you want, but how can you think of selling that Pinkham woman's poison?"

April's knife clattered to her plate. "Who told you?"

"Never mind who told me!"

"I know who it was! That snoopy doctor told you, didn't he! That interfering, sanctimonious—"

"Never mind who told me!" Riley thundered. "Doctoring's best left to doctors! No silly brew concocted by that Pinkham woman is going to fix women's ills. No vegetable compound is going to cure what ails them. People get sick and die, April. Living in a mortuary, you should know this. Mrs. Grimes died in childbirth. Mrs. Wazinski from influenza. Bertha Dickens from a burst appendix. Why, I've buried a half dozen women just this year—"

"Not from taking the compound!" April interrupted. "And if Ginny Grimes, Mary Wazinski and Bertha Dickens hadn't listened to some overzealous doctor, but tried to find other ways to treat their problems, they just might be alive today!"

"Hogwash! Not one of those women died from a doctor's neglect!" Riley's face was as red as the bowl of beets he was holding. "Young lady, you are to resign from the Pinkham 'circus' first thing tomorrow morning! Do you hear me?"

"Grandpa—"

"Tomorrow morning, April Delane!" A vein in his temple throbbed.

She knew better than to argue with him; it would be like barking at a knothole. He was such a stubborn old man!

Shoving her chair back, she pitched her napkin on the table and stormed out of the room.

Riley got to his feet, his hand automatically going to the left side of his chest.

"April Delane Truitt! You come back here, young lady! I'm not through talking to you!"

Entering her bedroom, April threw herself across the bed. Flipping onto her back, she stared at the ceiling, cursing the Fates that had brought Gray Fuller to Dignity. It had been a nice, quiet town until *he* got here.

Lydia Pinkham was helping women, and instead of working hand in hand to find solutions to problems, Gray and other doctors like him were doing everything they could to hinder her progress.

Women needed Lydia Pinkham's Vegetable Compound. Why, Henry had told her that a Connecticut preacher was actually murdered by his wife after she'd suffered for sixteen years with female complaints. That could have been averted if the poor woman had only had the elixir!

Mrs. Pinkham wasn't trying to lift Eve's curse, she

was only trying to ease a few miseries. April believed with all her heart that God wouldn't object to those poor women getting help. He'd given the formula to Mrs. Pinkham, April was sure of it. And she, herself, had felt His calling. She wouldn't be going behind Grandpa's back if she didn't believe that she was on a mission. Now, thanks to Gray Fuller, she had to choose between Grandpa or disobeying God. Life was so unfair.

It was a crime the way doctors routinely removed healthy ovaries, as they had done to her mother. Far too many women were dying from the process.

Rolling over, April buried her face in the pillow, recalling how her mother had died an untimely, unnecessary death.

Delane Truitt had been in the prime of her life when she was beset by female problems. A heavy menstrual flow put her to bed two out of four weeks a month. She'd gotten to the point where she couldn't appear in public for fear an "accident" would leave her red-faced with shame. In desperation, she'd finally consented to let the doctor remove her ovaries and uterus. The procedure had taken her life.

April was glad her father had not been around to witness the tragedy. He had died three years before Delane's death in a train derailment as he was returning from New York. "Dignity doesn't have anything good enough for my wife and daughter," he'd say, so off he'd go every December in search of the perfect gifts.

That December, he never came back.

April was obsessed by the thought that Mrs. Pinkham's compound might, just might, have saved her mother's life.

That hope was what fired her crusade.

If she could spare one woman her mother's fate, then her cause was justified, no matter what Grandpa thought.

Lydia Pinkham, far from being the quack Dr. Fuller called her, was truly a pioneer. She hadn't come by her trade easily. She'd been one of twelve children, her father a cordwainer and farmer. Twice married, he'd been a Quaker, but left the Friends because of a conflict over the slavery issue.

Lydia had graduated from Lynn Academy, then served as secretary of the Freeman's Institute. She was a schoolteacher when she married Isaac Pinkham, who had a daughter by a previous marriage. Their union produced five more children—Charles, Dan, Will, Aroline, and a baby who died.

Lydia confided that Isaac was a dreamer. Though he'd tried various real estate promotions and other business ventures, nothing had worked out. That's when the money problems began.

Unable to stand idly by and watch everything they had be taken from them, Lydia had decided to market her elixir. She chose botanical bases for the compound because she had so little faith in orthodox practitioners. She considered their medical treatment to be far too harsh.

And over and over again her skepticism proved to be sound.

Rolling onto her back once more, April stared at the ceiling, blinking back hot tears.

Grandpa had forbidden her to sell the compound. All because of Dr. Fuller.

April beat the sun up the next morning, anxious to tell Beulah about the doctor's betrayal.

Adjusting her hat as she entered the kitchen, she smiled at Datha, who was turning hotcakes at the stove.

"April girl! What are you doing up so early?"

After helping herself to a piece of sausage, April licked her fingers. "I wanted to get an early start."

"Well, breakfast is ready." Datha dished up three steaming hotcakes on a plate. "Sit down. I'll pour the milk."

It was just past seven when April left the house. On her way to Ludwig's Pharmacy she smiled at Fred Loyal, who was busily sweeping the sidewalk in front of his store, and called a greeting to Miss Thompson, the dressmaker and milliner.

Neldene Anderson was just unlocking the schoolhouse as Reverend Brown meandered slowly down the sidewalk, obviously rehearsing his Sunday sermon.

Crossing the street, April spotted Gray Fuller's office, and started a slow burn.

Dr. Grayson Fuller, General Practitioner, the script on the window read.

It should have read Dr. Busybody.

A pulled shade prevented curious passersby from looking in to see who might be seeking the doctor's advice.

April hurried past, determined to avoid a confrontation with him. It was early, and chances were he wasn't up yet.

Righteous indignation caused her cheeks to heat when she thought of what he'd done. The nerve of the man going straight to Grandpa, as if what she did was any of his concern!

Walking faster, she told herself to settle down. If his actions at the women's meeting were any indication, he'd *want* her to confront him, so he could tell her how foolish and misguided she was for working with the Pinkhams.

Well, just let him try to tell her anything. She walked faster. She'd give him a well-deserved piece of her mind!

Prompted by a sudden urge to throttle him, she stopped dead in her tracks, whirled around and started back. She could not let him get away with this. Other women might overlook his antagonistic attitude, but not April.

To her surprise, the door of his office opened easily, and she stepped inside.

The interior was freshly painted, but the furnishings were deplorable. A wooden coat rack stood in a corner. Hanging on it was the strangest hat she'd ever seen.

A medicinal scent and some other substance she couldn't identify were strong in the air.

The door to the examining room was closed, so she sat down on one of the half-dozen straight-back wooden chairs scattered throughout the room.

Tapping her fingers together, she waited.

She wasn't at all certain what she was going to say to him, but she would give him a piece of her mind. Someone needed to put him in his place, so it might as well be her. If he thought his good looks and arrogant manner could intimidate her, he was wrong.

The moments stretched. There were no sounds coming from behind the closed door.

*He's probably in there asleep,* she thought, and considered getting up and shutting the door again, with a loud slam.

Drumming her fingers, she shifted her gaze to the strange-looking hat on the coat rack.

*Pfft,* she thought. *His, no doubt.*

She studied the odd hat a moment or two, then curiosity drove her to get up and examine it more closely.

Silliest-looking hat she'd ever seen in her life. No brim. No shape to the crown. Just round and flat. What would possess a man to buy such a frivolous thing? She picked it up, turning it over in her hands. Why, it looked like a navy-blue, oversized pillbox!

Glancing up, she focused on the closed door of the examining room. Maybe it belonged to his patient.

No.

No self-respecting man in Dignity would be caught dead in this, nor anyone from Dallas, for that matter.

On impulse, April stepped in front of the small, gilt-framed mirror on the wall and removed her hat. Perching the foolish-looking thing on her head, she studied her reflection. The hat teetered atop her curls like a loose cap on a medicine bottle.

Utterly ridiculous.

Turning it first one way, then another, she laughed out loud at the picture she presented. Wouldn't you know that he'd wear something this absurd? Why, if the local men saw him, he'd be run out of town on a rail—

"Can I help you?"

"Oh!" She jumped, sending the ludicrous hat flying.

Dr. Fuller stood in the doorway, staring at her as she scrambled to pick it up off the floor.

"Sorry," she murmured.

His gaze slowly traveled the length of her sprigged cotton dress. For some insane reason, she was glad she had worn blue this morning. Henry said it was most becoming to her.

"It's you—the woman who sells Pinkham's compound?"

"You know very well who I am, *Doctor*." How dare he play innocent with her! Did he think he could tell Grandpa about her activities and expect her to roll over and play dead?

His implacable expression showed no indication of betrayal. "Do you want something?"

She did, but his unexpected appearance drove all thoughts from her mind. There he stood, leaning against the door frame as if he'd been there all the while observing her. His jacket was off, his shirt stretched across his broad shoulders in a distracting fashion. His hair was mussed, as if he'd run his fingers through it.

Studying her with heavy-lidded eyes, he waited.

What was it about this man that made rational women lose their minds? It was infuriating, that's what it was. Simply infuriating.

When she realized he was waiting for her to state her business, she blurted out the first thing that came to mind. "Is this your hat?"

His gaze was unwavering. "Yes."

A smug smile twitched at the corner of her mouth. "I thought so."

She hung the hat back on the rack, embarrassed that he'd caught her making fun of it. Now what she had to say to him wouldn't carry the same impact.

"Is there something you wanted?" His eyes refused to leave her, bringing a rush of color to her cheeks. "Other than to make fun of my hat?"

"Actually, I'm here on a personal matter." She adjusted her dress, repositioned her own hat on her head, then smoothed the sides of her hair, trying to bolster her courage. She hated confrontations, but this man *inspired* them. She could not, would not, allow him to think he could interfere in her life and get away with it.

Awareness dawned in his eyes, and he straightened. "Oh . . . I see. Step into the examining room, please."

She didn't have all day, and this wasn't a social visit. She could state what she had come to say out here just as easily. And she was about to do so when he took her by the arm and ushered her into a small room lined with cabinets and reeking of rubbing alcohol.

Wrinkling her nose, April glanced around the place, uneasy with his close proximity. "Aren't you with another patient?"

"No, just catching up on paperwork. Are you in pain?"

She met his gaze curiously. *Do I look like I'm in pain? If I am, mister, you're the cause of it!*

Reaching for a chart, he cleared his throat. "I'll step out while you disrobe."

Her gaze darted around the room to see who he was talking to.

They were the only two people in the room.

"Disrobe?"

"Yes. Take off your clothes, cover yourself with that white sheet, and I'll be back in a moment."

Her eyes narrowed. Disrobe? Why, the knave!

"You're not only a blabbermouth, you're disgusting!"

Already halfway out the door, he stopped and turned. "I beg your pardon, miss?"

*"Disrobe?"*

Wait until Grandpa heard what his precious Dr. Fuller had just suggested! Why, he would have him thrown out of the community! Dignity didn't hold with the likes of crude, ungodly men.

"Before I can examine you, you'll have to take off your clothes."

She stiffened. "I did not come in here to take off my clothes."

"If you have a female complaint, I'll have to—"

"Female complaint?" She stopped. Oh, yes, a *female complaint*. She couldn't have a simple ache or pain, no, it had to be a "female complaint."

"Yes, I do have a complaint and I am female, but the last thing I would do is disrobe for *you*."

Calmly closing the door, Gray returned to his desk and sat down. "Let's start over. Exactly what is your 'personal' problem?"

Planting both hands on the edge of his desk, she leaned close, glaring at him as she clearly enunciated each word. "What I do with my life, or what I take up as a profession, is absolutely *none of your business!*"

Leaning back in his chair to keep space between them, Gray frowned.

"And I'll thank you to keep your opinions to yourself, Dr. Fuller."

It was his turn to look over his shoulder to make sure she wasn't speaking to someone else.

There were still only two of them in the room.

"It's bad enough," April continued, "that I have to contend with your *archaic* views on the female population, but now you've really done it." Her tone dropped menacingly. "You've dragged Grandpa into this, and I cannot emphasize strongly enough that it is not *your* place to be telling Grandpa what I do, just because *we* do not see eye to eye on certain subjects!"

Pulling herself up to her full height, she felt weak with relief. This hadn't been as bad as she'd expected.

Readjusting her hat, she expelled a deep breath. "I believe I've made myself clear."

That said, she headed for the door and slammed it soundly behind her.

Gray's framed medical certificate fell to the floor, the glass shattering.

The doctor stared at the rubble, mystified. Getting slowly to his feet, he walked to the outer office in time to see the hem of her skirt whipping out the front door.

He opened the door and watched her flounce down the sidewalk and enter Ludwig's Pharmacy, slamming that door, as well.

What was that all about?

Stepping onto the sidewalk Gray peered at the closed door of the pharmacy, muttering under his breath.

More to the point, who was her grandpa?

The woman was an infuriating mystery, one he wasn't sure he wanted to unravel. She had a temper; the shattered glass of his medical certificate was proof. But she was angry because he'd told her *grandpa* what she was doing with Lydia. The question puzzled Gray. Who was her grandpa?

He narrowed it down to three possibilities, with Riley Ogden at the top of the list. Could she be the

"April" his friend talked about? It was more than possible, since Riley described her as stubborn, but beautiful. And if she was April, Gray couldn't argue with either description.

"A man, Beulah. That's what he is! A pigheaded, obstinate *man!* Doesn't that say it all?"

April was still fuming over Gray Fuller. The fact that she hadn't let him get away with it didn't help. The nerve of that man to expound about "modern medicine" at Lydia's rallies, when so many doctors still inflicted their obsolete opinions on women! The fact galled her.

"A most good-looking man," Beulah mused. "But not good enough for you to nearly break the glass out of Papa's front door."

"Handsome? I don't think so."

"Better have your eyes checked."

"Not all women are blinded by meaningless appearances," April reminded her. "There are some of us who judge a man for his character, which, if you recall, Dr. Fuller is sadly lacking."

"Dr. Fuller really gets under your skin, doesn't he?" Beulah carefully counted out fifteen pills before taking a knife and scooping them into a bottle. "I don't see what all the fuss is about. From what I can tell, the women in Dignity don't take every word the doctor says as gospel. They seem open enough for alternative help to their problems. Mrs. Pinkham is garnering her share of their attention when it comes to health issues.

Our laudanum sales have dropped off since she started selling her compound."

"Mrs. Pinkham cares about women," April said. "That's why she's so believable."

"Believable? Well, I didn't say that." Beulah set aside a bottle. "I just hope she knows what she's doing. I am, after all, taking my life into my own hands for you, you know. If Papa finds out I'm handing out Lydia Pinkham's Vegetable Compound to customers, I'll be lying in your grandpa's parlor, surrounded by baskets of stinking gladioli."

Turning around, April sobered. "How is your father feeling? I haven't seen him in the pharmacy this week."

"Papa has a frightful cold, and I made him stay home."

"I'm sorry. I'll have Datha bake him one of her chocolate cakes. That should have him feeling better in no time."

"He'd love that," Beulah agreed.

April's eyes lit with interest as she edged closer to the counter. "Has anyone said how the compound is working?"

"I haven't had any complaints, but the women I've handed it to don't know that's what they're taking. They think it's a tonic. So . . ." her friend leaned closer ". . . are you going to stop?"

"Selling the compound?"

"Isn't that what your grandfather told you to do? Stop working for Mrs. Pinkham immediately?"

April frowned, hating the thought. "Yes . . . that's what he said."

"Are you going to do it?"

"I guess."

"April," Beulah said warningly, "are you going to quit selling it or not?"

"Selling it, yes. Helping Mrs. Pinkham, no. I'm going to see if there isn't something I can do to promote the compound without blatantly going against Grandpa's wishes." She couldn't give up her cause. Grandpa might not believe in the tonic, but she *did*, and she had to help some way.

"Oh, brother," Beulah groaned. "Knowing you, this means trouble."

"I *can't* stop helping her now, not when Lydia is on the brink of success. Dan and Henry are at this very moment in Austin, trying to expand the market."

"When are they coming home?"

"In a couple of days," April said with a sigh. "I miss him."

"Dan?"

She swatted her friend playfully. "You have no reverence at all for love."

"For love I do. It's infatuation I have no patience for. And I, simple-minded cretin that I am, can clearly see that what you feel for Henry is nothing more than infatuation, pure and simple."

"No, it isn't. I care deeply for him. Besides, isn't it 'infatuation' you have for Dr. Fuller?"

Beulah ignored the question. "You've clearly lost your mind. You know what kind of man Henry T. Long is? He'll steal a woman's heart, then run off like a rabbit. It escapes me why, all of a sudden, you think that you're in love with him. You've known the knave since childhood, and until six months ago hadn't given him a serious thought. What happened?"

"I've recognized how charming, how utterly caring, he really is."

"He'll break your heart, then wonder why you're angry with him."

"He's wonderful, and I think he's on the verge of asking me to marry him."

"Deliver us all." Beulah pulled her apron off. "First you were worried about your grandpa finding out about the Pinkham compound. Now he knows, and his heart withstood the shock. But wait until he hears that you're actually entertaining the idea of marrying Henry Long—not that I think Henry will ever ask you to marry him, mind you. Henry isn't husband material. Never has been and never will be."

"Henry respects women," April said defensively.

"I know Henry likes women. *All* women, April, my dense but lovable friend. Open your eyes and be *healed!*"

"Henry enjoys the fairer sex, yes, but I know he's falling in love with me. Grandpa will just have to adjust to the fact, and he will, once he gets to know Henry, really know him."

"April Truitt," Beulah chided as she picked up her dust cloth. "If you believe that, and Lydia's compound cures insanity, you, dearest, should drink a full bottle of the stuff."

## Chapter Five

The marketplace was bustling with activity this morning. April and Beulah got there early, filling their shopping baskets as they sorted through fruits and vegetables.

"Better take advantage of the eggplant, April and Porky. It's the last of my garden," Mr. Portland said, adding several more of the plump vegetables to the display on the wooden tables outside the market.

"What a shame," April said, choosing one, sniffing, then holding it for her friend to smell. The aroma of warm sunshine and green vines still clung to the shiny purple skin. "I'll take three, two of the peppers, four tomatoes and—"

The rumble of a heavy wagon interrupted her. Turning to investigate the racket, April saw an ox-drawn wagon lumbering into town. A hired wagon—coming from Houston, no doubt. The weary, dust-covered animals plodded down the street, heads low as they strained to pull the load. Leading the entourage was a shiny black carriage with fringe around the top, drawn by two beautiful black mares high-stepping prettily.

Beulah, holding a large melon in the palm of her right hand, paused to look at the strange cavalcade. "What is that?"

April studied the fashionably attired young woman sitting beside the carriage driver. A middle-aged woman, so completely overshadowed she almost went unnoticed, sat behind them. The first woman, more beautiful than any April had seen in a magazine, smiled and waved at a passerby, while twirling a black satin-and-lace parasol.

"Mercy," Beulah breathed. "Whoever it is, I hope she doesn't stay long."

"Perhaps she's a street vendor." April's gaze traveled the length of the bizarre entourage. "Or a circus performer." The wagon creaked beneath the heavy cargo.

Squinting, Beulah shaded her eyes against the sun. "She doesn't look like any merchandiser I've ever seen."

The sound of a door slamming caught their attention. They glanced across the street to see Gray Fuller hurrying down the outside staircase leading from the living quarters above his office.

"Ooh," Beulah mused. "Must be someone he knows." The two friends stood elbow to elbow to watch.

The woman spied the doctor and stood up to wave. "Oh, Gray! Yoo-hoo! Gray, darling!"

"Gray," the girls mouthed to each other as the parade came to a halt in front of the doctor's office.

Dr. Fuller paused on the bottom step, scrutinizing the wagons. "What is all this?" Stepping off the sidewalk, he approached the buggy.

April watched as the driver assisted the raven-haired beauty down from the carriage. Snapping her parasol closed, the woman rose on tiptoe and kissed Gray flush on the mouth.

April looked at Beulah again, and they both raised their eyebrows.

"Hello, darling." Francesca brushed Gray's lips with her fingertip. "Surprised?"

"Very. I wasn't expecting you."

"Of course you weren't, darling. It wouldn't be a surprise otherwise."

Walking around the overburdened rigs, he frowned. "Francesca—you should have wired. You shouldn't be here at all . . ."

"If you insist on living here in this . . . this town, then I have no choice but to come to you." She smiled up at him. "Don't I deserve a more appropriate welcome? I am your fiancée. I am entitled to a kiss—"

"Was," Gray corrected. "Was my fiancée. The engagement is over. Done. Ended."

She wrinkled her nose. "Don't be absurd, darling. You can't break an engagement just like that."

Gray opened his mouth to protest, then stopped. "I can't?"

"Of course not," Francesca said firmly. "It just isn't done among people like us. Stop this foolishness and act like you're glad to see me."

He took her arm and steered her toward the door. "I'd like to speak to you inside."

She glanced toward the wagon and the waiting men. "Wait here. I'll be back in a few moments."

Gray eyed the heavily loaded wagon. "What is all that?"

"My clothing and personal effects. I've come to stay for a few days."

He stared, mesmerized, at the wagon. "Clothes? All those trunks?" He counted eight—enough for an army. A well-dressed army.

Francesca smiled. "But of course. Just because you're so rural doesn't mean I have to be."

Louis must own his own private mint if he could afford to keep his daughter in such style. One thing Gray knew—she was beyond the reach of a country doctor. He'd have trouble paying for the contents of *one* of those trunks.

Francesca perused the steep outside stairway. She paused. "Do you live up there? I thought you had a house."

"No, I told you that I live above my office. The living quarters are quite comfortable and convenient."

"Well . . ." She waved a lace handkerchief dismissively. "No matter. I'll return on the Saturday train and order new furnishings. I'll have your office looking so lovely you'll think it's a mansion."

Gray felt himself losing patience with her, something he did often lately. "I don't want new furniture," he said obstinately.

"Of course you do. Don't be stubborn, darling." Francesca smiled up at him. "Since when does a man know what will best suit an office? Besides, this will be my gift to you. Call it a wedding present."

Gray felt walls closing around him. No, make that a chain and collar around his neck. Apparently she hadn't heard a word he'd said.

She turned and walked toward his office door, and he followed. If she planned to change one thing, he wouldn't be held accountable for his actions.

April eyed the wagonload of trunks and boxes. "What on earth does she have in there?"

"Clothes, I'd guess," Beulah said. "She looks like the kind who'd travel with enough garments to outfit a mercantile."

"If you're right, she must have a small fortune tied up in them," April surmised. What a waste, spending money like that on clothing when it could be used for God's work among the needy.

"What do you think brought her to Dignity?" Beulah asked.

"A train." April turned away, pretending to examine a pyramid of potatoes. "And I couldn't care less."

"Of course you care. We all do, because, unless I miss my guess, she's after Dr. Gray Fuller, and no woman in this town can compete with her."

"You don't know that," April chided. "Maybe they're cousins."

"You don't kiss a cousin the way she kissed him. Or at least I don't." Her friend paused, a reflective look on her face. "But then I don't have a cousin who looks like Gray Fuller."

"Have you seen the McIntoshes today?" April

asked. "They look wonderful." The shiny red apples were far more tempting than the silly goings-on with Gray Fuller.

"And did you see that dress? Fifty dollars, if it cost a cent. And that hat."

"Look at that," April exclaimed. "String beans so late in the season!"

Beulah absently dropped a couple of apples into her basket. "Did you see the way she took charge of him? Mark my words, she's set her cap for our good doctor."

"Our doctor? Really, what difference does it make what the doctor does or with whom?" April stuffed a melon into her receptacle.

But she did happen to glance across the street to where heavy trunks were now lining the sidewalk. A crowd was gathering to watch the activity.

"Do you suppose they're betrothed?" Beulah mused. "Do you think . . ."

"It is really none of our concern."

"You may not be interested," her chum said, "but I, for one, am curious."

"You and every other single woman in town," April said dryly, then smiled as she turned to the waiting clerk. "I'll take a head of lettuce, also."

What Dr. Fuller and his fancy friend, who obviously had more money than common sense, did was of no interest to her.

She suddenly frowned.

But if that were true, why did she have a feeling of nausea in the pit of her stomach?

Francesca paused in the doorway to his office. Gray stood behind her, turning to glance at the carriage and wagon parked in front of his office. He saw the look Mrs. Perkins gave him; it withered him in his tracks. Her expression plainly said that she didn't know what was going on, but most God-fearing folks would disapprove.

"Darling, there is no need to discuss it further—"

"Dr. Fuller!" A breathless young boy nearly fell inside the door. "You've got to come quick! My Pa, he's cut his foot real bad!"

Gray grabbed his medical bag and started after the youngster.

"Gray . . . darling?" Francesca frowned.

"We'll discuss this later. Right now I have a patient." He heard her murmur something in French.

When Gray returned from stitching up George Dalton's foot, which the man had accidentally sliced open while cutting wood, he found the wagon and carriage parked in front of the hotel. He paused in midstep, not all that surprised that Francesca had shown up out of the blue. She hadn't packed all those trunks on the spur of the moment, he realized; this little trip had been in the works longer than overnight. She had understood when he'd told her the engagement was off; she'd just refused to accept it. He wondered how she could survive in Dignity with only one maid to dance attendance, the middle-aged woman she'd brought with her.

He made his way through the tangle of trunks and boxes and into the lobby. Francesca stood in front of the desk, badgering the bald-headed clerk cowering behind it.

"What is this you say? There is no room for my trunks? All my lovely dresses and hats? What do you suggest I do with them?"

The clerk looked as if he had a few suggestions if only he could bring himself to voice them. "Ma'am, I suggested . . . tried to suggest—"

Gray stepped over a hatbox to interrupt. "What seems to be the problem?"

"Oh, Dr. Fuller," the man gasped. "This woman, er . . . this lady—"

"Has way too many trunks to fit in one of your rooms."

"That's it." The man visibly wilted. "I tried to tell her, but . . ."

"She wouldn't listen."

He nodded. Sweat glistened on the shiny dome of his head. "Never heard a word."

Francesca shot Gray a look from beneath lowered brows. "You're the one who insisted on living in this horrible place. Now you must decide what to do."

"Must?" Gray started to rebel, then realized it would do no good. He glowered at her, then turned to Clarence Coghill, the hotel clerk. "Any suggestions?"

Clarence nodded, his Adam's apple bobbing in agitation. "Yes, sir, Doc. There's an empty room behind the millinery shop. She can store the trunks there."

"Impossible," Francesca protested. "I must have my clothes with me."

"Then I suggest you load them in the wagon and take them back to Dallas," Gray murmured.

She stiffened visibly. "I will do no such thing. I must have my personal belongings with me."

"I'm sure Louis would prefer you return."

Her mood changed in a twinkling, her eyes sparkling with malice. "You're wrong, darling. My coming here was his idea. After all, he has invested in your career. He sent me to keep an eye on you."

Gray bit back words of anger. "You're here to keep an eye on me? Why?"

"To persuade you to give up this quixotic venture. I'll stay until you accompany me back to Dallas."

"Then you're going to be here for a while." He led the way outside, where the men from the wagon and the carriage driver lounged, oblivious to the stares of passersby. "All right, let's get these trunks loaded in the wagon."

"Loaded?" The burly man with the long black beard glared up at him. "We just got them unloaded."

"They have to be moved." Gray watched as a tall, amply built elderly woman threaded her way through the stacked trunks and boxes.

"Inconsiderate," he heard her mutter as she passed. "Vanity of vanities."

Even strangers were amazed at the amount of stuff Francesca thought necessary for her comfort. Gray helped load the trunks, helped unload them, gave directions to the livery stable and then plodded back to the hotel. He didn't care if Francesca had a room or not. She could sleep on the settee in the hotel lobby for all he cared, but he did owe Louis. Back at the hotel, he made arrangements for a room for Francesca and another for Nelly Hoover, the maid cum chaperone.

Francesca pouted prettily. "Gray, what would I do without you?"

"You'd manage," he said dryly.

"And now we will eat dinner here at the hotel, *oui?*"

"No. I've neglected my patients long enough."

She smiled. "All right for now, darling, but once we're married you must keep regular hours."

"We're not going to get married, Francesca."

"Ah yes, you told me, but you'll change your mind, eventually. It's just a matter of time until you come to your senses."

Gray turned on his heel and strode out of the hotel.


"I don't know about you," Beulah said as she and April strolled toward the pharmacy, "but I'd say the good doctor doesn't make those trips to Dallas simply for medicines." After the market, the two friends had shopped for dresses, then had tea at the hotel.

"I fail to see that what the doctor does in Dallas, or here, is any of our business."

April had tried to get Beulah's mind off Gray Fuller for the past four hours, but she was obsessed with the new turn of events in the doctor's personal life.

"You're not disappointed that he's taken? Don't you think he's incredibly handsome?"

"Of course he's handsome. He probably knows exactly how good-looking he is, and uses it to his full advantage. Just like that woman uses her beauty to wrap him around her little finger."

"Who? Frenchie?"

"Frenchie. You wouldn't want a man like that."

"Oh, yes, I would. In fact, I'd take any man I could get."

"You would not."

"I would, too."

"Henry says—"

"Oh, Henry, Smenry. Henry isn't nearly as smart, or as handsome, as Dr. Fuller."

"Or as *talkative*." April's tone rang with implication.

"True, he shouldn't have told on you," she agreed.

"Beulah, that's enough about Dr. Fuller."

She frowned and glanced back over her shoulder. "It's obvious she means something to him. Did you see her kiss him? And at high noon—on Main Street."

"Surely that's their business." The subject of Gray Fuller and his mystery woman was wearing a bit thin.

"She's gorgeous, isn't she?"

"Far too self-assured, I'd say," April snapped, wishing she could forget the dark-haired woman standing on tiptoe to kiss Gray Fuller.

"Self-assured." Beulah laughed. "Poor Rachel Brown won't like hearing our fine doctor has a lady friend from Dallas."

"Why should Rachel care?"

"Because she's set her sights on him but good. Are you working this afternoon?"

April was relieved Beulah had finally changed the subject, albeit suddenly. "I have a meeting with Mrs. Pinkham at two."

"Was she disappointed when you told her you'll have to be less conspicuous in your work?"

"She understood my concern for Grandpa's health."

Consulting her locket watch, Beulah sighed. "I have to cover again for Papa in the pharmacy this afternoon—" she grinned wickedly "—though I doubt the good doctor will be writing any prescriptions."

"You're incorrigible. You don't know anything about that woman." From what April had heard, the doctor was a Christian man with strong values. The past few hours were suspicious, but then she was judging by outward appearances. Admittedly, appearances didn't favor the doctor, but for now she would give him the benefit of the doubt. She was not one of those Bible thumpers who rebuked without good reason. Not when it came to a man's belief. Now his ignorance regarding the Pinkham compound was a different matter entirely. There was no excuse for medical blindness—from which the good doctor surely did suffer.

April firmed her lips. "We don't know anything about Gray Fuller."

"Except that he's partial to French ladies."

Granted, Gray Fuller was infuriatingly male. The puzzling paradox made him that much more intriguing.

He may have come from Dallas, but April had to admit that he'd settled into Dignity as if he'd been here all his life. The residents seemed to like him, especially Grandpa, and Riley was usually a good judge of character.

The suits he wore were good—not new, but comfortably broken in. Nora Stonehouse washed and ironed his white shirts, and he always looked fresh. April remembered how good he'd smelled that day in his office. As if he'd just stepped out of a hot tub, scrubbed clean and smelling nicer than a warm rain.

Datha told her that all the single women and their mothers were making fools of themselves over him, bringing endless baked offerings to attract his attention.

Judith Hawthorn had taken him an entire baked turkey last week.

A baked turkey!

Had the woman no shame?

It seemed that everyone in town, women especially, thought the doctor was superb, and that every word he spoke was true. It was exactly the sort of distorted thinking Lydia was trying to discourage.

April stopped in a couple of stores on the way home, once to look at a hat, another to consider a pair of brown shoes that would go well with her new heavy cloak.

By the time she reached home, it was well past noon and she was hungry. The house was strangely quiet this afternoon. Thinking Grandpa was asleep, or in the mortuary working, she put the fresh vegetables in a pan for Datha to wash, then went in search of him.

"Grandpa?" she called. Pushing open the screen door, she stepped onto the side porch. "Grandpa?"

The smoking porch was empty.

Going back through the house by way of the kitchen, she checked the mortuary office, even went into the dressing room. No one. Now she was concerned.

As she was walking back through the house, Datha burst in through the front door.

"Miss April!"

The girl's hair was coming loose from tight braids, and her eyes were as big as saucers.

"Datha—what's wrong?"

"It's Mr. Ogden. He got sick . . ." She panted. "I didn't know what to do. I took him down to Dr. Fuller. He said to come get you."

"Dr. Fuller?"

"Yes'um. He said for you to come right now."

April followed the young woman out the back door, her heart pounding in fear. Sick? How sick? Was it his heart, or something else? She prayed harder than she had in years. God wouldn't take Grandpa. The town needed him—she needed him! Her heart beat in her throat and her thoughts kept pace. Why had she deceived him? Why was she a thorn in his side?

*Please, God, spare him. I know I'm unworthy to ask, but I'll change—I'll do better. Please . . .*

By the time they reached the doctor's office, she was out of breath and had a painful stitch in her side. Going straight past the two women seated in the waiting room, she entered the examining room after a brief knock.

Riley was lying on the examining table, his face pale and damp. Dr. Fuller bent over him, listening to his heart with a stethoscope.

"Grandpa?"

Riley raised a hand in greeting, and April took it between her own.

"He's doing fine," Gray said. His eyes darkened as he glanced up and recognized her.

Glowering at him, she silently warned him not to make a scene.

"What happened?"

Giving her a feeble wave, Riley smiled. "Law, they won't let an old man rest."

Leaning over him, April examined his ashen features. His eyes drifted shut, his mouth went slack and his breathing was shallow.

"The heat . . . must be getting to me today," he whispered.

Pressing her hand to his forehead, she said quietly, "Was it another spell?"

"I . . . just a . . . weak spell," he managed to reply. "I'll be fine. Just need to lie down a bit. Datha got scared . . ."

"I'm glad she acted quickly."

"I brought him here fast as I could," the young woman said, hovering nearby.

"You did well, Datha. Thank you." Stepping back, April cleared her throat. "Doctor, may I have a moment, please?"

"It's too hot for October, that's all this is. . . . I'll be fine. I need to be home—Sadie Finley is only half-done. . . ."

"Doctor, may we speak?"

Setting the stethoscope aside, Gray ushered her to the small dressing alcove at the other end of the examining room.

"All right, what's happened to my grandfather?"

"First, I'd suggest you calm down—"

"I'll calm down when I know what's wrong with Grandpa!"

He studied her a moment as if prudently weighing his answers.

"I didn't think you liked doctors. We're quacks, remember? Unethical fools who don't know the difference between a scalpel and a butter knife."

"You don't, as far as I'm concerned. If I had been home, I would have dosed Grandpa with herbs and put him to bed. But I wasn't there, and Datha was, so here we are. I can hardly jerk him off the examining table and take him home, so we'll just pretend I go along with your diagnosis."

Crossing his arms, he stared at her. "But you don't. You know more than I do when it comes to the heart."

"Not more, but probably as much."

"Fortunately, most sane people don't agree with you."

"Are you saying I'm not sane?"

"I'm not saying anything."

"That's wise, because most people haven't had the experience I have with the egos of the medical community."

He stiffened. "Miss . . . ?"

"Truitt. April Truitt. Riley's granddaughter."

"I *knew* I'd seen you somewhere before."

Stepping closer, she seethed. "You know perfectly well who I am. You told Grandpa about me selling the compound with Mrs. Pinkham, and don't deny it. Because of you, I can't sell it anymore!"

His eyes turned glacial. "I don't know where you got that idea, but I haven't said a word to your grandpa about your activities with the Pinkham woman. How could I? I didn't know who you were until five minutes ago!"

April rolled her eyes in disbelief. "Oh, really, Dr. Fuller."

He met her defiant tone and matched it. "Yes, *really,* Miss Truitt. I don't give a fig what you do—got that?"

"Dr. Fuller." She drew herself upright, facing him. "I may not like it that my grandfather is here, but I trust you to do the best you know how—"

"Meaning you think someone else could do better?"

"Meaning that I want to know what's wrong with him."

"Then what?"

"Then I'll determine what course of action to take."

After shooting her an angry glance, he studied his notes. "Your grandfather has a heart problem. Today's episode may have been an attack, or it may have just been a warning. In any event, he needs rest. I'll want to observe him."

"For how long?"

"At least through the afternoon."

April was against leaving him here, but she supposed she must. If she caused a scene, it would upset Riley more. The extra time would give her the opportunity to consult with Mrs. Pinkham and old Mrs. Blake as to what herbal treatment would be most beneficial for him.

Meeting his eyes, April whispered ominously, "I'll be back for him late this afternoon."

Gray's face tightened. "And I'll release him as soon as I feel confident it's safe."

Did he actually think he could take that tone with her?

Apparently he did.

He walked off before she could call him back.

Datha was waiting for April when she stepped outside the office. "Is Mr. Ogden all right?"

"He'll be fine," she reassured her. "I'm glad you were there to take care of him."

"I was so scared," Datha admitted, her shoulders slumping in relief.

"The doctor wants to observe him for a little while, but he'll be back home by this evening."

"I'm so glad."

It was nearing four o'clock when April returned. Gray was standing in the doorway of the examining room, studying the tall vase Francesca had purchased for the waiting room. No matter where he put it, it didn't look right.

When he heard the door open, he turned to greet the new arrival. His smile faded when he saw who it was.

"How is he?"

Setting the vase back in the corner, he said calmly, "He's doing very well. Color is good. He had a little soup to eat."

"I'm doing just fine," Riley grumbled, pulling his suspenders up over his shoulders as he emerged from the examining room. "I see you've met April. My granddaughter worries too much."

"Why, Dr. Fuller knows every woman in town. Isn't that right, Doctor," April said in a goading tone.

"If you say so, Miss Truitt."

Riley chuckled. "So that's where that delicious pie came from. Some woman baked it for you."

"Pie?" April glanced at Gray.

He shrugged, looking guilty. "He was hungry. It was less stressful to feed him than to enforce his new diet at the time."

"He's trying to starve me," Riley groused.

"Don't be in a hurry to leave," Gray said, directing

his patient back into the examining room. "I want to listen to your heart one more time."

April started to follow, but he closed the door in her face.

Sitting down in one of the padded chairs, she leafed through a magazine, listening to the muffled sound of men's voices behind the closed door. That was just like a doctor, thinking women didn't "need" to be involved in medical discussions.

When she heard Riley's laughter over some story the doctor was telling, she almost envied them their camaraderie. Dr. Fuller didn't find anything amusing when he was with her.

Tossing the magazine aside, she studied the office, finding it not much different than it had been when Joe McFarland had it. Evidently Dr. Fuller wasn't concerned about impressions. A vase, three feet tall, in shades of blue, purple, green and brown, didn't seem to fit the rest of the decor. She'd seen prettier. Maybe his French friend could lend some advice on decorating. The idea disturbed April so much that she snatched up the magazine and started leafing through the pages.

Straightening, she sighed, wishing Henry would get back. Obviously, she had too much time on her hands if she was thinking about Gray Fuller's personal life.

Her gaze returned to the closed door of the examining room as the sound of laughter drifted out again. What could Riley and the doctor find to laugh about?

Getting up, she started to pace. Finally the door of

the examining room opened. Riley came out, buttoning his shirt, followed by Gray.

"Well?" April demanded, trying to decide if the flush on her grandpa's face was from exertion or laughter.

"Your grandfather should rest for a few days. Don't let him do anything strenuous."

"I have a business to run," Riley reminded him.

"Let someone else do it for a while. Your health is far more important."

"Well, that's nice, but I don't have anyone who *can* do it. Most folks are skittish about letting someone new take care of their loved ones. I'll be just fine," Riley said.

"Grandpa, the doctor said *rest*. And that's what you'll do," April said. "Beginning now. Thank you, Doctor. What do I owe you?"

His gaze swept over her and she flushed. His eyes were the most unusual shade of green. Like pictures she'd seen of the ocean, just before a storm.

"A dollar."

She paid him, then steered Riley toward the door.

"I like that young man," her grandfather said, as they started down the sidewalk. The spring was out of his step this afternoon. "Seems to know his business. Nice office. Fancy."

Dr. Fuller might be a barrel of laughs, but he hadn't given her a diagnosis of Riley's condition. It occurred to her that he'd not said anything definitive about it, and she wondered why.

Her own heart nearly stopped with fright. Was there something seriously wrong? So bad that he didn't want to frighten Riley by mentioning it?

Escorting her grandfather down the sidewalk, April realized she had to go back and talk to that infuriating man alone. Her gaze fell on the fancy buggy parked in front of the hotel.

*If* he could spare the time.

"Where's the fire?" Riley blustered, trying to keep up with her.

"Sorry, Grandpa," April murmured. She slowed immediately, aware that he couldn't be rushed. She wanted to get him out of Dr. Fuller's hands and into more competent care. Hers.

## *Chapter Six*

After breakfast the next morning, Riley went straight to the side porch with a stack of journals and stayed there throughout the morning. Apparently he was taking the doctor's order to rest seriously. Jimmy Peters, a neighboring teenager, agreed to help with the heavy work. Other than Sadie Finley's service that afternoon, business was quiet.

The nagging suspicion that Dr. Fuller hadn't told her everything wore on April's mind. Midmorning she gave up trying to concentrate. She simply had to know if Gray Fuller thought Riley's weak spells were getting worse. Being as he was a doctor, his opinion wasn't of much value to her, but if she were to treat

Grandpa effectively with herbal medicine, she needed to know what she was fighting.

Dropping what she was doing, she changed into a pretty, lavender cotton dress with matching hat and gloves. The change wasn't intended for Dr. Fuller's approval, she assured herself as she checked her hair once again in the downstairs hall mirror. She had made it a practice to look her best when she conducted business.

"I'm going out for a while," she called to Riley as she passed the door to the side porch. "You stay right where you are until I get back."

"What am I, a child?"

"Yes, and you're being punished." She laughed at his indignant growl. "Jimmy's here if you need him."

"I'll be fine. Stop your fussing."

He seemed to be himself this morning, and April was relieved. Still, she was concerned about him, and Dr. Fuller was the only person who had the answers she needed.

A brisk wind rolled off the water as April walked toward the center of town. The weather was cooler this morning. A distinct touch of fall was in the air. Low, pewter-colored clouds building in the west promised rain by evening.

Making her way along the cobbled street, April breathed in the smells of burning leaves and fresh bread from the bakery.

Tall ships crowded the port. Casks of whale oil and bundles of whalebone were piled high on the bustling piers. Not many big vessels came in this time of year, just enough to create a good business for everyone in town.

Weathered houses built seventy-five to a hundred years earlier lined the roads that intersected the main thoroughfare coming inland from the wharf. The houses were small and unassuming, with one room for cooking and dining, plus living and sleeping quarters adjacent for the husband and wife. Children and servants made do with a loft above the main room.

Toward the center of town, near the square, shop windows were filled with jewel-colored glassware, copper pans, drapes of fabric, ready-made dresses and millinery. Wonderful aromas drifted from a spice shop, exotic goods that came to Dignity from faraway places. Larger cargo ships passed by and put in at the Houston port, but many smaller ones stopped here first.

April paused at the shoemaker's window to look at a pair of red leather boots. Henry didn't like red, but Gray and his Frenchie friend obviously would. What better reason for April to pass up the boots?

Stepping around fresh mounds left by a flock of sheep being herded down the street in front of her, she heard the schoolhouse bell ring, and quickly moved out of the way of a young boy who was in a desperate race to make it to his seat before the last peal.

"Milk, cheese, butter. Get your fresh milk, cheese, butter churned just this morning." A ruddy-faced farmer was making his morning rounds, hawking farm goods from a wooden cart. More than likely his wife had been up before dawn to help him milk, churn butter and wrap cheese for him to sell to the grocer, and then peddle what was left on the street. Grandfather's profession provided a comfortable income, and when she married Henry, he, too, would provide for them well.

The sight of the doctor's office set her heart to racing. Oh, how she dreaded facing his piercing gaze and his holier-than-thou attitude. She hated even more the way he could start her stomach fluttering with one careless look. What did she care if the new physician was the most sought-after man in town? Henry wasn't a troll.

Beulah's earlier words suddenly colored the pleasant walk. *Henry will never ask you to marry him.*

Her best friend was wrong. April wasn't a fool. She knew Henry had faults, but who didn't? He would make a fine, solid family man, who would rear his children to believe and trust in the Lord. True, she'd never paid particular attention to him growing up. He'd favored the girls too much, preferring to play one against the other. But he was different now, just as she was older and more appreciative of his outgoing nature. At least he didn't kiss women on Main Street in broad daylight. But then, Henry could use a little more spontaneity—the sort the good doctor had in abundance. . . .

Admittedly, Henry had taken her by storm when

he'd decided to court her. Unaccustomed to such undivided attention, she was caught up in the excitement of having a man like Henry openly vying for her favors. Like Beulah, April wouldn't have thought she would be magnetized by a man with his propensity to flatter, but she was.

Too much so, she was afraid.

Dr. Fuller's waiting room was empty when she opened the door. She could ask her questions and leave. The hum of voices coming from the examining room told her the doctor was in and busy. She stared around the place, deciding again that she liked the way it looked. Plain and functional.

She moved around the room, studying the decorations. A wooden hat rack that dated back to Joe McFarland hung on one wall. She looked at a lithograph entitled *The Stag at Bay,* and a picture of two children standing on a bridge over a dangerous-looking chasm, with angels hovering around them with outstretched arms. Probably came with the office. She couldn't see a pigheaded man like Gray Fuller choosing anything so sentimental.

The ugly vase was in a corner, but somehow looking out of place.

Curious, April bent to study the piece. Three feet tall, it had an intricate pattern of crouched figures in purple and blue, entwined with ropy green and brown vines and tree branches. Noticing it was already dusty, April extracted a handkerchief from her bag and wiped the vase clean, looking closely at the small, intricate drawings that made up the design circling the base.

When the bell over the door rang, she turned, expecting to find a neighbor arriving. Instead, Gray's lady friend swept in on a cloud of expensive-smelling perfume.

Snapping blue eyes in a pale, heart-shaped face framed by a cloud of sooty black hair scanned April imperiously.

*Whoever she is,* April decided, *she's absolutely gorgeous. And rich. Extremely rich, if those stones in her earrings are real.* The dress she was wearing must have cost a fortune, and the ruby brooch pinned to her bodice was most certainly genuine.

"Oh, I'm glad you're here."

April lifted an eyebrow questioningly.

Closing the door, the woman crossed the room to run a gloved finger over the mahogany table serving as a receptionist desk—the only piece of good furniture in the room. "I expect this to be dusted properly every day and oiled once a month. The carpet is to be taken out and beaten at least once a week. And that vase. You do realize what it is?"

"I believe I do," April said hesitantly, aware the woman had her confused with the cleaning lady.

"It's of the Ming dynasty. It must be handled very carefully. It's museum quality, you know. I'm sure even *you* understand that. Is the doctor in?"

"I believe he's with a patient," she said, not bothering to correct the woman.

"Well, remember what I've told you about caring for the wood." The outer door opened again. "Oh, excellent!"

Two men came in, one carrying framed pictures, the other two potted plants.

"Put them down by . . ." Laying her fingertip on her cheek, the woman frowned. "Oh dear, it is a bit crowded, isn't it?"

The door to the examining room opened, and Gray emerged ahead of a young boy and his mother.

"Don't be putting anything else up your nose, young man," he admonished, ruffling the lad's hair affectionately.

"Thank you, Doctor," Freeda Brown said. "Come on, Robert, you'll not be missing school because of this." She ushered her young son out of the office in a flurry.

"Francesca," Gray acknowledged, closing the door behind the pair.

"Good morning, darling."

When he glanced at April, his expression tightened. "Is your grandfather feeling worse this morning?"

Ignoring Francesca, who was suddenly busy directing the men on where and how to hang the new pictures and where to position the plants, April raised her voice to be heard above the fray. "He seems more like himself today, but I—" She glanced at the other woman, who was dragging a chair across the floor. "I'm concerned about him. You didn't say what you thought . . ." She gave up trying to talk above the noise of the men hammering nails into the walls.

Gray regarded her quizzically, waiting for her to continue.

Suddenly feeling awkward and out of place, April wished she'd waited to speak with him. Apparently this wasn't the best time to garner his concentration.

"I—I noticed yesterday that you didn't actually say what you thought about Grandfather's condition."

Gray suddenly shouted, "Francesca. Can't that wait?"

The hammering temporarily ceased. Her eyes wide, the beauty blinked back at him. "Sorry, darling. Go right on with whatever you're doing. You won't bother us."

Turning back to April, Gray indicated for her to continue. "You were saying about your grandfather?"

"Just . . . is there a reason why you didn't elaborate on his condition?" She found herself extremely conscious of him this morning. He had this special way of focusing on her as if she were the only person in the room. No wonder single women found any excuse to visit him. Why, if she didn't have Henry, she might be tempted. . . . But she did have Henry, and Gray Fuller was a doctor, the last man she would be interested in.

"As I indicated yesterday, your grandfather needs to take it easier. Rest. Eat more vegetables and fruit. Take a long walk every day." Gray leaned closer, lowering his voice to a whisper. She detected a faint whiff of soap and water—French soap, no doubt. "And have him stay away from that elixir you're selling."

April felt a flash of anger. "Because of you, that won't be a problem. Grandpa has forbidden me to sell the compound."

"Good."

When she stiffened with resentment, he continued. "Joe McFarland's diagnosis, in my opinion, was correct. Your grandfather isn't a young man. He needs to slow down."

"I've told him that, but he won't listen."

The workmen were making so much noise again it was practically impossible to carry on a normal conversation.

"Do the best you can," Gray said, smiling at her with candor, the corners of his eyes crinkling with amusement.

She was stunned by her reaction. Her heart thumped like that of a foolish schoolgirl in the throes of her first crush. Why, she was no different than the other besotted women in town.

"Thank you, Doctor."

"You're most welcome, Miss Truitt."

He smiled again, as if he knew the effect his smile had on her.

"Gray, darling, come tell me what you think about putting this plant here—"

Turning on her heel, April strode quickly out of the office and closed the door firmly behind her. The giggle that had been threatening burst into full-blown laughter. *You might be a fancy Dallas lady, but you have no idea what it takes to be accepted in Dignity,*

April thought. *And Gray Fuller's an even bigger fool if he believes the people of this town think fancy paintings and plants will make him a good doctor.*

April giggled again, and Mrs. Handleman gawked at her as she walked past the bank.

Remembering her manners, April forced a straight face. "Morning, Mrs. Handleman."

The banker's wife nodded, looking as if she thought April had lost her mind.

Swallowing another giggle, April set off for the pharmacy, anxious to tell Beulah about Dr. Fuller's lady friend, who seemed bent on making him the laughingstock of the town.

Riley was playing checkers with Jimmy on the side porch when April arrived home. Realizing she hadn't spoken with Lydia Pinkham in a couple of days, and wanting information on Will and Henry and their efforts in Austin, she decided to visit her that afternoon. The woman wasn't in the first flush of youth, so would likely be resting. But April would make the visit brief.

Satisfied Riley would be fine for a few hours, she told Datha she'd be back by supper.

"He wouldn't eat his fruit at lunch," Datha complained. "Says it gives him a stomachache."

"I'll talk to him."

"Yes, April girl. That would sure help."

As she passed Dr. Fuller's office for the second time that day, April noticed the Ming vase that had been of such concern to Francesca was now sitting on the sidewalk in front of the office.

Slowing her pace, she wondered how the piece had gotten out there. Had a young patient played a prank on the new doctor? She hoped not.

Not with a Ming vase.

The object was conspicuous by its shape and color. She noticed Jackson Myers swaggering down the sidewalk with his hands in his pockets, whistling a tuneless ditty. When he reached the doctor's office he leaned over and spat.

Into the Ming vase.

She winced. He had used the vase as a spittoon. Francesca would have apoplexy.

As Jackson continued on down the walk, April hurried to rescue the vase. Gingerly picking up the expensive decoration, she carried it into the waiting room. The door to Dr. Fuller's private office was open, and he was bent over a ledger. He glanced up as she entered, frowning when he saw the vase in her hands.

Leaning back in his chair, lacing his fingers behind his head, he regarded her with a half smile, his gaze sweeping her carelessly. It wasn't hard to see she wasn't making any points with him today.

"Forget something?"

"Fancy spittoon you have here, Doctor."

"Spittoon?" His gaze moved to the vase. "That's not a spittoon. That's Francesca's vase."

Shaking her head, April tilted it and peered inside.

124

"No. Jackson Myers just walked by. It's definitely a spittoon now."

Gray paled as he straightened, his feet thudding against the wooden floor. "Francesca will have my head on a platter."

"Ooh, is the doctor scared of the mean ol' woman?"

Ignoring her taunt, he got up to circle the desk and take the vase.

"I'd suggest, Doctor, that you take better care of your gifts. Have you any idea what this 'spittoon' is worth? Your lady friend informed me it's museum quality."

"Her name is Francesca DuBois."

"How fancy."

He took the vase from her and carried it back into the waiting room, looking as if he didn't know what to do with it.

Trailing behind him, April realized that she was enjoying this. Francesca had the poor, hapless man in a dither. "I understand you were having difficulty fitting it into the waiting room, but I don't suggest leaving it outside. It makes a terrible spittoon, and I have very specific directions from Francesca on how it, and your other furniture, should be cared for."

He turned, a scowl on his face. "I beg your pardon?"

"You should." Her eyes hardened. "Francesca thought I was the cleaning woman."

"I'm sorry. Francesca . . ." He appeared to be searching for the proper term.

"Is presumptuous?" April supplied.

"That, too," he agreed, still standing in the middle of the room uncertainly.

"Use it as an umbrella stand," she suggested. Then, curiosity overcoming manners, she blurted, "Exactly how *presumptuous* is she?"

Gray's mouth curved in a smile, the corners of his eyes crinkling in that distressingly attractive way.

"Sorry," April murmured. "I guess that makes two of us, being presumptuous, I mean. I apologize. And I think I know a place it would fit."

"There's actually a spot left?" His smile was captivating, and she found herself smiling back. She hadn't meant to, but he looked so appealing with his shirt-sleeves rolled up.

"Over there." She pointed to a tiny alcove beneath the wooden hat rack. Heat flooded her cheeks as she started for the door.

"Does Riley use refined sugar on his morning oatmeal?"

"Yes—" she turned back "—he does. Why?"

"Does he use jam and jelly on his biscuits?"

"Of course."

"And he favors biscuits and gravy?"

"Yes." Her pulse jumped. "Why? Is there something wrong with that?"

"Well, that sort of eating habit isn't healthy for him."

"But he's eaten those things all his life."

"I know, but your heart is the engine for the body. It's what makes everything work. The heart needs proper nourishment to pump efficiently. Refined sugar, gravy, biscuits all clog the working parts of the body and slow it down, until one day it stops altogether."

Moving back to the desk, she waited for him to go on. "Are you saying my grandpa is about to die?"

What would she do without him? She'd lost nearly everyone she loved. Riley was so important to her, and she loved him so much. Sagging against the desk, she let the frightening possibility sink in.

The doctor stepped toward her, his hand closing around her arm as if he was afraid she was going to faint. "Are you all right?"

"I-I'm fine. What about Grandpa—"

She forgot to breathe. The doctor was so close that her stomach started to flutter. She tried to attribute that to his warning about Riley, but deep down she couldn't deny it was him. There was a softness in his warm eyes that melted her.

Gray stepped back, as if realizing she was about to pull away from him. "I'm saying that your grandfather needs to eat more vegetables, and honey instead of sugar. In fact, get him to take two teaspoons of honey with each meal, and walk a couple of miles a day. You'll find he feels better, sleeps better and has fewer stomach complaints."

April was skeptical. "What good is honey, other than it tastes good?"

Moving to a metal cabinet, he filed a document he'd picked up off the desk. "It's part of getting back to nature. I've done quite a lot of study in that area."

She tilted her head to one side, deciding that while

127

he was an adversary, he was a well-educated one. Her admiration was grudging.

"Yet you charge Mrs. Pinkham with being a quack?"

He smiled. "Honey is pure, untouched. The body assimilates it easily, and uses it well. The 'elixir' that Mrs. Pinkham puts in those bottles is questionable."

"You're wrong about Mrs. Pinkham. I truly believe she is helping women, and I feel it is my calling from God to serve with her."

He quirked a brow. "From God?"

"Yes, from God." April felt a rush of blood to her cheeks, but lifted her chin. "God calls each of us to special service, and this is mine. Are you a Christian, Dr. Fuller?"

"As a matter of fact, I am, Miss Truitt. I believe God has called me to attend the ills of the citizens of Dignity, using the best medical knowledge available, not by using herbal compounds made up of who knows what."

April straightened, crossing her arms as she faced him smugly. "You, good doctor, are jealous of Mrs. Pinkham's results."

He laughed. "You, dear woman—"

The outer door suddenly burst open, and they turned in unison.

"There you are, Doctor!"

Two wide-eyed young women, assisting a third between them who leaned an arm heavily on each of them, came into the office. April recognized the Gibson twins, Marilyn and Carolyn.

Manhunters.

Molly Nelson was the injured party.

"What's the problem?" the doctor asked.

April could tell him the problem, but he'd know soon enough himself. The Gibson twins wanted husbands. They'd even sniffed around Henry, when it was plain he favored her. Marilyn and Carolyn each supported Molly with one hand, and held a freshly baked pie in the other.

Their intent was evident. It was hunting season.

"Why, we don't know, Doctor." Marilyn handed him a gooseberry pie. "We were walking by when Molly suddenly felt faint. We thought perhaps we should bring her in here to rest and . . . perhaps you could look after her?"

Gray glanced at April, and she couldn't help grinning at his discomfort. "Why, Marilyn, the doctor was just saying how he was trying to cut down on sugar and lard. Good diet, you know, is very important to the digestion."

"Let's get your friend into the examining room," Gray suggested, sending April a look of both censure and amusement.

April was still grinning as the women led Molly into the other room.

*Pies,* she thought. *How transparent.*


She spent the afternoon with Lydia Pinkham. Together they wrote advertising copy for the newspaper and assembled new flyers for Will and Henry to use in their sales efforts.

On the way back home she stopped by the pharmacy to tell Beulah about Marilyn and Carolyn's outrageous behavior. Pies. She wondered who'd made them. Everyone in Dignity knew the twins couldn't peel potatoes.

"A couple of teaspoons a day, now. You'll be feeling like a new woman before you know it," Beulah was explaining to a woman with four young children tugging at her skirts. "One in the morning, and one after supper."

"Well, I guess it won't hurt to try it. Thanks, Porky." The woman held up the small brown bottle to inspect it. "Just two teaspoons a day, you say?"

"Just two."

April held the door open as the woman shooed her rowdy brood out the door.

"Was that Mrs. Pinkham's compound you gave her?" April asked as she closed the door.

"Isn't that what I'm supposed to do? Give women a sample and tell them it'll solve all their problems?"

"Yes, but you could be more enthusiastic about it."

Beulah shook her head. "All that poor woman needs is rest. Four children in five years, and she hasn't recovered from the last one, two years ago. How's your grandpa today?"

"Dr. Fuller says he needs to change what he's eating, and take a long walk every day. I don't know how Grandpa is going to take to that. He loves his biscuits and gravy every morning, along with all the rest Datha insists on fixing. She cooks enough to feed a milling crew."

"Speaking of Datha, people are saying that she and Jacel are seeing a lot of one another lately."

"Let's hope Flora Lee doesn't hear anyone saying it. But Datha's awfully crazy about that boy."

"You think she's too crazy? You know, do you think she knows how babies are made?"

"She's sixteen—and the last of a whole line of children. I'm sure she knows. Why?"

"I was just wondering." Beulah absently straightened a row of salves. "Jacel comes in once in a while. He's been buying stoneseed root lately."

Stoneseed root? April had heard the herbal remedy was used by Narragansett women to cause sterility. What use did Jacel have for it? Jacel knew and loved the Lord. He knew the marriage bed was sacred, and intimacies between a man and woman were reserved for marriage. Yet he was young and the young were impetuous, Grandpa said. And Datha had stars in her eyes for the handsome young man. . . .

"That's odd. Do you think I should say something to her?"

"No. It's probably nothing. . . . It just seems to me that Datha's awfully young to be so serious over a boy. Knowing how Flora Lee is so dead set against the relationship, I worry about her."

"Jacel's hardly a boy. He's what? Seventeen now?"

Coming around the counter, Beulah wiped her hands on her apron. "Eighteen, actually. You know, most girls in this town are married before they're seventeen. They don't wait as long as we have—though it hasn't been exactly our choice," she finished with a grimace.

The news was disturbing. Jacel and Datha were terribly close. "I know Datha's loyal. Once she gives her heart, nothing sways her."

"Well, let's just hope Jacel is mature enough to know the consequences of . . . well, you know, living outside of the Word."

April had seen the consequences of young love, shame, babies born out of wedlock. She knew it was best to keep God's commandments, though admittedly it was most difficult when a young couple fell in love. "Yes, let's hope," she said pensively.

"Back to Dr. Fuller," Beulah said, "I hear half the ladies in town have suddenly developed fainting spells." She grinned. "Seems they could at least be creative."

"Mmm-hmm. That was Molly's ploy this morning."

Beulah laughed as she pulled down the Closed sign on the shade of the pharmacy door.

"Have you heard what the doctor's French friend did with his living quarters?"

"Her name is Francesca," April stated. "Francesca DuBois."

Beulah looked mildly impressed. "How do you know that?"

"Dr. Fuller told me."

Her friend gazed at her wryly. "Did you have a 'fainting spell,' too?"

"No, I was on the way to meet Mrs. Pinkham when

I noticed Miss DuBois' Ming vase sitting out in front of the doctor's office. It was being used as a spittoon at the time."

"A spittoon?"

"Jackson Myers initiated it, and I nicely took it back inside. I don't think the doctor has any idea what a vase like that costs. I found a place for it in his office, and in the course of the conversation he told me that the lady's name is Miss Francesca DuBois from Dallas. And while I was there, she brought in a bunch of paintings and plants. You can hardly get a live body in that waiting room now."

Removing her apron, her friend hung it on a hook. "Wouldn't you love to know what she's done to his personal quarters?"

"No."

"You would, too."

"I would not, Beulah. Stop being so nosy."

"She went back to Dallas this afternoon."

"Who did?"

"Miss DuBois."

"How do you know that?"

"Thought you weren't interested."

"I'm not. Just idle curiosity."

"Mmm-hmm. You know what curiosity did."

"Killed the cat. How do you know Francesca left today?"

"I saw her. She rode out of town in her fine black buggy, preening like a peacock. Want to know what she did to his bedroom?"

"Absolutely not."

"You do, too," Beulah insisted.

"Do not."

"Liar."

"All right." April surrendered. "What is the new decor?"

"No. You're not interested, and far be it from me to bore you with the details. Ready to go?"

"Beulah!"

She laughed. "Well, since you've twisted my arm. The rumor is, and it's from a very reliable source, that the doctor's fine lady has redone his quarters in a shocking shade of lavender! Can you imagine? Little frilly curtains at the windows. The sofa is lavender with lacy pillow covers. And I understand his collection of fine furniture now includes a dressing table complete with silver brushes and a 'charming' little chair with a lavender seat cushion. Can you just imagine Gray Fuller perched on that tiny chair?"

They broke out in giggles, and April felt foolish. They were acting like schoolgirls. She cringed when she thought about what Beulah would say if she knew how she'd reacted to a mere touch by the doctor. Of course, she wouldn't admit to acting like an adolescent, and give Beulah more fuel for her fire.

"And," her friend continued, "he has a fine table with a complete new set of bone china dishes. Plus, I'm told, with silver plate flatware. There's also a magnificent china hutch, the bottom of which now holds the finest linens money can buy. Irish linen, it's suggested."

"You can't be serious. I've noticed the wagons coming into town . . . Why, in order to accomplish so much in so little time, she would have had this planned all along."

"True. The woman is a shark."

"Beulah, that's judgmental."

"All right, a land predator, then. It's shameless the way the doctor is letting her take over."

"Hmm . . . yes, shameless, but maybe he can't stop her." April was sure Henry would never permit such a thing, and if Gray Fuller had any gumption about him, he wouldn't, either. The scandalous talk starting to pop up would hurt his business and his personal reputation. Last Sunday, the reverend had looked straight at him when he'd preached on sin.

"I suspect Dr. Fuller doesn't mind."

"Why, Miss Beulah! How you do go on," April drawled dramatically, laughing while ignoring a sudden, irrational spurt of jealousy.

"She is a beautiful woman," Beulah admitted. "Beautiful, rich, sure of herself."

"Yes," April concurred, sobering. "Perfect."

She sighed.

## Chapter Seven

The frightful heat that imprisoned the town slowly began to dissipate. Fall brought more bearable temperatures to Dignity. But the promise of rain was yet to be fulfilled; a good soaking would wash everything clean and fresh by morning.

A round harvest moon bathed the woodshed in light as Datha paced back and forth, worrying that Jacel couldn't get away to meet her, and praying he wouldn't come about the time Flora Lee woke from her evening nap and came looking for her.

Peeking between the cracks in the door, she nervously chewed her fingernail as she looked out. Her grandmother would tan her hide if she knew she was meeting Jacel almost every night. At the mere mention of his name Flora Lee flew into a tirade, preaching about "uppity folk" and how they ought to have enough sense to know their place.

Jacel wasn't uppity. He had big dreams—dreams of being a lawyer someday and helping people who needed him. Why was that so hard for Flora Lee to understand and respect?

It wasn't as if Jacel hadn't already done more than most men his age, black *or* white. He'd read every book in town, and ordered books from Boston whenever he had enough money.

Mr. Ogden loaned him books from his own library and even promised to get Jacel into law school and pay his tuition when he was accepted. But that hadn't convinced Flora Lee that Jacel wasn't uppity.

Datha had learned to ignore it when Flora Lee's aches and pains made her unreasonable, but sometimes it made her downright mad that her own grandmother disapproved so much of the man she loved.

"Uppity, he is," Flora Lee said far too often. "And ain't no good gonna come of it. He'll hurt you, girl. Hurt you powerful bad with his fancy ideas."

Datha was tired of hearing her complain about Jacel and his dreams. He had a right to dream; what eighteen-year-old didn't?

It wasn't much comfort to know Jacel's folks weren't happy about the situation, either. While Flora Lee had her strong opinions about him, the idea that Jacel's parents might have bad thoughts about Datha didn't sit well with her.

Truth was, the Evanses thought Flora Lee had lived with rich white folks too long.

"Nothin' good will come of you two seein' one another," Flora Lee said again and again. "Mark my words, girl, that boy's gonna get you in trouble someday."

Well, Datha loved Jacel, and he'd die before he saw her hurt. Why, she loved him more than life itself, and she'd do anything to see that he got a chance to go to law school. Even if it meant they couldn't think about marrying for years.

A rap on the shed door pulled her from her litany of

worry, and she hurried to open it. "Hi, baby," she whispered.

"Datha, honey," Jacel murmured. "I've waited all day to see you."

"I missed you, too." She nestled in his strong arms. "I wish we didn't have to slip around like this."

Jacel chuckled. "We're like Romeo and Juliet. If it were just you and me, we'd be fine."

Her fingers traced his features lovingly. "Why can't our families leave us be? My grandmother's forgotten what it's like to be young and in love."

"No, she's not forgotten," Jacel said, a smile in his voice. "She remembers, all right, and that's why she's worried. But she's got no reason to be afraid. I'd never hurt you, Datha. I know we're young, but there won't ever be anyone else for me. I'm going to take good care of you, always."

It was all right to let him love her—God would understand. Once they were married no one would ever separate them. God loved them. He would forgive them. . . .

Riley lingered at the supper table as April finished putting away the remains. They'd decided to eat in the kitchen tonight. For the past week, Datha had cooked fresh vegetables and roast chicken for their evening meal. Grandpa complained that the chicken wasn't fried and the creamed gravy was missing, but April noticed the bland fare hadn't affected his appetite. He ate like a harvest hand.

"I'm glad to see you're adjusting without a lot of fuss," April said.

"My belly thinks my throat's been cut, but I guess I'll live." Striking a match, Riley lit his pipe. "I'm surprised at you, though. You're not putting up a fuss over the doctor's orders. Why not?"

"I don't disagree that it's a sounder way of eating. It doesn't take a doctor to know all that grease and sugar isn't good for you." Dipping a skillet in hot water, she added, "Even a doctor can occasionally come up with sound advice."

Chuckling, Riley pushed back from the table. "What have you done all day?"

"Oh, visited with Beulah. And I stopped by to chat briefly with Mrs. Pinkham—"

"April . . . !"

"I only visited, Grandpa. I haven't sold an ounce of the compound. I promise." She quickly changed subjects. "Beulah says hi."

Drawing on his pipe, he grunted. "Don't know why your friend doesn't insist everyone use her real name."

"Everybody's called her Porky so long, she thinks that *is* her real name."

"She'll never get a husband if she doesn't put a stop to it. What man wants a woman called Porky?"

"A smart one. Someday the right man for her will come, and he won't care about her dress size. He'll see how her eyes shine like black agates, and he'll notice the way she lights up like a Christmas tree when she laughs, and makes you feel good all over."

"Humph. How many men want a Christmas tree for a wife?"

"Well, obviously not many," April conceded, thinking of her friend's noticeable lack of male companionship. The last man who'd courted Beulah was married now and had two children.

A smile curved April's lips when she thought about her friend's crush on Dr. Fuller. April purposely hadn't teased her about it. Not much, anyway, because she hoped the infatuation would pass. And she didn't want to hurt her feelings. Gray Fuller had his pick of every single woman in Dignity, not to mention Francesca DuBois.

To Gray's credit, he did nothing to encourage Beulah's affections, or any of the other women's. But the last thing April wanted was for her friend to be hurt. She was good as gold. There wasn't another woman in Dignity as caring or as giving as Beulah Ludwig, but she wouldn't stand a chance against Dr. Fuller's wealthy French lady.

Grandpa glanced around the empty kitchen. "Where'd Datha disappear to?"

"She asked to be excused early tonight. I told her I'd clean up."

Smoke formed a wreath around his head as Riley chuckled. "She off with Jacel again?"

Storing a tin of flour in the pantry, April answered over her shoulder, "I didn't ask."

When the kitchen work was finished, April retired to the back porch, taking her book with her.

140

Lying back in her chair, she breathed deeply of the evening air. Fall was her favorite time of year. Yet loneliness filled her when she thought about Henry. She missed him. But his work was important, as was hers, though she couldn't be as open about it as he could.

Her visit this afternoon with Mrs. Pinkham had been inspiring. April felt useful and productive in Lydia's company. Advancing the cause of something she believed in so completely was satisfying. It was so very gratifying to know she was serving God by helping others. *Keep me humble, Father, the better to serve You.* She hesitated. *And if it's not too much trouble, show that stubborn doctor that he's wrong about Lydia Pinkham and her compound.*

Resting her head against the back of the chair, April thought about the new flyers they'd designed this afternoon on bright blue paper printed in black ink.

A Sure Cure for all FEMALE WEAKNESSES. Pleasant to the taste, efficacious and immediate in its effect, it is a great help in pregnancy, and relieves pain during labor. For All Weaknesses of the generative organs, it is second to no remedy that has ever been before the public; and for all diseases of the Kidneys it is the Greatest Remedy in the World.

Well, maybe not the "greatest remedy in the world," April silently admitted, but it did help women in a variety of ways.

Opening her eyes, she stared at the darkening sky, thinking about how Dr. Fuller had prescribed a proper diet and exercise for Grandpa.

She wondered if the doctor recognized the similarity between his advice and her convictions. The two of them appeared to agree on some things, at least.

But despite Lydia's claims that her compound produced amazing results, sales were not good. The Pinkhams were expanding the advertising campaign. In order to create a consumer demand and to convince Texas druggists to carry the compound, Dan, Will and Henry would be distributing hundreds of thousands of pamphlets to potential customers as well as pharmacists.

Newspaper ads were effective, and many daily journals, hungry for advertisers, accepted merchandise in payment for advertising space. More than one such firm had a good supply of Lydia's compound lying around the office. The newspaper publishers acted as a sales force. They took the product and turned it over to local wholesalers and druggists, who accepted it because they could count on a retail demand stimulated by the newspaper ads. With Henry's marketing ability, the next few months should prove more successful, April mused.

Voices from the side porch interrupted her thoughts. Frowning, she sat up as Gray Fuller's voice drifted to her. He and Grandpa were playing checkers.

Opening her book, she took out the letter she'd received from Henry late this afternoon. Spreading it on her lap, she reread the untidy script. Henry, charming rake that he was, had handwriting that would do credit to a physician.

It has been raining and we've been forced to stay inside. I am anxious to get out and start selling again. We are in a back room and little air circulates, even when we open the one window. Also, Will snores.

Money is short. If you could, put in a word to Lydia. We have not been extravagant. We've spent less than $2.00 a day. Fortunately, I have a few dollars of my own put aside or I would not have the funds to send this letter.

We have much to discuss when I return.

Love, Henry.

*Love.* Closing her eyes, April rested her head on the back of the chair. What, she wondered, did Henry want to discuss with her when he returned? Matrimony, perhaps? She caressed the missive as if touching it would bring her closer to him.

"Letter from an admirer?"

She jumped, her eyes flying open in surprise. "Oh! I didn't—" She sat up in concern. "Is something wrong?"

Gray Fuller stood in the doorway. "Wrong?"

He had taken her completely by surprise. She'd thought he was on the side porch with Riley. "With Grandpa?"

"No, he's fine." The doctor's gaze moved questioningly to an adjoining chair. "Mind if I sit a moment?"

*Why would he want to sit with me?* she wondered, but politely nodded her consent.

"Riley says you're starving him to death. Vegetables, fruit, baked chicken. Says he'd really like a plate of biscuits and gravy."

She shrugged, relaxing. "He complains too much. I assure you, he still has a healthy appetite."

"Good. Has he been walking?"

"No, I'm not a miracle worker."

Gray glanced at the letter in her lap. "Mail?"

Refolding it, she put it back in her pocket. "News from a friend."

Dr. Fuller's presence unnerved her. She had been deep in thought about Henry, but since Gray had sat down she couldn't even picture Henry's face.

"Someone special?"

He had the hands of a doctor, long fingers, nails neatly trimmed. Manly looking hands. She couldn't explain the effect he had on her. She didn't like him, of course. The man was stubborn, hardheaded, ignorant of women's complaints, just like all doctors, but . . . there was something about him. Not even Henry affected her the way Gray Fuller did.

"Why do you ask?"

"The way your hand lingered on it."

Embarrassment warmed her cheeks. "Well, he is . . . rather special."

"Someone from here?"

144

"Yes."

"Serious?"

"I don't think that's any of your business."

"It is, if it affects my patient."

April frowned. "Your patient? Grandpa? Why would my relationships affect him?"

"Because he worries about you."

She studied the doctor's face a long moment. "He's discussed something with you? Something about me?"

Leaning back in the chair, Gray studied the sky. She thought he looked tired tonight, as if he'd worked long hours. "He was very upset when he learned you were selling the tonic."

"That's your fault."

"I did not tell your grandfather you were doing that." His tone was testy now.

"Then who told him?"

"Have you asked him?"

She had, and he said never mind who'd told him. "What's that got to do with my relationship with—"

"Everything you do affects Riley. He takes his responsibility for you seriously."

"He shouldn't. I'm a grown woman."

"Well—" Dr. Fuller smiled faintly "—apparently he thinks he does need to worry about you, for whatever reason. I'm only suggesting that you try not to worry him overly much."

Anger flooded April at the man's audacity. "Dr. Fuller, you take care of your own business, and I'll take care of my grandfather—"

"Your grandfather *is* my business," he interrupted. "He's a patient. I worry about my patients—"

"Then stick to worrying about Grandpa, and leave me alone."

Gray stood up. "I assure you, nothing would suit me better. But remember what I said. At this point I'd rather Riley wasn't under any undue stress. That includes anxiety about you, and any man you might be involved—"

"Doctor," April said, standing also. "Good night!"

"Good night . . . but I suggest you and I call a truce."

"I wasn't aware we were engaged in a war."

"Neither was I, but since we can't carry on a conversation without firing a shot, apparently we are."

Turning her back to him, she studied the sky. Clouds skittered across the moon, darkening the porch. "What are you suggesting?"

"Let's agree to disagree. I believe modern medicine is what people need most—"

"And I believe the natural way to health is better. Did you know there are herbs that—"

"Let's not argue."

His smile was charming, and she felt her temper begin to cool. "You're right. We're not going to agree, and we do have to live in the same town. A small town at that."

He seemed relieved with her acquiescence. "It *is* a small town."

She stepped to the porch railing and leaned against it, watching the moon slide in and out of the clouds.

"Why did you come here? I mean, after all, Dallas has so much more to offer a doctor."

"I didn't want that. I like Dignity."

"How does your lady friend like Dignity?"

Gray shrugged.

"I hear she, ah, helped decorate your living quarters as well as your office."

"That's gotten around town already?"

"Mmm-hmm. It doesn't take long in Dignity—one of the negative aspects of living in a small community."

Joining her at the railing, he stood for a moment, looking at the sky. "There seems to be an epidemic of fainting going on."

"Light-headedness, that sort of thing?"

Closing his eyes, he smiled as if a little embarrassed. "Yes. . . ."

Grinning, she rested her head against a post. "Must be something in the water."

"Yes, very puzzling. Half the eligible women in town seem to be coming down with it."

She met his smile.

"I don't suppose there's going to be a box supper or a bake sale anytime soon?"

"Not that I know of. Why? Planning to make a bid on someone's box?"

"No, planning to contribute. It appears the mothers of Dignity are under the impression that a single man lives on baked goods alone. I've got a wagonload of pies going to waste, at least a half-dozen cakes, and I haven't even bothered to count the tins of cookies."

April chuckled at his consternation. When he smiled, his green eyes crinkled at the corners and shone with boyish mischief.

"There must be something about a medical license hanging on a man's wall that makes him nearly irresistible."

"Speaking of Mrs. Pinkham . . ."

April couldn't help laughing. As much as she hated to admit it, he could be charming when he wanted to be. "I didn't know we were."

"I wanted to. Not too subtle?"

"Not nearly enough. I warn you, Dr. Fuller, I like Mrs. Pinkham very much, and I believe in what she's doing."

"I would think a woman with your intelligence might have reservations about a product that promises to be a cure-all for women's ills."

April stiffened. "Then you've misjudged me."

"The compound isn't proven to be effective. Aren't you concerned that you will mislead a woman into thinking she can cure something she can't?"

"No. I believe women are astute enough about their bodies to know when something is working and when it isn't. The compound works, Doctor. You and your colleagues refuse to admit it."

"The claims are misleading, Miss Truitt."

"It's an alternative, Dr. Fuller. A very good one. If you suffered with painful problems during and after childbirth, you'd be singing the elixir's praises."

"There's nothing in that elixir that can do what she claims it will."

"Then why does it work?"

"I'm not convinced that it does. Show me solid proof."

"I can't do that. I can only point you to women the compound has helped."

He bent closer and whispered, "You're letting your prejudice toward doctors and men color your objectivity."

"You're thinking like a typical man, Doctor."

Leaning even closer, he caught her eyes. "That's a reasonable assumption, Miss Truitt, since I am a man and you're acting like a typical woman."

"Really now? And exactly what do you mean by that?"

"Letting your emotions rule your thoughts. You have decided to believe in Mrs. Pinkham and you don't want to let a few facts get in the way." His eyes twinkled with good humor. "That's not a bad thing. The world needs the loving compassion of women to temper the harshness of life."

His smile was so engaging that she smiled back in spite of herself. What was there about him that made her so angry she would gladly shoot him where he stood one minute, and the next, have to pray he wasn't able to see the way he affected her? Suddenly April knew quite clearly what the women of Dignity saw in Dr. Fuller, and it made her wary.

"Then we agree to disagree?" he asked.

"Yes. We certainly do," she retorted, lifting her chin in defiance.

"Good evening, Miss Truitt. Remember what I said about keeping Riley calm."

"I'll try to do that."

With a nod, he stepped off the porch and disappeared around the corner of the house. His unique scent was left hanging lightly in the air.

Sighing, April rubbed goose bumps that had suddenly cropped up on her arms.

*Oh, yes, Dr. Fuller*, she conceded. *You are very much a man.*

That's what bothered her.


## Chapter Eight

Beulah was dusting the shelves of the pharmacy when April came in the next morning. She was clearly annoyed with someone, and that someone was Dr. Fuller. Her friend turned to look at her. "What's wrong?"

"Dr. Fuller, that's what. The gall of that man."

"What's he done now?" Beulah stuffed her dust rag into the pocket of the large apron she wore to cover her dress while in the store.

"He was playing checkers with Grandpa again last night."

"So? He does that at least three times a week. It's never bothered you before."

"Well, this time he cornered me on the back porch

and warned me—*warned* me, mind you—that I should make sure Grandpa isn't upset about anything!"

Beulah frowned. "Warned you? What does that mean?"

"It means he's sticking his nose into my business! He told me to make certain that what I do doesn't upset Grandpa. That includes my association with Mrs. Pinkham, as well as my relationship with Henry."

"Dr. Fuller knows about your relationship with Henry?"

"Not everything, but he saw Henry's letter lying in my lap."

"Well, you know how Riley feels about Mrs. Pinkham, and about Henry." She flicked her cloth over a row of bottles. "Why all the fuss when the doctor says something about it?"

"What's wrong," April replied, "is that he told me to be careful of my 'relationships' so Grandpa wouldn't be upset. It's not his place to tell me what to do."

"I suppose he thinks that anything to do with a patient is his concern."

April paced the crowded aisle. "Then he's mistaken. I might have expected you to defend him. You're like every other woman in town, thinking Gray Fuller walks on water. Well, he doesn't, and he'd better keep his nose out of my affairs. My 'relationships' are none of his business."

She took a deep breath to stay her temper. She'd

fumed over that man all night, trying to come up with a way to prove to him that Mrs. Pinkham's elixir *was* a "wonder cure," but she'd failed. Nothing she thought of was overwhelmingly conclusive.

"Have you been getting comments from women you've given the elixir to? Are they feeling better?"

Beulah turned pensive. "Well, some are. I'm not sure how much of it is due to Dr. Fuller's prescriptions and how much to the elixir. But three of them have specifically mentioned they have more energy."

Rubbing her hands together smugly, April grinned. "Good. Now, if I could only get the doctor to try it himself—"

"Beulah, it's time to get busy."

"Yes, Papa," Beulah called out to her father, who was settling onto the high stool behind the counter. "His cold is better," she whispered to April. "He insisted on coming in today even though he's still feeling poorly."

"Maybe you should give him the elixir," April suggested softly. She laughed at Beulah's shocked expression. "I'll talk to you later." She smothered another laugh. "Good morning, Mr. Ludwig," she called out as she opened the door.

"Humph," Mr. Ludwig grunted, sparing her a brief glance.

Beulah spent the morning filling prescriptions and advising new mothers on how to treat the first colds of the season. When young Mary Benson left the store, she was toting the obligatory bottle of tonic.

While Beulah didn't completely agree with what April was doing, she suspected there was something in the elixir that did make women feel better. Now, if only she could find a way to recommend the elixir to the doctor. If it worked, then perhaps he would rethink his objections.

Aware that nearly every woman in town was trying to make an impression on Dr. Fuller, she decided she would have to use a practical approach. She didn't want to make an idiot of herself. Gray Fuller would not be attracted to an idiot—no, wait: there was Francesca.

The solution came to Beulah that afternoon.

*Gefüllte Klösse.* It was a safe assumption Dr. Fuller had never tasted her grandmother's recipe for this German delicacy. Nor *brombeerkuchen,* the black-berry cake her father loved. Not sweet like dessert, it went wonderfully with coffee at breakfast. Not one other woman in Dignity could offer the doctor such a wonderful treat, and, while she was plying the good doctor with *gefüllte klösse* and *brombeerkuchen,* she would casually mention the elixir.

Sometimes her brilliance shocked her.

That afternoon she opened a jar of blackberries and mixed up a batch of dough. That evening she made the desserts for her father, with extra portions for Dr. Fuller.

The next morning she dressed with care, wrapped the dumplings and cake in a clean cloth and put them in a basket, along with a bottle of the elixir. Then, gathering her courage, she strode quickly down the sidewalk to Dr. Fuller's office.

The waiting room was full, and from the assortment of boxes and towel-covered items held securely on laps, few of the women were patients.

Beulah felt a little foolish carrying her shopping basket, fearing she would be counted among those enamored of the physician. Even if she was, she didn't stand a chance with someone like him. But if she could get him to dispense the tonic for April, that would be appeasement enough for her hard work.

Locating a chair in the corner, she perched on the edge, hoping she wouldn't have to wait long. A young man seated in a corner of the room nodded at her, before shifting his gaze back to the picture hanging on the wall behind her. She hadn't seen him before, but he was nice looking. Brown hair, round face, kind blue eyes. She studied him a moment, until he glanced at her again, and she quickly looked away. Undoubtedly he was part of the new family that had moved from Galveston last month.

The examining room door opened and Mrs. Greenwood came out, followed by Dr. Fuller. At once, fully half the women in the office stood up and advanced on him.

"Doctor—"

"Dr. Gray—"

"Dr. Fuller—"

"Just a moment, please." He walked to the door with

Mrs. Greenwood, bent close to finish his instructions, then gave her a reassuring pat on her shoulder.

As the door closed, he confronted the sea of anxious faces before him. "Who was next?"

Chairs scraped noisily as he was set upon as if by a plague of locusts.

Ten minutes later he was staggering under the weight of pies, cakes and bread fresh from the oven, appearing overwhelmed. Only Beulah and the young gentleman remained seated.

"Uh, who's next?" the doctor asked in a strained voice. He still clutched a plate bearing a chocolate cake.

"He was here first," Beulah said, nodding toward the quiet young man.

"I'm here as a representative of Claxton Medical Supplies," the young man said quickly.

"Sorry, I buy my supplies from—"

"I'm aware you may already have an established supplier," the young man interjected, "but I'd like the opportunity to show you what I have, give you a few prices, and if you like something—or, if not—" he swallowed "—then keep my card in case there is something you need in the future. I'm through here every three weeks."

Gray took the card, still balancing baked goods on one arm. "Thank you, Mr. Grimes. I'm busy at the moment, but perhaps next time you're through town we can talk."

"I'd appreciate that. I'll let you get back to work now. I'll be back in three weeks."

"Thank you." Gray tucked the card into his mouth as he shifted the chocolate cake to his left hand.

Mr. Grimes nodded at her, then left the office.

"Now, Miss Ludwig, what can I do for you?" the doctor muttered.

Clearing her throat, Beulah got up. "Can I help you with those pies?"

The consternation on his face turned to relief. "Thanks . . . just put them in there." They carried the offerings into his office, and he kicked the door closed behind him. He glanced at her basket.

She laughed. "Well, it looks like my thoughts aren't original," she began. "I do have more than a pie for you, though." She helped him heap the baked goods on his desk.

"What is it?"

"April said you left this on their porch last night."

He took the light jacket she offered, smiling at the look of chagrin on his face.

"It is yours?"

"Yes, I'm bad about leaving it wherever I go." He pitched the jacket toward the coat rack, hooking it expertly on a wooden peg.

"You're good at that."

"I've had a lot of practice."

"Oh, I have something else for you."

"What is it?"

"Some of Mrs. Pinkham's Vegetable Compound."

He frowned, and she could see he was going to be a hard sell.

"I know your objections, but I think you will find the tonic useful." She set the jug on his desk. "You can't say it doesn't work when you've never used it, now can you?"

"I don't prescribe anything I don't personally believe will help."

"And I say you can't form an opinion without trying it."

"You're a friend of April Truitt's," he guessed.

"Yes. Did she tell you?"

"No. You're just alike. You're suggesting I try the compound?"

She studied him a moment. "If I tell you something, will you keep it in confidence?"

"If I can."

"I've given it to several women as a tonic only. Three out of four women have said they felt better after trying it."

He looked surprised, but not convinced. "Does your father know about this?"

"No! And if you tell him, he'll tan my hide."

"Well, I appreciate your generosity, but I don't want the tonic."

"The women really do feel better. I can tell by the way they act. Addy Menson is actually singing in the choir again."

Gray studied Beulah a moment, amusement lighting his eyes. "You and Miss Truitt are really sold on this elixir, that's apparent."

"It works."

"But it doesn't cure anything."

"We'll never know for certain unless we use the product and study the results. I'm hoping you're the man who will make women's lives easier—maybe not cure everything, but make midlife complaints more tolerable." She nudged the jug closer to him. "Just think about it. All right?"

Shrugging, Gray walked to the medicine cabinet. "I don't think so, but you've made a sound argument."

She thought about not leaving the *gefüllte klösse*. It was her favorite and if he wasn't going to cooperate . . . "Oh, and here." Taking the baked goods out of her basket, she made a place for them on his desk.

"Not more desserts," he muttered.

"Certainly not." She straightened, refolding the cloth and putting it back in the basket. "They're German delicacies."

"Oh." He sat down. "Good day, Miss Ludwig."

"Good day, Doctor."

When the door closed behind Beulah Ludwig, Gray stuck the bottle of Mrs. Pinkham's elixir on a shelf behind his office door.

There was no way he was going to prescribe the elixir to his patients.

Not ever.

Henry, Will and Dan returned from Austin on Friday, disgruntled about their trip but still dedicated to the mission.

"I missed you," Henry said, drawing April into his arms. "It's been the longest two weeks of my life."

She gazed up into his face, resting her fingertips on his lapel. "What a wonderful surprise! Lydia didn't expect you back until Sunday."

Mrs. Pinkham's hotel room was full of luggage and boxes of compound brochures. After greeting Lydia, Henry had pulled April into the hallway, where they could be alone for a few minutes.

"The rain never let up, and we didn't see the sense of staying another two days crowded into a single room together." He smiled. "But more than that, I couldn't wait to get back to you. Dinner tonight?"

"Of course." She frowned. "Are you limping? Have you hurt yourself?"

He looked a little chagrined. "No. Just a . . . Well, my toe is a little sore. Probably all that walking we did handing out pamphlets."

Stepping back into his arms, she embraced him, but discovered something missing today. The excitement—the sheer elation she usually felt— wasn't there. She excused the reaction to a hectic week and Henry coming home two days early. His arrival had taken her by surprise, and she was distracted.

"I will look at it if you like."

"It's nothing, really." Consulting his timepiece, Henry frowned. "I really must run now. I promised to meet a business contact shortly after noon."

"So soon?" They hadn't seen each other in two

weeks, and already he had another meeting. They'd barely spent five minutes together.

"Will seven be convenient for you?"

Nodding, she absently leaned forward to receive the kiss he brushed across her lips.

"Seven," she agreed.


They ate in the dining room just off the foyer of the Kingston Hotel. The menu was limited, but that wasn't important. Henry's company was all that mattered. Strangely enough, April had to remind herself as she'd dressed for the evening.

Henry dominated the conversation with stories of his recent adventures in Austin. April was determined to make a trip there soon herself, believing a woman could make inroads in placing the vegetable compound where the three men had failed.

When Henry suddenly paused, lifting the tablecloth to look under the table at his foot, April frowned. "Is your toe still bothering you?"

He grimaced. "Somewhat."

"I can recommend an herbal treatment or . . ." she couldn't believe she was going to say this ". . . perhaps you should see Dr. Fuller."

Glancing up, Henry grimaced. "Fuller?"

"The new doctor."

"Oh, yes. Would you care for dessert?"

"No, thank you. Grandpa and I have been going without sweets. Dr. Fuller won't let him eat refined sugar, so I've been doing without, too."

Henry frowned. "You've been discussing health issues with Dr. Fuller? You haven't been ill, have you?"

"No, Grandpa had another one of his dizzy spells. A bad one. Datha was frightened, and she took him to see the doctor."

"Ah, yes, Dignity's new medical man. I recall seeing him on occasion at the meetings." He quirked his eyebrow questioningly. "Is your grandfather well?"

"Yes, but I worry about him. Dr. Fuller suggested a change in diet and a walk every day. Surprisingly, Grandpa's stuck with the diet, though he complains a lot. I haven't been able to persuade him to walk yet."

Henry tilted his head to study her. "I can't believe you're trusting your grandfather's care to a doctor. The man must be extremely persuasive."

April smiled. "If it had been my choice, Dr. Fuller wouldn't have seen Grandpa. But he seems to be doing well with the doctor's supervision, though I have had a tonic made up for him."

"It sounds as if the good doctor is doing a fine job."

"If the daily parade of eligible women marching through his office with baked goods is any indication, the doctor is doing *very* well."

Henry laughed. "He's single?" He leaned forward, his smile teasing but confident. "Dare I ask if he's made an impression upon you?"

"Only a bad one," she parried. "He's all for 'modern

161

medicine' and says prescribing the elixir is the same as calling in a witch doctor."

"But Riley likes him?"

"Unfortunately, yes. They visit on the side porch every evening."

As they emerged from the hotel an hour later, Henry glanced up at the sky. Clouds scudded swiftly overhead. "Are you in the mood for a stroll?"

"I'd like that."

They walked slowly around the town square arm in arm, enjoying the beautiful night. A large harvest moon sat in the night sky like a huge dish, bathing the town with a white glow.

"Ah, what a lovely sight," Henry said, patting her hand.

Breathing deeply of the crisp air, she smiled. "It is a lovely evening."

"I was referring to the lady on my arm." He stopped and turned her into his embrace.

His kiss was warm, comfortable. He didn't stir up butterflies like Gray did. Were butterflies what she wanted? Henry believed in the same things she did, the importance of changing lives through the God-given mission of restoring health.

Of course, Gray thought he was serving God, too. She pushed the unwanted thought away. Gray Fuller might mean well, but he was a stubborn, hardheaded man who couldn't, or wouldn't, see the truth.

Voices of others strolling in the square floated to her,

and April was uneasy. They were in a public area, making a spectacle. She pulled back. "Henry, we shouldn't."

"I know, but I've missed you."

"I've missed you, too."

But it wasn't seemly. If Grandpa were to hear she was encouraging the attentions of a suitor in public, he would be troubled. Gray Fuller's voice, repeating his earlier warning about upsetting Riley came back to her. Reluctantly removing herself from Henry's arms, she sighed. "It's late. I must be getting home."

"I'd rather take another turn around the square."

"That would be nice, but I really must go. Grandpa is waiting for me. He worries if I'm out too late."

By the time they arrived back at the mortuary, Henry was limping again.

"I do think you should have the doctor look at that toe," April said as he kissed her good-night.

"If it's not better in the morning, I'll stop by and meet your new doctor."

"He's not *my* doctor," April retorted.

"Only teasing." Henry laughed. "I know I'm the man in your life."

"You are," April confessed, unable to shake the feeling that Riley was watching from the upstairs window.

"Ah, my love." Henry pressed her tightly to his wool jacket. She breathed in the faint scent of tobacco, the lingering hint of cologne. He smelled nothing like Gray . . . nothing at all.

"I don't want to leave you. I thought about you every waking moment while I was away. There in that room, listening to Will and Dan snore—"

"How flattering."

"I didn't mean . . ." He held her away from him, his gaze capturing hers affectionately. "You're teasing me."

"I am, but I do appreciate that you were thinking of me."

"I merely meant—"

She lay her fingertip across his prickly mustache. "I know what you meant. I'd best say good-night."

"Will I see you at Lydia's tomorrow?"

"Yes, I promised I'd help with the pamphlets."

Taking both her gloved hands into his, Henry held them tightly. "The hours that separate us are endless."

She smiled up at him. "Really, Henry—you're not in too much pain, are you?"

"I barely noticed it, darling. Just a little sore to the touch."

"But you will see the doctor first thing tomorrow morning?"

"If I think of it, dearest."

"Good night, Henry."

"Good night, my love."

Upon entering his room, Henry ripped off his shoe and yanked his foot up on his knee so he could look at the swollen appendage. It felt as if someone had seared his toe with a red-hot branding iron.

You could count on him being on Dr. Fuller's doorstep. At the crack of dawn!

Rolling out of bed the next morning, he examined his toe. Overnight it had doubled in size and it was throbbing painfully!

"How am I going to get my shoe on?" he murmured, staring at the pulsating extremity.

Loosening the laces of his shoe as much as possible, he gritted his teeth and gingerly edged his foot inside, at the last moment clamping his eyes shut and jamming it in the final inch. Groaning, he fell back across the bed, sweat rolling off his forehead.

Several minutes passed before he could muster enough gumption to sit up and lace the shoe. Making his way slowly down the stairs of the boardinghouse, he straightened his coat, then attempted to stride naturally down the street.

As he entered the doctor's office, he smiled at the many women, all packing baskets of fresh baked goods. They looked him over like a piece of meat, and he remembered what April had said about them setting their sights on the single doctor. Henry could almost feel sorry for the man. But then he was single, too.

Nodding to the ladies, he hung his hat on the rack and sat down.

The waiting room was well furnished except for a three-foot-high vase tucked in a corner. The good doctor had excellent taste. Henry liked nice things. One day he was going to own fine furnishings himself.

The door to the examining room opened, and the doctor appeared. "Next?"

Glancing at the women, Henry waited for someone to get up. When one by one they smiled at him and said, "You go on, we're waiting to see the doctor on a personal matter," he didn't quibble. He needed relief, and he needed it fast.

Getting up, he moaned, straightened and limped behind the doctor into the examining room.

Closing the door, Fuller asked, "What can I do for you today?"

"My toe is killing me. You've got to do something."

He smiled. "Let's have a look at it."

Henry noticed the examining room was small, but the equipment was new.

"Sit on the table, and remove your shoe, Mr. . . ."

"Long. Henry Trampas Long." He climbed on the table and untied his left shoe. After a slight hesitation, he yanked it off. "Aghhh!"

"Sock?"

Henry carefully pulled off his sock and let it join the shoe on the floor.

"Prop your foot up here, Mr. Long, and I'll have a look at it."

Henry gingerly rested his foot on the towel across the doctor's knee. "You've got to do something. It's killing me."

"How long has it been this way?"

"Two . . . three days."

"Um, angry-looking."

"What's wrong with it?"

"Ingrown toenail. Been doing a lot of walking lately?"

"Nothing but. Can you fix it?"

"Yes, a little minor surgery, a little trimming. Then we'll need to treat it for a few days, and you'll be good as new."

Fear flooded Henry's chest. He sometimes fainted at the sight of blood.

Fuller smiled, moving to the glass-fronted medicine cabinet. "It'll be a little uncomfortable for a few minutes."

"Can you give me something for the pain?"

The doctor laughed. "I'll heat some water and let you soak it before we start."

Henry met the doctor's eyes expectantly. "This is going to hurt, isn't it?"

"Like fire," he admitted. "I'll get the water."

A few minutes later Henry's foot was soaking in a tub of hot water while the doc laid out his instruments.

"How are you liking Dignity?" Henry asked.

"I like it fine. It's a nice town, and I'm settling in comfortably."

"Folks treating you all right?" he asked, trying to get his mind off the upcoming surgery.

"The people are very accommodating. You from around here?"

"Lived here all my life."

"Mmm." Fuller selected a small scalpel.

"Do you miss Dallas?"

"No, can't say that I do."

"Really?" Henry said. "I'd think you'd miss the conveniences, the theater, the restaurants."

"No, I like Dignity. I plan to make it my home."

"Not me." Henry winced as the doc probed his swollen toe. "I've been in Austin the last couple of weeks. I'm looking forward to working there full-time one day."

Fuller bent over, blocking the view. Henry was relieved. He would just as soon not see what was going on.

"Dignity too familiar?" the physician guessed.

"Boring," Henry replied, wincing as the probing became sharper.

"Odd, I haven't found it to be so."

"Ouch!" He shot up from the table. "What are you doing?" Gritting his teeth, he gripped the edge harder.

"Just looking. Relax," Fuller murmured. "It'll be over in a few minutes."

Lying back, Henry clamped his eyes shut. Sweat again beaded his forehead. "You haven't lived in Dignity long enough. You'll see I'm right. In a year you'll be wishing you'd never left Dallas."

"Perhaps. . . . This might hurt a little."

Henry groaned, getting a firmer grip on the sides of the table. That meant it would be excruciating. *Yowww!*

Fuller straightened, tossing a wad of cotton aside. "That should do it."

Henry closed his eyes. "Are you finished?"

"I'm finished."

Swiping his forearm across his dripping forehead, Henry croaked, "April said you knew your business."

"April?" Fuller was wrapping Henry's toe with a piece of white gauze.

"April Truitt. She said you'd treated her grandpa."

"Mmm," he murmured. "I'd suggest you stay off the foot for the next little while, keep it elevated. Come back in a couple of days and let me check it again."

"Sure thing, Doc."

Both men looked up as the door of the examining room burst open. "Gray, darling!"

The woman framed in the doorway wore a tiny hat perched over her forehead, atop an enormous cloud of curls. Her Dolly Varden dress, fashioned of a brightly patterned fabric in colors of blues and maroon, fit closely at the bodice and waist, with rows of lace running down the front of the skirt. On anyone else the bright colors would have been overwhelming, but on Francesca DuBois the effect was smashing.

"Francesca?"

"It is I!" Gliding across the room, she planted her hand on the front of Gray's coat and looked up into his face demurely. "Have you missed me?"

"I can't believe you've made another trip here. . . ." She was paying a fortune in rail services.

"But I told you I would only be gone a short while—long enough to buy more suitable furnishings for your office. . . ."

Her gaze swept to Henry, who was openly ogling

169

her, and she gave him a withering look. "I was hoping to whisk you away for a while, for an early lunch, perhaps?"

Sitting up, Henry straightened his jacket, grinning at her as he tried to hide his big toe under the towel.

"Sorry." The doctor walked over to close the door.

"Oooh, Gray! I've come all the way from Dallas, and you can't spare a moment to have lunch with me?"

Impatience tinged Fuller's features. "I have an office full of patients. Your efforts are in vain—give it up, Francesca!"

She clicked her tongue in a show of impatience. "Oh, Gray. Don't be such a bore. I'll wait for you in the dining room at the hotel."

"Francesca . . ."

"Papa sends his best wishes and says he sincerely hopes you profit greatly from your little adventure."

Her eyes met his and he got the message. He still owed Louis money—a lot of money. He quietly conceded. "The hotel. Noon."

"My goodness," Henry said when the door closed behind her. "Now *that's* a woman."

Gray clenched his jaw. "You like her? You're welcome to her."

## Chapter Nine

Gazing up at the sky, Datha listened to the wind moving through the trees. She felt a sense of anticipation, knowing the hot summer was over, and winter hadn't yet closed. She loved fall, but then, anytime was good as long as she was with Jacel.

They lay on their backs, side by side, the long grass waving above them, forming a pretty pattern against the azure sky.

"Are you my woman, Datha?"

"I'm your woman, Jacel Evans. Forever—till death part us."

Jacel propped himself up on his elbow, gazing into her face. A half smile curved his lips.

Datha let her hand drift over his chiseled features. How she loved this man! Surely God couldn't object. They were young and deeply in love, and the world was at their feet. Nothing could mar this love, nothing destroy it. Jacel could move more raw lumber than the most seasoned worker. Problem was, Mr. Jordan didn't appreciate his work, or his loyalty.

But before long Jacel would be going off to college. When he described the school to her, she felt small and insignificant. He'd told her that Harvard had been established not long after the Pilgrims landed at Plymouth Rock, and she just couldn't comprehend anything being that old and still serviceable.

Already it was over two centuries old, turning out lawyers and doctors and scientists who made a difference in the world. And in a few years Jacel would be one of those who helped change folks' lives. Just thinking about it gave her goose bumps.

"I love you, Datha Gower." He clasped her hand and held it tightly. "I'm sure going to miss you when I go off to Harvard."

"I'll miss you, too, but it'll be worth the wait."

"One of these days we won't have to sneak out to be together. One day we'll be married. I don't like sneaking around this way."

"Me, either," she whispered. She didn't want to keep anything from her grandmother, but she wouldn't understand. Datha had tried to talk to her about Jacel, but she refused to listen. Once they were married, she would see what a fine, knowledgeable man God had given Datha. Then Flora Lee would know why her granddaughter had to sneak around.

"Before you know it I'll have a law degree."

"And you'll be the finest lawyer around."

"I'll be making lots of money, and we'll get married, have lots of babies and live like rich folks."

They laughed at the extravagant thought. Rich? That was pretty funny, all right.

"I don't want to live like rich folks," she whispered. "I just want to be with you—even if that would mean that we don't have a penny in our pocket."

"Has your grandmother been questioning you again?"

Datha shrugged. "No more than usual. She don't like us seeing each other."

A frown put a crease between his brows. "She's got no call to feel that way."

Datha turned her head, looking away from him. "She says you'll go off to school and forget all about me."

He pulled her into his arms, laughing away her fears. "Don't you be worrying your pretty head about that. You're my woman. No way could I forget you. We're going to be together for always, and when I'm finally a lawyer no one can say anything about what we do. We'll get married, buy us a place for ourselves and do exactly what we want. It won't matter then what folks say."

Early Monday morning, Henry limped into Dr. Fuller's office, nodding to two women already seated in the waiting room.

Sitting where he could stretch his foot out in front of him, he settled down for a wait. This was his fifth visit for treatment, and he'd yet to come in when the waiting room was empty.

No doubt about it, Gray Fuller was carving a nice little niche for himself in this town.

Well, that was just fine. Henry planned to carve a niche for himself—only it wasn't going to be in Dignity.

The door of the examining room opened, and Gray followed Mary Rader out. "Remember, Mary. Rest.

Get some exercise, and I want to see you in two weeks."

"All right, Doctor."

Gray watched her leave, then turned to the waiting patients.

Grinning, Henry stood up. "Good morning, Doctor."

"Henry. How's the toe?"

"Better, I think."

Gray smiled. "Let's take a look at it."

Glancing around the crowded waiting room, Henry frowned. "I think there are others ahead of me."

The doctor's eyes grimly assessed the baskets resting on the women's laps. Smells of roast beef and dumplings wafted from beneath the checkered cloths. "I'm sure the women won't mind a small delay."

Henry followed Gray into the examining room. "How are things going, Doc? I see the ladies are still flocking in to see you."

"I'm not going hungry," he admitted as he unwrapped the toe. He paused a moment, examining it. "Seems to be coming along fine."

"It's better," Henry agreed.

Gray cleaned and dressed the injury.

"Heard you live upstairs." That wasn't all Henry had heard. He'd heard that that fancy Frenchwoman came to visit him on a regular basis. Henry winced as the doctor worked, then he grinned knowingly. "What is it about us professional men that attracts women like flies?"

"I don't know—what do you think it is?"

"It's the aura of success. That's been my experience."

"You don't say."

"Women are easily influenced. A man with the determination to succeed draws them like honey."

"You've experienced this personally?"

Henry laughed. "Man to man? I have found women fascinated by success. Careful, Doc. It's still tender."

He winced as Gray rebandaged the toe.

"When my partners and I were in Austin, I was in a café, having a cup of coffee, and a woman came over to my table and invited me out. I must say, she was a pleasant diversion."

"Hmm," Gray murmured.

"I find ladies in the city more adventurous, don't you? This one in Austin is something. More worldly than the girl I'm seeing here. The one here's beautiful, gentle, genuinely caring, but innocent." He punched Gray on the shoulder. "Know what I mean?"

Gray straightened and reached for a brown bottle of medication. "You're seeing a woman in Austin and one in Dignity?"

"Well, the woman is actually from Burgess, but yes, ungentlemanly of me and—" Henry shrugged "—foolish. If one should ever learn of the other . . . Well, you know what I mean."

"I believe I do."

"I don't like to think about it," Henry conceded. He was playing with fire, no doubt. "I shouldn't be seeing the other woman, but when I'm with Grace—" he winked "—my best intentions fly right out the window."

"What about the woman you're seeing here?"

"Sweet innocence. My bluebonnet belle."

"Is that wise? Courting two women at the same time?"

"Ah, that's the problem. Yes, it is foolhardy, but I find myself overly fond of both. I've known one all my life. She's been the flower in my life in this otherwise colorless garden. But she isn't Grace."

"She's Bluebonnet Belle."

"Yes, my innocent little flower. No doubt after I've sown my wild oats I'll settle for April. She's a wonderfully bright woman. And just as lovely as Grace. But Grace . . . Grace makes me feel alive, good. I find myself in quite a dilemma."

Gray finished wrapping the toe and indicated he could sit up.

Henry pulled on his sock and reached for his shoe. "Think my foot will be healed in time for me to return to her next week?"

"I don't see any reason it shouldn't. Just wear comfortable shoes, and allow plenty of air to the wound."

"Good. I'm looking forward to getting back." He winked slyly. "And not just for fun. The Pinkham formula is about to take off." He raised a hand, palm toward the doctor. "I know your opinion of the elixir. April's been very clear about your position. But your opposition doesn't stifle our enterprising spirit."

Henry preceded Gray from the examining room.

"Thank you, Gray—you don't mind that I call you Gray? You seem more like a peer than a doctor."

Fuller's expression sobered. "A friendly word of advice, Henry. I'd be careful not to find myself caught between two very angry women."

"That would be awful, wouldn't it?" Laughing, he clasped the doctor on the shoulder. "See you when I get back."


Henry Long was an idiot.

Leaning back in his chair, Gray relished one of the few quiet moments he'd had lately. His mind kept turning over Henry's troubling revelation of that morning, trying to absorb the ramifications.

The man was seeing a woman near Austin, as well as Riley's granddaughter, April. Bluebonnet Belle.

Henry was playing with a loaded gun. It was evident that neither woman knew about the other. Christian principles aside, the man was out of his mind.

April was enamored of Henry Long. Gray had recognized that the night he'd found her on the porch with Henry's letter in her lap.

April had been so quick to talk about her faith that he wondered if Henry was a Christian, too. The way he was behaving, treating women like toys, was definitely not Christlike. In Gray's line of work he saw all kinds, but he tried to show God's love to everyone on an equal basis, regardless of that person's social or financial standing. He thought of Francesca and what she expected of him. At first he'd been strongly attracted to her, certain that he wanted to marry her, and he'd been happy enough to take Louis' money to help start his career. Now he wished he'd never met father or daughter. God would have provided a way for him to meet his needs without becoming entangled with the DuBois family. Gray had tried to be honest with Francesca, tried to break her smothering hold, though she stuck tighter than a sandbur.

But he wasn't openly lying as Henry was. It was shabby, not to mention foolish, of Long to court two women at the same time. But it wasn't Gray's place to inform Riley's spirited granddaughter of what the man was doing.

She didn't want Gray's opinion about anything.

His previous encounters with her had been confrontational, and he didn't intend to goad her further by butting into her business. Her grandfather's health was too important; the last thing he wanted was her feeding Riley herbal remedies and refusing Gray's help. She'd made it clear that what he thought didn't matter.

April and her "vegetable compound."

She had called him a quack. Far be it from him to cross her again by telling her she was involved with a skunk.

Picking up a chart, he turned to the more pressing problem of Mary Rader. Studying his notes, he shook his head.

Mary had been one of his first patients. In her late twenties, married, she suffered with cramps so severe she was reduced to bed nearly two weeks out of the month.

The situation was even more frustrating in that Mary's husband had no understanding of the difficulties she was experiencing. Severn Rader was becoming increasingly more belligerent that his wife had not conceived.

The situation had worn Mary down. Her face often had a waxen cast, a look of despair. Gray never concluded a situation was hopeless, but he was beginning to suspect this one might be.

He leaned back in his chair, his gaze passing over the large bottle of Pinkham's Vegetable Compound. It sat there on the shelf where he'd left it earlier. He had intended to dispose of it, but had never gotten around to it.

Leaning forward, he reached for the jug and uncorked the bottle. He sniffed it. His eyebrows lifted. Definitely a high herbal content, but Pinkham claimed there was nothing in it to harm a person.

Still, he knew the mind was a strong influence. If the brain were convinced the elixir was helpful, then the body often believed it. He'd tried everything he could think of to treat Mary's problems outside of surgery, which he didn't want to do.

Studying the jug of compound, he toyed with an idea. It wasn't his first choice, but he wasn't as closed-minded as April Truitt thought him to be.

Lacing his fingers behind his head, he leaned back in his chair and studied the bottle pensively. She accused him of being headstrong and narrow-minded about women's problems.

Was he?

He focused again on the jug of amber liquid.

Why not prove Miss Truitt wrong? Why not conduct his own studies on the effectiveness, or lack of effectiveness, of Pinkham's elixir? A couple of spoonfuls a day couldn't hurt Mary and might even convince her she was being effectively treated, which in turn would allow her to relax.

If she relaxed, her situation might alleviate itself.

Reaching for the jug, Gray took a small brown bottle from a lower shelf and filled it with compound. Printing Mary's name and the dosage on a label, he affixed it to the bottle and set it on his desk to await her next appointment.

Leaning back in his chair again, he crossed his arms, grinning.

*There, April.*

*Now who's the bigoted one?*


"How are you feeling this week, Mary?"

Gray's hopes that Mary Rader was feeling better faded the moment she came into his office two weeks later. If possible, she looked paler than before.

Tears pooled in her eyes. "I don't know anymore, Doctor. I've forgotten what feeling good is like."

They were sitting in Gray's office, he behind his desk, she in front of it, twisting a lace handkerchief into a tight knot.

Gray knew there was no need to examine her. He'd done so, from head to toe, and found no definitive problem that he could fix. Mary had female problems, and other than surgery that would dissolve all hopes of having a family, there wasn't a thing he could do about it. He had never felt so frustrated by a medical condition in his career.

"Well, Mary, I know we both hoped to avoid surgery, but it looks as if that's our only alternative."

Twisting the handkerchief, Mary stared back at him, frightened, near tears again. "When?"

"As soon as I get you built up a little." Reaching for the small brown bottle of Pinkham's compound sitting on his desk, he smiled reassuringly at her. "There's something I'd like you to try, Mary. A tonic. Frankly, I don't know how much it will help, but I know it won't hurt."

He wasn't going to hold out false hope to her. If it helped in any measure, it would enhance her physical condition for the surgery. Handing her the bottle, he instructed her on the dosage.

She viewed the compound with lifeless eyes. "Will this stop the misery?"

"No, Mary. I'm only trying to get you stronger before I perform the surgery. Take a couple of tea-spoons a day for the next few weeks, and then come back. We'll set up a time."

Wiping tears from her eyes, she got up and followed him to the door. "Two teaspoons a day?"

"Three, if you like." It couldn't hurt.

"Thank you, Doctor."

Taking her hand, he held it momentarily. "I know you're scared. I would be, too."

Tears rolled down her cheeks. "I wish there was another way."

"I've done all I know to do, Mary. I'm as frustrated as you are, but there's no alternative."

"Severn is going to be angry. He wants children."

Patting her shoulder, Gray said quietly, "I'm sure he's more concerned about your health. If he wants to talk to me, have him stop by the office. I'm here every night until late."


"Ah, indeed, we're leaving first thing in the morning," Henry confessed as he and April ate dinner that evening. The hotel dining room was quiet tonight, affording them much-needed privacy. "Dan and Will want to get in a full day, if they can. We might have to travel as far as San Antonio—even Brownsville this time."

"I wish you didn't have to leave so soon," April admitted.

Taking her hand, he stroked it gently. "We must make progress on marketing the compound soon, or I'll be out of a job."

"I know. I was hoping the trip to Austin would be more successful. I hate the times we're apart."

Henry's forehead furrowed. "As I do, dearest. We're doing everything possible, but women are reluctant to try something new. You know that."

"Lydia and I have written more advertising copy and

pamphlets. Poor Isaac traveled here, sick as he is, to help fold the pamphlets and pack them. He's so supportive of Lydia's work."

"He should be," Henry muttered. "If the compound isn't successful, the Pinkhams will meet financial ruin."

"You will faithfully write, won't you?"

"Of course, darling. Have I ever failed?"

Later, as Henry walked April home, he drew her close to his side. "I am going to miss you dreadfully," he whispered.

Warmth flooded April's cheeks. "So will I. I was thinking. Perhaps I can come for a visit—"

"No!" Henry said quickly. "No," he repeated more gently, when he noted her shocked countenance. "I won't hear of it. It's much too far—you would need a chaperone— No, it's out of the question."

As they approached the mortuary, he pressed another benign kiss on her forehead, whispering, "How I am tempted to linger, but we'd best part quickly, my love. I wouldn't want to upset Riley."

"You'll be so lonely! Perhaps I could travel to San Antonio and take a train to—"

"Such a lovely thought, but I will cloak myself in loneliness and count the moments until we are together once more."

"You promise to write?"

"Of course, dearest. Every day."

April stopped by the pharmacy late the next afternoon. With Henry gone, she had time on her hands.

The smells of herbs and liniment filled the shop. April always liked coming here. The creaky wooden floors, whitewashed walls and plain shelves were friendly. Beulah's plants hung in the windows, the southern light and her green thumb keeping them healthy as their trailing vines framed the wide windows. Over the years many a homemaker had pinched a start from Beulah's plants.

"Hi. Doing anything later?"

"Me? Nothing. Why?"

"Oh, I'm just lonely."

"Henry off again?"

"Yes." She sighed. "He left for Austin this morning."

"Well, I've got a remedy for your melancholy. Just let me finish up, then we'll eat dinner out tonight."

"We should go to the quilting bee. We haven't been in a while."

"I don't want to go sew on some old quilt. Let's splurge and eat at the hotel."

"I don't know. I haven't had dinner with Grandpa hardly at all lately."

"He doesn't mind, does he?"

Actually, he didn't. April knew he would eat quickly and retire to the porch to play checkers with Jimmy.

As the two women walked home after a late supper, April filled Beulah in on her day.

"Did Will and Dan accompany Henry this morning?"

"Yes. I hope they're successful. We can't afford many more setbacks."

"Speaking of Dan Pinkham, what do you think of him?"

April shrugged. "He's nice. He has some political ambitions."

"Mmm-hmm."

"Why?"

"Just wondering." Beulah sighed.

"I think Will is much nicer. He has kind eyes, though I don't much care for the long muttonchops."

"Dan's beard is nice."

April laughed lightly. "I don't know why our opinion matters. Both men are married."

Beulah released another long sigh. "All the good ones are, except Dr. Fuller, of course. But I did notice a nice young man in the doctor's waiting room a few weeks ago. A medical equipment and supplies salesman."

"Oh? And did you happen to notice whether he was married and what his name was?"

"I might have, but since you're being so snippy, I don't think I'll share it with you. I did notice that *woman* was back to visit Dr. Fuller the other day."

April's eyes rolled toward the sky with exasperation. "Haven't you anything better to do than spy on people?"

"Not really. Aren't you the least bit curious about what she's done to his living quarters?"

April stopped short. "No, nor should you be. You're becoming obsessed with Gray, and it has to stop."

Beulah wasn't listening. "Shameless . . . she's utterly shameless!"

"Surely Gray—"

Beulah stepped in front of April. "'Gray'? He's 'Gray' now?"

April realized that some time in the past month she'd ceased thinking of him as Dr. Fuller and started referring to him as Gray. Oddly enough, she no longer thought of him as an adversary. He had been helpful with Riley, and she couldn't deny he was intelligent and informative to talk to. But so what? That didn't mean she thought of him in a personal nature, even if he was the most attractive man she'd ever seen. And so what if her heart skipped a beat at the very sound of his voice?

"He comes by the house nearly every evening to see Grandpa, you know."

"But you call him 'Gray'?"

"Don't try to make something of it. He's Grandpa's friend, not mine."

Falling back into step, Beulah laughed. "Wouldn't it be funny if you two became friends? Or better yet, what if you were to take a fancy to each other! That would be so *so* romantic!"

"Not a chance. I don't dislike him, but I don't like him, either."

Her friend grinned. "Wouldn't you just die to see his personal living quarters?"

"Beulah! What an outrageous thought. Why, if your papa or Reverend—"

"Oh shush. Let's do it!"

April suddenly halted, leaving Beulah to walk on for several steps before she turned and looked back at her. "What's wrong?"

"You're *not* serious."

"Of course I'm serious. Why not?" She glanced in the direction of his office. "No lamp on upstairs. This would be the perfect time."

"To *break* into his office?"

"Certainly not," Beulah stated, lifting her chin. "To *look* into his living quarters. Come on. Enis Matthews keeps a ladder behind his store. We can use it."

"Definitely not," April said, intent on walking right past the doctor's office.

"It'll only take a minute. What happened to your spunky spirit?"

"It left at the mention of peeking in windows."

"Well, I'm going to look." Beulah started toward the narrow alley in back of the doctor's office.

"Beulah!" April whispered in horror.

"It'll only take a minute," she whispered back. "Who's to know? It's obvious he's not there. Come on, scaredy-cat!"

"No—"

Beulah's eyes darted down the alleyway. "See? There's the ladder."

"Leave it alone. I refuse to take part in this . . . this idiocy!" Sneaking around in alleyways, staring into men's bedrooms! It was shameful. Sure she was curious, but Beulah was going too far.

"We can lean the ladder against the back wall, climb up, sneak a peek in the window and leave."

"No!" April whispered. "It's pitch-dark. How are we going to see in his bedroom?"

"I'm going to try anyway. If I don't see anything, then no harm's done."

"You have lost your mind—" April found herself talking to thin air as Beulah disappeared down the alleyway. Cringing, she listened to faint bumping and scraping sounds as her friend dragged the ladder into place.

"For goodness' sake! You're going to hit the window and break it," April declared in a harsh whisper. Stealing a second glance at the alleyway entrance, she dropped her reticule on the ground and hurried to help Beulah balance the ladder. "This thing must be fifty feet long!"

"Stop complaining. It's worth the effort."

"We're going to look ridiculous, not to mention be put in jail, if we're caught."

"There. Put it right next to the upstairs window. We can peek in . . . see? He's left the curtain open. How thoughtful of him."

April closed her eyes with frustration. "I must be mad to let you talk me into this."

"Not mad, curious. I'll go first."

April held the ladder while Beulah hiked her skirts up to her knees. Holding the fabric with one hand, she clasped a rung with the other, slowly making her way up the steps.

The climb took forever. April's eyes darted toward the street to make sure they weren't attracting attention. Stubborn, pigheaded Gray Fuller was not worth the fuss!

Glancing to her left, she spotted a round, black shape lying on the woodpile next to the building. Standing on tiptoe, she peered at it more closely.

*Why, that was his hat!*

The hat Francesca had brought him from Paris! What was it doing lying on the woodpile?

Steadying the ladder with one hand, April leaned to the side and reached for it. She felt the ladder sway beneath her hand, and glanced up just in time to see Beulah lean to the other side.

The ladder began to wobble, then tip.

"It's going to fall!" April hissed.

But it was too late. Her friend leaned too far out and, before April could do anything, the ladder tilted grotesquely to one side.

Hands flailing, Beulah grabbed for the window ledge.

Grunting, April tried to shove the ladder back into place. It wavered, wobbled, then fell with a loud thud, leaving Beulah hanging.

"*Now* what do we do, smarty?" April snapped in a harsh whisper.

A lamp sprang to life in the window, and she mentally groaned.

Oh, wonderful.

Forgetting Beulah's predicament, she bolted to the

corner of the alleyway as the door to Gray's personal quarters burst open and the doctor descended the stairs two at a time.

April knew her presence in the alleyway at this time of night was not going to be easy to explain. Leaving Beulah hanging, she quickly stepped around the corner to confront Gray as he reached the bottom of the stairs.

His eyes clouded with confusion when he saw her. "April?"

Taking a deep breath, she grinned, motioning behind her back for Beulah to stifle her whimpers. Her friend was dangling from the ledge beneath the doctor's window like a broken puppet.

"Good evening, Dr. Fuller. What are you doing out this time of night?"

She smiled up into his eyes, hoping he couldn't see far enough into the alley to notice her friend in her Peeping Tom mode. If they got out of this with their reputations intact it was the last time she would let Beulah Ludwig drag her into anything. If a word of this escapade reached her grandfather's ears, or even worse if Henry heard about it . . . Her heart stopped when she thought of her fiancé learning that his intended had been caught peeping into Gray Fuller's window.

He stared at her, his expression bewildered. "I heard something . . . a cry and a thud, like someone was hurt." He peered closer. "What are you doing in the alley at this time of night?"

"Me? Nothing." Swallowing her pride she stepped forward to take his arm, steering him back to the stairs. April cringed when she heard Beulah fall to the ground with a soft thud. Gray stiffened and started to turn back, but she tightened her grip on his arm. "Lovely night, isn't it?"

"It's as cold as a Texas blizzard. What are you doing here? Is Riley ill?"

"No, Grandpa's fine. In fact, I've talked him into taking Mrs. Pinkham's tonic—although he doesn't know that's what it is—a couple of times a day, and he's feeling much better, thank you."

Gray allowed her to propel him along, staring at her as if she had lost her mind. "I was just walking by when I heard you coming down the stairs," she explained. "I hope I didn't disturb you."

"You were just walking by in the alley at ten o'clock at night and you wanted to say hello? Is that it?"

"Yes. I like walking at night. Here." She handed him the hat. "I found this on the woodpile. What, may I ask, was it doing out here?"

"I put it there."

Shaking her head, she smiled and wagged a finger at him. "Francesca would be upset if she knew you were treating your hat this way."

April gave his arm an indulgent pat, then turned him toward the steps and made herself stroll slowly on down the sidewalk hoping Beulah could collect herself. Glancing over her shoulder, she noted his expression. Stunned. So she'd surprised him. Good.

He was far too full of himself, in her opinion.

Walking faster, April prayed Beulah hadn't broken every bone in her body, but it would serve her right for being so nosy!

## Chapter Ten

"Well, that looks to be it," Gray said, rechecking his medications list. "Thanks, Ray. Your coming by every three weeks has been a tremendous help to me."

"Glad to do it," Ray Grimes said, repacking his sample case and closing it.

"It's late. Are you staying in town tonight?" Gray shut the door of his medicine cabinet.

"I'd planned on it. It looks a bit like rain out there. How's the hotel?"

"Nice enough. We're having a preholiday celebration. If you're not busy, drop by. I'll introduce you to some people, and you'll get to know the town."

Raymond Grimes smiled and nodded. "I'd like that. Being on the road all the time, I don't get to meet many people, except doctors like you."

"Good. You get your room, and I'll come by for you around seven."

"Thanks."

In the two months since Ray had begun calling on Gray, the two men had formed a friendship. Gray was glad to have Ray as a supplier. His list of available medications and equipment was very good, and the personal delivery more convenient than traveling to

Dallas every two weeks. Best of all, it allowed Gray to see less of Louis and Francesca. The woman was a constant thorn in his side, showing up unexpectedly, staying a few days, then leaving in a huff. If business continued to increase, Gray would soon be able to send another hundred dollars as payment on the loan. Another year, and the debt would be paid, and he could stop saving every penny and use his funds toward expanding his practice. That was a day he looked forward to.

Gray knocked on Ray's door precisely at seven o'clock that evening.

"I can see why you favor Dignity," Ray commented as they strode across the town square.

A cool wind came up, a portent of the winter ahead. Both men pulled up their collars against the chill.

"I've fallen in love," Gray admitted.

"Oh? You're referring to your ex-fiancée, I assume?"

Chuckling, Gray rephrased the statement. "With the town and its residents. They're good, hardworking people."

"Ah, then they have accepted you. That speaks well for you."

"They've accepted me too much." He laughed. "The women have taken me under their wing, determined to keep me fed. I've had enough cookies, cakes, pies and pot roasts to feed two armies."

"Guess that's the way with friendly towns."

"Yes." Gray smiled. "That appears to be their way."

Light spilled from the town hall windows into the

square. The decorating committee had removed most of the benches and shoved chairs back to the walls. Already the room was full. A fiddler was tuning up, and two guitar players plucked at the strings of their flat tops.

The refreshment committee put the last tray of cookies on a table that held a variety of food, along with lemonade.

"Dr. Fuller!" Mazie Bennett hurried over with a wide smile on her face.

"Mrs. Bennett. How nice you look tonight. I'd like you to meet a friend of mine. Raymond Grimes."

Mazie looked the stranger up and down. "Pleased to meet you, Mr. Grimes."

"Mrs. Bennett is in charge of the celebration tonight."

"Quite an undertaking," the salesman said.

"Oh, I enjoyed doing it. The festivities are in honor of our new doctor. We feel so privileged to have him in our town."

"I'm sure you do." Ray's gaze shifted to the door when Beulah and April walked in. "I appreciate being invited tonight."

"Any friend of the doctor's is a friend of ours. You just make yourself at home. I've got to greet these folks coming in." With that, Mazie Bennett bustled off to spread cheer and goodwill.

"Lemonade?"

"Thank you," Ray said, his eyes straying again to the two young women, who were now making the rounds of the room.

The two men stood to one side, sipping their drinks as the musicians began the first song. Soon the floor was full of couples reeling to the quick tunes, which began melting one into the other.

"I think I'll meander around a little," Ray said.

"Of course . . . and the girl you've got your eyes on is Beulah Ludwig. Her father's the pharmacist."

Blushing, Ray set his cup of lemonade on the table. "Thanks." He threaded his way through the crowd to where she was standing.

Gray's eyes lingered on April as she slipped off her shawl and hung it on a hook beside the door. Riley wandered off to join some of his cronies while she spoke to friends.

Lamplight shone in her hair. The dark green dress she wore made her look older, and he realized that she was the most beautiful woman in the room. She was one woman who didn't need to bake a pie in order to catch his attention. Every time he saw her, he felt that all too familiar urge to pull her into his arms.

The next song began and couples formed a reel. Gray slowly made his way across the room to where April was standing with friends. He had almost reached her when James Nelson swung her into his arms and joined the couples on the floor. Stepping back, Gray accepted a dance with Meredith Nelson instead.

When the dance ended, James returned April to her friends. Snapping open her ivory-and-lace fan, she laughed at something someone said.

Excusing himself, Gray made his way back to her. "I believe this is our dance."

April turned in midlaugh, her brows lifting when she saw him. "Why, Dr. Fuller, I didn't notice you here."

"May I have this dance?"

"Of course."

As they approached the floor, the music changed to a slow waltz. April's hand rested lightly on the front of his jacket. He held her loosely, aware that she was conscious of his palm resting at her waist, the warm clasp of his other hand around hers.

"I wasn't sure you'd dance with me," he stated as they slowly fell into step.

"Why not?"

"I have the distinct feeling you don't like me, Miss Truitt."

Smiling up at him, she made a face. "Why ever would you think that? If we disagree, it's on how to treat women, not on waltzes."

"Where's Henry tonight?"

"He's away on business."

"He's gone a lot, isn't he?" His gaze skimmed her flushed features. Couldn't she see how Long was playing her for a fool?

Her smile faded, and she didn't look gullible, just lonely. "Yes, far too often, I'm afraid."

Gray grinned. "Let's be civil to each other tonight, all right?"

"I think that would be lovely, Doctor. Please keep it in mind when I say anything that annoys you."

· · ·

"Miss Ludwig?"

Beulah turned. "Yes?"

"My name is Raymond Grimes. I'm a friend of Dr. Fuller's."

She smiled. "Yes, I've seen you in his office, haven't I?"

"I'm a salesman, medical supplies and equipment. Dr. Fuller was nice enough to invite me to the celebration tonight."

Beulah's gaze scanned the young man from head to foot. Brown hair brushed back from a wide forehead, kind blue eyes, white shirt and brown suit, his boots freshly polished . . . He wasn't outstandingly handsome, but he looked nice.

"Could we visit?"

She hesitated. She seldom took time to socialize at these affairs. She usually minded the refreshment table. "I—I shouldn't leave my post."

He looked disappointed. "Couldn't someone watch it for you a moment?"

Glancing around, Beulah spotted Mrs. Steel, smiling and nodding encouragingly. Thelma's eyes seemed to be urging her to enjoy herself.

"Well, I guess it won't hurt," she finally said, taking the hand he offered.

She was glad for a break. A nice-looking young man had actually sought her out!

Her, Beulah "Porky" Ludwig!

She smiled, hoping to make pleasant conversation.

"Do you travel through town often?"

"Every two to three weeks, depending on how things go."

Oh, dear. Did he notice how thick her waist was? Did it matter to him? Why hadn't she worn a corset! Drat! She would have suffered through the atrocity if she'd had any idea a man would ask her to chat!

"This your hometown?"

She nodded. She wasn't good at small talk. Never had been.

"It's a nice place."

"I think so."

They watched the others, saying nothing, and she didn't mind. This was comfortable. Of course, he was a stranger in town and probably taking pity on her, but she didn't mind. It was worth it to see the look on Janie Anderson's face.

"Gray tells me your father runs the pharmacy."

"Mmm-hmm. I work there with him."

Oh. That was it. He saw her as a potential account. It didn't matter. For now, she was actually being accompanied by a man.

"What do you find to be the fastest-selling medications?"

For the next two hours they talked about medicines, over-the-counter treatments and even Pinkham's elixir. Ray didn't agree that it was a miracle cure, but he did say that for some people it seemed beneficial.

"Would you like some refreshment?"

"Yes," she said, though she was reluctant to move.

This didn't happen that often, and she wanted to make it last as long as possible.

Ray handed her a cup of lemonade and they stood at the edge of the crowd while they sipped their tart drinks.

"Hello, Porky."

"Hello, Melinda."

When the young woman lingered, Beulah remembered her manners. "Melinda Barnes, this is Raymond Grimes."

"Raymond, I'm glad to meet you." Melinda's adventurous eyes devoured her escort, but it didn't matter. He would be gone in the morning. "Are you new in town?"

"Just passing through."

"I see." She smiled ever so charmingly. "Well, I certainly do hope you'll come back soon."

Melinda's attention was caught by a friend, and she hurried off.

"Did she call you . . . Porky?"

Beulah blushed. "That's my name."

"Surely not."

"Well, it's a nickname that's stuck since I was a little . . . since I was a child." She'd never been a 'little' anything.

"Why?"

"*Why?*"

"Yes." His eyes softened. "I don't see that it fits."

Beulah blinked; then her eyes suddenly welled with tears. That was the nicest thing anyone had ever said to her. He didn't mean it—she looked like a cow in this dress—but it was still a nice thing to say.

"You're serious?"

"Yes."

"You're really serious?"

"Miss Ludwig, I—"

"Because I'm a large woman, Mr. Grimes, or are you blind?" He was making fun of her. Of course. And she had almost fallen for it.

"I assure you, I'm not blind. Do you mind if I call you Beulah? You can call me Ray."

"I do not appreciate being made fun of, Mr. Grimes." Taking her skirt in her hand, she started to walk off, but he reached out and stopped her.

"I wasn't making fun of you, Miss Ludwig." His eyes met hers, and she was hopelessly caught by their sincerity. "Forgive me if you thought I was."

Now she felt foolish. The first man who'd ever shown an inkling of interest in her, and she'd accused him of poking fun at her.

Hanging her head, she said softly, "Do you mind if we just talk?"

"I'd be delighted, Beulah."

"How did you know my name?"

"The doctor told me."

They spent the entire evening talking, and by the time the musicians took their break, Beulah was sure that the angels in heaven had finally smiled on her. Even if she never saw Ray Grimes again, she'd remember this night for the rest of her life.

On the opposite side of the room, Gray visited with one young lady after another.

It seemed the women of Dignity had despaired of earning his favor through culinary bribes and had turned to charm to gain his attention.

As he tried to make small talk, his gaze kept drifting to April. Henry was absent, but she had more than her share of suitors.

Around ten, he excused himself from a young girl of seventeen and made his way quickly across the room. "Miss Ludwig, may I have the pleasure of sharing some refreshments?"

Beulah's eyes widened. "Me?"

"You, Miss Ludwig."

"Bring her back to me," Ray called with a friendly grin.

Taking her arm, Gray escorted her to the punch bowl.

"You look lovely tonight, Miss Ludwig."

"I'm having a marvelous time." Her smile stretched across her face. "Want a cookie?" she blurted.

"A cookie?"

"Actually, I'm supposed to be tending the refreshment table, but Mrs. Steel said she'd watch it for me."

"Thank you, no cookies." Smiling down at her flushed face, Gray commented casually, "I see you have an admirer."

Beulah's gaze traveled to Ray, who was standing

on the sidelines. "He's taking pity on me. What do you know about him? He's new to the area, isn't he?"

"I just know what he's told me. He has no family to speak of. Got into the sales business in Illinois about five years ago. Likes to travel because he likes people, but hates being on the road all the time. Seems to be an honest man. Sells good equipment, doesn't try to take advantage. I like him."

"Yeah," she said wistfully. Her eyes returned to the medical equipment salesman and she sighed. "Me, too."

"Mary?"

The woman who stood before Gray the following week was luminous. Bright color tinged her cheeks and she was smiling.

Actually smiling.

"Dr. Fuller! Look at me! I feel wonderful!"

Gray walked across the room to greet her.

"You *look* wonderful!" He assessed her healthy glow. "What have you done to yourself, Mary?"

She practically floated into the examining room. "It's that elixir you gave me. It . . . Well, I haven't felt so good in I don't know when. I have such . . . *energy!* Why, I'm cleaning my house again, doing laundry. And Severn . . . he says he's got his wife back." Grasping Gray's hand, she smiled up at him. "How can I ever thank you, Doctor? I feel like a new woman!"

"The heavy flow?"

"Much lighter. So much so, I don't think surgery will be necessary."

Gray sat back and stared at her. The change was astonishing. Surely Pinkham's compound wasn't responsible. "Well, I can't say I'm anything but pleased that we finally found something that works for you. You look radiant."

Mary leaned forward anxiously. "I need more of the tonic."

"Well . . . yes, certainly. I'll get another bottle for you."

"Oh, good. Severn says I'm never to be without it ever again."

Gray moved to the shelf, poured more of the elixir into a small bottle and printed Mary's name on the label. With a slight hesitation, he handed the vial to her.

She looked at the tonic as if it were nectar from heaven. "Oh, thank you, Dr. Fuller! You don't know what this means to me."

"Just stay healthy, Mary. Follow the diet we discussed, as well as take the . . . tonic."

"You want to see me again in two weeks?"

"That's up to you—"

She suddenly looked frightened. "What about my tonic? I'll need more by then?"

"Whenever you run out, come back."

Clasping the compound to her chest, Mary skipped out of the office.

Dropping into his chair, Gray watched her disappear through the front door, singing.

*Singing!*

His eyes focused on the jug of compound, and he shook his head. Surely not . . . there was no way Pinkham's tonic had produced this wonder.

Was there?


Two days later, Charley Black sidled in the door of the waiting room just as Gray was about to pull down the shade and lock up for the night.

"Doc?"

"Charley. Something I can do for you?"

Charley was the town blacksmith, a great burly man who moved slowly and deliberately. Riley had laughingly commented once that he suspected Charley fell asleep between strikes of his hammer on a horseshoe.

"My Delilah says you gave Mary Rader some elixir that cured her. She says I should come and get some from you."

Gray's brow lifted with concern. "Are you ill?"

"Well, not so pert. I work long hours, you know. Just like Severn Rader."

"Severn Rader?"

Charley nodded. "Yeah . . . you know." He winked. "Severn."

"Are you saying you're tired all the time?"

"Delilah says so," Charley mumbled, his skin flushing crimson beneath its deep bronze tone. Gray was aware a man didn't like to discuss his personal life.

He hesitated, then decided there'd be no harm in giving Charley some of the elixir. The change in Mary was amazing; maybe it would give Charley a needed boost.

"Wait here. I'll get a bottle for you."

Charley shifted from one foot to the other, making the floor creak beneath his considerable bulk. Gray poured elixir into a smaller bottle and printed Charley's name on the label.

"This should help. One spoonful, twice a day. Come back in a week and let me take a look at you. All right?"

"I work long hours. Just like Severn," he reiterated.

Gray assumed Charley, like most men in Dignity, didn't want to be seen coming into the office. "Tell you what. My horse is favoring the right front. I'll bring him by later this week to have you take a look at him."

Relief flooded Charley's face. "Sure thing, Doc. Thanks."

Charley nodded his way out of the office, and Gray wearily rotated his head and shoulders. What made a man choose medicine as a vocation? His day started at first light and rarely ended before dark. At least once a week he was called out in the middle of the night, and often didn't get back home before dawn.

Well, Gray knew why he had taken up medicine and why he was practicing in Dignity. A man had to step out in faith, following where he believed God led. Sure, the hours were long, and the pay wasn't as good as it would be in Dallas. But this was where he belonged; he'd fallen in love with the town. God was good to allow him to serve in a place where the people gave in return.

"Is that a letter from Henry?"

Beulah caught up with April as she emerged from the post office Friday morning.

"Finally." She could hardly contain herself. Henry had been gone three weeks, and this was the only letter she'd received. Her eyes scanned it quickly as they walked along the street.

"How's the work going?"

"They've taken a room in San Antonio." April glanced up. "Things are going so well that Dan has written home to persuade the family to come there."

"San Antonio? What does that mean?"

"It means I'm out of a job, and Will will want to move there, too."

"Do you think the Pinkhams will actually go?"

"I'm sure Lydia won't want to."

"Henry really likes a big city."

"Well, it would seem that he does." She read on. "It's exciting, I guess. He went to hear Henry Ward Beecher preach, and he's attended political rallies. Henry says Dan sees the opportunity to make good contacts with druggists and patent medicine men. He thinks the business could be worth thousands if they explore the new market. It seems that finally we're making progress. Praise the Lord."

"But what if *Henry* wants to move there?"

April was forced to consider that eventuality. "I don't know. I'll wait to cross that bridge when I get to it."

"Coward."

"Me? What about you?"

"I don't understand."

"That young man you spent all your time with the other night."

"Ray?"

"Ray?" April's eyebrows arched.

"Ray Grimes. An equipment salesman. Dr. Fuller says he's a very nice young man."

"Uh-huh. What do you think?"

"I think . . . that I've never had such a wonderful time. He's coming back in two weeks and, well, we're going to have supper together." Her cheeks turned pink. "He . . . he really didn't understand why I have the nickname Porky."

"I'm glad," April said, and she was. It was about time some man appreciated Beulah's finer qualities. "You just make sure he treats you right."

As she walked home, April thought about the possibility of the Pinkhams moving. What would she do if Henry wanted to move? San Antonio was exciting, but she wasn't sure she'd want to live there. Nor did she like to think about leaving Grandpa, and Dignity. But if Henry were to decide to move . . .

For some reason, she didn't want to think about it.

207

• • •

Gray glanced out the window of his waiting room late that morning to see April and Beulah crossing the square. The sun glinted on April's light hair, and he wondered if, when his debt to Louis was paid off, he would pursue April. He laughed. If Francesca thought he was interested in another woman, she'd insist her father call for the entire balance owing at once, if not sooner.

Of course, there was one other minor problem: April was infatuated with Henry Long.

The door opened and Delilah Black came in.

Turning from the window, he greeted her. "Mrs. Black, how are you?"

"I'm fine. Just fine. Well, I think I'm fine. I don't know . . . for sure. It's my first, you know."

"Whoa," Gray cautioned. "Slow down."

Delilah flushed as prettily as a young girl, though she was well past thirty. "I . . . I . . . well, I want to talk to you."

"Certainly. I finished with my last patient fifteen minutes ago. Come into the examining room."

Delilah followed him, twisting the strings of her handbag tightly around her fingers.

"Have a seat," Gray invited, pointing to a straight-backed chair.

The woman perched uneasily on the edge of the seat.

"What can I do for you?"

"Well . . ." she flushed a deep red ". . . it's a little difficult for me."

"Just relax."

"I wish I could. It's just that this is so . . . well, personal." She twisted her bag nervously.

"How is Charley?" Gray asked, hoping to make her feel more at ease.

"Oh," she practically trilled, "Charley is just *fine!*"

"Good. The tonic I gave him—"

"Is *wonderful!*"

Sensing there was something he was missing, Gray paused, trying to form his next question. "I gather he's feeling better?"

"I've never seen him feeling *better.*"

"Are you and Charley having difficulty?"

"Oh, no! Morning sickness."

Gray nodded. "Morning sickness."

"You don't understand. If I am . . . with child, I'd be most happy to spend the entire day with my head in a chamber pot." She flushed a deeper crimson.

"So, you think you're with child?" Gray asked.

Delilah grinned. "Yes!"

"You're here to . . ."

"Have you confirm that I am in the family way. You see, Charley and I have been married twelve years, and I've always wanted children, but the good Lord never sent any until now. Oh, God is good!"

Mentally shaking the cobwebs out of his mind, Gray tried to follow her. "Well, before we get all excited, let's take a look."

Fifteen minutes later Delilah Black floated out of Gray's office a happy woman. She was, indeed, with child, and was rushing over to the livery to tell Charley the good news.

Gray slowly climbed the stairs to his rooms, shaking his head in disbelief.

*Interesting,* he thought as he pulled his boots off and lay back across the bed. He hoped Delilah Black would keep the news of Charley's incredible rebirth to herself, or he would have every man in Dignity flocking to his office for the compound.

## *Chapter Eleven*

"Dr. Fuller," the proprietor exclaimed as he entered the hotel dining room. "I have a nice window table waiting for you."

Francesca's gaze swept the diners with a haughty air. She had arrived late this afternoon to spy on Gray. Her monthly surveillance was wearing thin; it was all he could do to maintain a civil air.

He settled Francesca into her chair, and noticed that April and Riley were dining across the room. Struck by Riley's granddaughter's presence, he raised an eyebrow. The soft lamplight turned her hair to finely spun gold. She was laughing at something Riley was saying, her face animated, happy . . . so different from the opportunistic woman opposite him.

"Excuse me a moment."

Rancor tinged Francesca's voice as she glanced up. "Gray, you are not going to abandon me."

"No, I need to speak to someone."

Her mouth firmed, but Gray ignored the warning that she was on the verge of a temper tantrum.

After pausing to speak with a young couple sitting to their right, he crossed the room to Riley's table.

"Gray," the older man said, getting to his feet when he spotted him. "How nice to see you."

Gray shook his hand, his gaze assessing April. "Enjoying a special occasion?"

"No, no," Riley said. "Datha was gone tonight, so April and I decided to treat ourselves." He looked about the room. "Are you alone?"

"No, I'm with someone. I just wanted to say good evening." His gaze focused on April. "Miss Truitt."

She glanced toward Francesca sitting at a window table, and her smile was almost like that of the Cheshire cat. "Dr. Fuller."

"I've missed our checker games, but I hear you've been busy," Riley said.

"Very busy, but I hope to see you one night this week."

"Good. I'll look forward to it."

Turning back to April, Gray smiled. "I trust you are well, Miss Truitt?"

"Never felt better, Doctor. And you?"

"Very well, thank you."

Conspicuously consulting her menu, she parried softly, "Isn't that Miss DuBois with you?"

Gray turned around to look. "Why, yes, I believe it is. You have met, haven't you?"

"We've met." She burrowed her head deeper into the menu.

He was surprised to see the blush that crept into her cheeks. He should be ashamed of teasing her, but her looks—not always friendly ones—amused him. If it wasn't for that infernal compound separating them, April Truitt would have him worried. He'd never met a woman who quite captured his attention like this. . . .

"How is Henry? Is he still away on business?"

"Yes. He wishes he could be here, but duty calls."

"How distressing. Are you expecting him back soon?" Gray had never noticed it before, but she was gorgeous when she was furious.

"I'm expecting him back any day now, thank you."

"You and *Henry?*" Grandpa blustered. "What's this?"

"Grandpa, you know I see Henry on occasion," April murmured, shooting Gray a confrontational look.

"Perhaps you and Henry and Francesca and I can make an evening of it soon?"

"I don't think so, Doctor." She snapped the menu shut. "We're busy."

He smiled, accepting the parry.

"April!" Riley scolded. "Where are your manners?"

With a disarmingly generous surrender, Gray said, "It's all right, Riley. I understand when a person is busy. Please give Henry my regards, Miss Truitt."

She sent him a scornful glance.

Chuckling, he clasped Riley warmly on the shoulder, and returned to Francesca.

"What's this about Henry?" Grandpa was saying as he walked away.

Gray grinned. That would teach her to mess with him.

The following month the community was struck down with colds and congestion. Gray was up half the nights and worked long days. His temper was frayed as he made the long trip to Dallas midmonth. Louis had summoned him. Did he intend to demand repayment of the loan now that Francesca had informed her father the marriage was off? If he did, Gray would have no choice but to close his practice and move to a larger city. The loan was sizable and must be repaid. Citizens in Dignity did not always have the funds to pay for medical services in cash, and he kept his fees nominal.

The air had a bitter feel. Gray wouldn't even be surprised to see snow, he decided, as the buggy pulled up in front of the DuBois mansion. The house was outrageously ostentatious, and he didn't have time for dalliances.

A party was in full progress, light streaming from every window. He was shown inside by a black-suited servant. Francesca saw him immediately and latched on to his arm.

"Darling!"

"Francesca."

"Gray, my boy," Louis boomed from across the room when he saw them. "Come over here, son. There's someone I want you to meet."

Crossing the room with Francesca on his arm, Gray approached the senior physician.

"Hampton, I want you to meet Gray Fuller. Gray, Hampton Brinkman. Gray has recently opened a practice in a nearby coastal town. Dignity. Ever hear of it?"

"Can't say that I have."

Louis laughed. "Don't feel bad. Nobody else has, either!"

Gray shook hands with Hampton.

"Hampton is interested in having you join him in his clinic. You two might want to discuss—"

"Not this evening," Gray interrupted with a polite but firm refusal. When Louis frowned disapprovingly, he softened his stance. "I've had a long trip, and an even longer week, and I don't wish to discuss business this evening. I'm afraid I would be a poor conversationalist."

Louis looked perturbed, but recovered sufficiently to give Hampton a jovial slap on the back. "Perhaps tomorrow at dinner, Hampton. I'm sure Gray can—"

"Sorry, but I'll be leaving before noon."

"Oh, Gray, I've made plans for tomorrow evening," Francesca protested. "Surely you can stay a *few* days. Adele Mason's having a holiday soiree Sunday evening, and I told her we would attend."

"I'm sorry, Francesca. I have a patient who is running a high fever. I have to return immediately."

"Gray—"

"Louis. Hampton? Perhaps another time."

Gray threaded his way back across the room. Francesca would be furious, but he couldn't do it. He couldn't spend another night in the company of swine who swore to uphold the medical oath based on the principles and ideals of the ancient Greek physician Hippocrates, but thought of nothing more than lining their pockets at the expense of the ill.

"Your hat and coat, sir," the butler said.

"Gray, you were *rude* to Mr. Brinkman," Francesca murmured as she caught up with him.

"It was rude of your father to summon me all this way only to waylay me. I will not go into a clinic. Do you understand me, Francesca?" He paused, his eyes meeting hers directly.

"I don't know what's happened to you—I barely recognize the Gray I once knew."

"I am the same man. You have chosen to ignore every word I've said to you since I moved to Dignity."

"My father wants the best for us!"

"Come with me, Francesca. We'll walk in the park and discuss this. I can't stay here."

She gazed at him, sure of her power to control. "No. You stay, and we'll discuss our differences later."

"Don't make this more difficult, Francesca. Come with me now."

With a shake of her curls, she dismissed him. "You know I can't leave. Papa would never forgive me. He has important associates here tonight, Gray. He expects you to mingle and help entertain. Why are you acting this way?"

He gazed at her intently. "In the future, I suggest you consult with me before you plan my life." He opened the door. "Are you coming?"

Her eyes were filled with angry humiliation. "No."

"Then I bid you good night."

"Gray!" she called as he strode quickly toward his carriage. "Gray! I will *not* have you walking out on me like this. What will people think?"

He stepped into the waiting buggy, picked up the reins, and the horse trotted off.

## Chapter Twelve

The wind was sharper than April had anticipated. Drawing her cape tighter, she slapped the reins against the horse's rump. Usually she didn't mind the five-mile trip to Burgess, a neighboring community, but at the moment she wished she'd picked another day to hand out pamphlets on Mrs. Pinkham's elixir.

Riley didn't know what she was doing. He thought she was visiting, which, of course, she planned to do before the day was over.

She spent the morning handing out pamphlets. The response was good, and she considered the long hours in the cold wind productive.

By noon she was chilled to the bone. Hurrying down the sidewalk, rubbing her hands together, she saw the sign she'd been searching for: Clara's Chocolate Shoppe. A cup of hot chocolate and a piece of short-bread were exactly what she needed.

A woman in bright taffeta crossed the street and stepped onto the sidewalk in front of April.

The woman, though beautiful, was wearing a dress far too colorful for daytime. The girl, for she was hardly more than a girl, wore heavy makeup—eyes outlined with kohl, rouge too red for her milky skin.

"Excuse me," April murmured, stepping around her.

"Oh, Miss Truitt!"

April turned at the sound of her name.

"Yes?"

She recognized the small boy who had loitered around the table she had handed out pamphlets from. Approaching her, he extended a stack of pamphlets.

"You dropped these."

"Thank you." Patting the lad on the head, April stuffed the brochures in her bag and walked on. That young woman's hat was all wrong, too. Dark green with a large plume that dipped over her forehead.

As April stepped inside Clara's, a bell over the door announced her arrival. The warmth felt won-derful. Shivering, she smiled at all the delicious smells. A morsel to eat and a nice warm place to rest after the long, cold morning were just what she needed.

"Miss?"

"A table for one, please."

"This way."

She followed the server to a table in the center of the room, admiring the crisp white cloths and blue china.

"Thank you. A cup of hot chocolate, please."

Slipping off her gloves, she studied the small room. Dignity had nothing so lavish. She must bring Beulah the next time she came; they could drink hot chocolate and shop to their hearts' content. Smiling, she recalled the young woman she'd seen on the sidewalk. Though her makeup had been too heavy, she was quite beautiful. Worldly, unlike any woman April knew. She wished Beulah were here to share the adventure.

The server returned with a pot of chocolate. Picking up the menu, April tried to decide whether she wanted a sandwich, as well, as she listened to the babble of talk around her.

"Here you are, miss. That will be ten cents."

April handed the girl fifteen cents and received a light curtsy as a thank-you. She sipped the chocolate, letting its warmth flow through her.

The bell over the door tinkled again, and a woman sitting behind her gasped. Turning to look over her shoulder, April was surprised to see the heavily made-up young woman she'd encountered on the sidewalk earlier entering the place.

"Look at that. Can you believe it?" the woman behind her whispered to her friend.

"Isn't that one of *those* women?"

"It is, I'm sure of it. She works at Emogene's Pleasure Palace."

"No! Why would *she* come in here?"

"Yes, why? How brazen to parade in as if she owned the place."

"How do you know she's one of Emogene's girls?"

"I saw her coming out of that . . . that establishment yesterday. Do you know they dance nearly naked over there, as well as . . . well, I don't need to tell you what else they do in there." The woman sniffed. "Disgraceful, it is."

Curious, April glanced up as the young woman gazed directly at her.

Not knowing where to look, she smiled timidly back.

The girl headed in a beeline for her table. Stopping in front of her, she asked, "Are you April Truitt?"

Glancing around, April realized she was speaking to her. "Why . . . yes," she admitted hesitantly, wondering how the young woman knew her name.

"I'm Grace Pruitt."

Nodding, April smiled at the similarity of their names, but failed to see how that concerned her.

"Henry Long's intended."

Her smile faded. "Henry's what?"

"Henry's intended." The girl stared at her. "I gather he hasn't mentioned me to you?"

Shaking her head, April searched for her voice. When she found it, she hastened to correct the woman. "You're mistaken. *I'm* Henry's intended."

"No, you're the one who's made a mistake." Grace slid into the opposite chair, fixing her eyes on her.

"*I'm* engaged to marry Henry Trampas Long. We're planning a fall wedding."

"See here—"

The girl's face hardened. "*You* see here, sister. *You leave him alone.* Understand?"

April not only didn't understand, she was thunderstruck by the girl's assertion. Her Henry? Engaged to this woman? Why, that was ludicrous. Henry would never associate with a woman from Emogene's Pleasure Palace!

"I don't know who you are, but there must be a mista—"

"The only mistake is yours," Grace whispered urgently. Leaning forward, she gripped the edge of the table. "Henry is *my* intended, and I want you to leave him alone!"

As the allegation started to sink in, April felt ill. The room was suddenly too hot, and she could feel the eyes of the other patrons on her.

"How do you know who I am?" she murmured, humiliated by the scene the girl was making.

"I heard the boy call your name. It dawned on me you must be April Truitt, and I remembered the tintype Henry showed me. The one you had made when the traveling photographer came through Dignity last summer?"

She *had* given Henry a picture made by a traveling photographer. April's heart sank.

"Have I made myself clear? Henry is mine. You leave him alone."

April nodded, numb now.

Grace looked around the café, glaring at the two women sitting directly behind April, who were eavesdropping.

Suddenly unable to breathe, April reached blindly for the bag containing the pamphlets, got up and walked regally out of the café, her cheeks on fire.

As the door closed behind her, she broke into a run, covering a full three blocks before slowing to a fast walk. It had to be a mistake. That was it, a silly mistake. The young woman had confused her with somebody else.

No, she said she'd recognized her by her picture.

Then someone was using Henry's name.

Yes! That was it. Some cad was using Henry's name!

But how had the girl known *her* name? How had the impostor gotten her picture?

"It doesn't make sense," she murmured.

Henry wouldn't dream of seeing another woman. He wasn't the sort of man to trifle with two women's hearts. He worked day and night to make the Pinkham compound a success; he didn't have time to court two women . . . even if he did have the inclination, which she knew, absolutely *knew,* he didn't.

She relaxed. He'd told her he loved her, and she believed him.

It was all some horrible mistake.

Glancing over her shoulder, she shuddered. Some big, horrible mistake.

• • •

"Beulah, what if it's true? What if Henry has been seeing that woman?"

Henry was still in San Antonio, but April wouldn't have discussed the matter with him anyway. The young woman's claims were just too preposterous! He would be embarrassed and angry with April for even listening to the girl, much less casting doubt on his gentlemanly conduct.

And she didn't believe this Grace Pruitt, whoever she was. It was a mistake, pure and simple, and she was going to put the incident out of her mind.

"How did she know who you were?" Beulah asked.

"She said Henry had shown her a picture of me. That one I had made last summer." April paced the pharmacy, feeling upset. She hadn't slept all night for thinking about the bizarre turn of events. Henry, a philanderer? Impossible. In his youth, perhaps, but not now. He was too responsible. Too decent to involve himself with another woman.

"I don't know, perhaps she isn't quite right. Maybe she just picked me out of the crowd—"

"But she knows Henry."

"I don't know what the explanation is, but I'm certain there is one. Henry would never do something like that. Never."

"Well, it's simple enough to find out."

Pausing, April looked at her warily. When she got that tone in her voice, her brilliance was about to surface.

"How?"

Scooping up another bit of ice cream, she grinned. "Make Henry set a wedding date. He's been dilly-dallying far too long. You claim he wants to marry you, so make him officially announce the engagement."

April felt sick at the thought. She wanted his proposal to be romantic and straight from the heart, not forced upon him, to prove his loyalty.

No, she couldn't make Henry propose to her. Besides, she didn't necessarily want to get married yet.

"I can't do that."

"Why not? If he intends to ask you anyway, what difference will it make if you hurry the process along?"

"We've talked about it," she admitted, "but it doesn't seem right. Obviously this Grace Pruitt has me confused with someone else."

But by the end of the week, April's nerves were taut from suspicion. True, Henry hadn't asked her to marry him, but Grace Pruitt concerned her. Was Grace mistaken, or was Henry seeing two women at one time? If he was playing games, she intended to find out.

She reread Henry's recent letter.

*My dear April,*
*Our efforts are finally being rewarded. Dan and I have nearly walked off the soles of our shoes, but*

*we convinced three pharmacists to make the compound available in their places of business. The weather has been cooperative. Cold, but no rain or snow as yet. I look forward to seeing you soon.*
*Love,*
*Henry*


April let the letter fall to her lap. One letter in two months.

One measly letter.

They were working hard, and it hadn't snowed yet. Not much to hold her until he got back.


Gray looked up from his desk the following week and saw Henry Long standing in the doorway to his office.

"Henry, you're just the man I'm wanting to see."

"Me?" Closing the door, he limped into the room.

"Toe bothering you again?"

"It's even worse than it was. I can't stand to touch it," Henry replied, taking off his hat. "What did you want to see me about?"

Gray ushered him into the examining room and closed the door. "Can we speak in confidence?"

Frowning, Henry nodded. "Certainly. What is it?"

Gray cleared his throat. "I need some Pinkham compound. A good deal of it."

Henry stared at him for a moment, then threw his head back, laughing.

"Did I say something amusing?"

When he finished laughing, Henry just looked at

him. "I thought you were adamantly against the elixir."

"I have been, but I've been conducting an experiment on my own regarding the tonic. I must say, it does seem to have limited success among my patients."

Henry broke out laughing again. "I assume you don't want April to know about this."

"I'd rather she didn't," Gray conceded.

"Don't worry, I understand. We men have to stick together." He punched him in the arm. "Know what I mean?"

"Can you provide me with the tonic on a regular basis?" Gray asked.

"I can get you a barnfull. But why me? Why not purchase it from your original source? Was it April? Oh, that's rich. She's been selling you the tonic!"

"Certainly not."

Henry chuckled.

"It was Beulah Ludwig. She brought me some to try, and I said I wouldn't, but I ended up using it. Now I'm out, and my patients are demanding more."

"Why not just tell your patients to buy it from us? It's readily available."

"I can't do that." Gray was at his mercy, much as he hated the thought. "As you might suspect, I would look like a fool in their eyes if they found out I am prescribing a tonic I've adamantly advised against. I plan to endorse the elixir—but gradually."

Henry grinned. "I see your problem. Well, don't

worry, I can supply you with all the tonic you want. Unfortunately, our prices have recently gone up." He climbed onto the examining table.

Gray calmly removed Henry's shoe. "How recently?"

Grinning from ear to ear, Henry said. "About sixty seconds ago."

"Well, that is unfortunate timing for me," Gray admitted, removing his patient's sock.

"Careful, Doc, it's sore as a boil."

"I can see that."

"You understand about the price hike. A man's got to make a profit when he can."

Gray nodded. "Oh, I understand." Glancing up, he smiled. "As you will understand when I tell you, much as I hate to put you through it, I'm going to have to do some in-depth work on that toe, Henry."

Henry suddenly paled as the implication of the words sank in.

"And unfortunately, it's going to get real nasty." Gray grinned.

Henry emerged from Gray's office a half hour later, obviously shaken.

Spotting April coming out of Ludwig's Pharmacy, he called her name. He limped across the cobblestone street and caught her by the hand, his cheeks ruddy from the trials of the past half hour. "I just got back and stopped to talk to the doctor. Look at you! You look wonderful!"

April fought the insane desire to snub him and enlighten him at the same time. "Thank you, Henry. I didn't know you were back. I take it your trip was successful?"

"Extremely so, my love. Lydia is pleased with the progress." He smiled. "I also just picked up a large account right here in town."

"Oh? Who?"

"I'm not at liberty to say, but it's a nice one." Taking her arm, he steered her away from the damp, foul winds coming off the water, insisting they spend a private moment having tea at the hotel before he returned to work.

"How have you been, love?" he asked as he gave their order, then settled back in his chair to gaze at her.

They were seated at a window table, overlooking the square. April should have felt elated; Henry was back, and the silly misunderstanding about Grace could readily be cleared up. But the heaviness in her chest was like a millstone.

Taking her hand between his, he smiled at her. "You grow prettier with each passing day."

"When did you get back?"

"An hour ago. I believe we made some real progress."

"That's nice." Distractedly, she cast about for a casual way to bring up the subject of weddings.

"Did I mention three apothecaries have agreed to carry the elixir and highly recommend it?"

"Yes, in your . . . brief letter. That should go a long

way toward convincing others to carry it, as well."

Tea was brought, and a plate of tiny sugar cookies.

"Did you hear Sylvia Smitts and Ben Logan have set a date for their wedding?" she asked.

"No, I hadn't," Henry said, munching on a cookie.

April toyed with her spoon. "They're planning a spring event. Isn't that romantic?"

"I suppose so. Did Lydia tell you we needed more pamphlets?"

"Yes. We're having some made up this week." April casually took a sip of tea. "Priscilla and Jeremy have set a date for their wedding, too."

"Have they?" He chose another cookie. "I think we should have a larger printing this time."

"I'll tell Lydia. Priscilla and Jeremy have decided to get married in June. Priscilla wants a garden wedding."

"Uh-huh. Where's our waitress? The tea is cold."

Henry signaled for service as April tried to think of a way to catch him in his duplicity—if that was what he was practicing.

"Henry?"

"Hmm?"

"Isn't it wonderful when two people care deeply for one another, and marry?"

He smiled at her, his eyes cajoling. "Of course, love. Now, drink your tea before it gets cold."

She wasn't letting him off the hook that easy. "Henry—"

"You look very lovely today, my dear. Is that a new dress you're wearing?"

"No, Henry, it's old," April whispered miserably, realizing he wasn't taking the bait.

"Henry!" Dan Pinkham crossed the dining room floor, apparently in a big hurry.

Getting to his feet, Henry frowned. "Dan?"

"I've been looking everywhere for you. Mother wants to talk to you. . . ." Glancing at April, Dan said apologetically, "I hope I'm not interrupting."

"Not at all," Henry told him. Kissing April's hand, he smiled. "We weren't discussing anything important, were we, love?"

Later that afternoon, April pushed the door open to Gray's clinic. She was relieved to see the waiting room empty.

Calling, "Dr. Fuller?" she waited.

"In here."

Closing the outer door, she followed his voice to the office. "Hello," she said, holding something behind her.

"Miss Truitt?" He dropped an instrument in a drawer. "Slumming this afternoon?"

"No." She gave him a singularly sweet smile. "I have something for you."

"I'm in no mood for games." He frowned. "What is it?"

"This." She held out the pillbox hat. "Funny how you keep misplacing it. Datha found it in our trash this morning. Wonder why?"

"Because I put it there." Slamming the drawer, he

muttered, "That thing is like a homing pigeon."

Laughing, she tossed Francesca's gift onto a chair in the corner.

"Did you stop by just to annoy me?"

"Yes. You're on to me, aren't you?"

Why had she stopped by? The hat was a pretense. Datha could have brought it to him.

"Too bad, because, unfortunately, I have you figured out."

"I doubt that." Perching on the edge of his desk, she watched him work. "A man never has a woman figured out—don't you know that yet?"

"Where's Riley today? I stopped by the mortuary this morning, and he was gone."

"You're not going to believe this, but he's walking. Two miles after breakfast every morning."

Gray looked surprised. "That's good news."

"Yes." April ran a gloved finger lightly along the edge of his desk, frowning when it came up dusty. "I say this with great trepidation, but maybe modern medicine isn't so bad, after all."

He gazed at her, grinning. "This from the Pinkham camp?"

"No, this from a woman who is open to new ideas, as you should be."

Moving to the window, she heaved a long, pent-up sigh. She was here because she needed a shoulder to cry on, and his was the broadest, most available one in town.

"Is something wrong?"

"No, why do you ask?"

"You just blew my curtains out the window."

"I'm restless, that's all. Now that I can't sell the compound, I don't have enough to keep me busy."

Gray leaned back in his chair. "I saw Henry this afternoon."

She turned from the window, to find him observing her. "Did you?"

"His toe was giving him trouble again."

"Yes—we had tea earlier." She glanced out the window again, watching the fading light cast shadows through the town.

"Is something bothering you? I know you don't find my company that stimulating, but you seem a little distracted this afternoon."

Rubbing her arms, she softly said, "I tried to get him to propose to me."

There was a short silence. "Who? Henry?"

"He wouldn't do it."

Why was she telling him this? It certainly wasn't Gray's "bedside manner" that prompted her to confide in him. She longed to tell him about the woman in Burgess who claimed to be engaged to Henry, but feared he would only laugh at her.

"And that concerns you?"

His dry humor made *her* laugh. At the moment she wanted so badly to tell him about Henry's infidelity, but how could she when he wasn't taking her seriously? She couldn't talk to Grandpa, and Beulah's perception of Henry was slanted. What was she to do?

"He says he doesn't want to get married until he is financially able."

"Sounds reasonable. What's the big hurry?"

"I want to make certain he's not playing me for a fool," she murmured, her fingertips resting against her lips as she watched a young couple strolling across the street.

The doctor's tone was somber, more evasive now. "Do you have reason to suspect he's playing you for a fool?"

"No, of course not."

"Then why worry about it?"

April turned again from the window, embarrassed that she had bothered him with her problems. Francesca would not appreciate another woman crying on his shoulder.

"I'm sorry. I've taken up too much of your time."

She grabbed her bag and swallowed against the lump in her throat. "Take better care of the hat."

Waving goodbye, she walked out to the waiting room.

"Miss Truitt!"

She turned to find him standing in the doorway of the examining room.

"Yes?"

"Next time you find my hat?"

Her brows lifted.

"Lose it for me. All right?"

She grinned. "You lose it—properly for once."

She turned to leave, then suddenly turned back. "Dr. Fuller?"

"Yes?"

"Thanks for listening to my blathering."

A smile formed on his lips. "I'm always here, Miss Truitt."

"That's very gracious of you," she admitted. Their eyes met, and she sensed he knew that she was troubled.

"If you change your mind and want to talk, I'll be in the office late tonight."

Gray stared at the closed door, wishing he'd had enough courage to press April for more information. He had a fairly good idea what was wrong. Something had happened to make her doubt Henry, otherwise she wouldn't have come in here to talk. He knew that irresponsible rogue couldn't avoid discovery for long.

Gray pulled out a chair and sat down, remembering how vulnerable she had looked. He didn't want her hurt.

*Lord, help me to help her. She's young and impressionable, and men like Henry should be—* He wanted to say *shot,* but didn't. *He should not prey on innocent women.*

## Chapter Thirteen

Holiday festivities came and went and winter got down to business. Gray thought he'd seen the last of Francesca until spring, but during a mild spell in late January she arrived, looking half-frozen from the journey, but bearing gold-embossed party invitations.

He listened as she prattled on about some plan—a party, the largest Dignity had ever seen. When he protested, she shook her head and accused him of not wanting to reimburse "dear papa" for the time and money he had invested in Gray's career.

"A party—to express your gratitude to your patients, darling. Why do you fight me when it's only your welfare I'm concerned about?"

"The last thing I want is a party."

"But you will see, *chéri*—the town will bless you." That said, she motioned for the two men to unload the overburdened wagon.

Gray stood back, bit his lip and silently vowed he would never borrow another cent the rest of his life.

Francesca was reluctant to invite "everyone in town"—she wanted the riffraff excluded. But Gray said everyone or no one.

She agreed, though testily, and he reserved the town hall for the event. A winter festival, he called it, and she corrected him: a reception. It was a *reception*.

"Didn't I tell you it would be wonderful?" she enthused as they watched the decorations go up.

Gray looked at the ceiling of the large room, which was draped with bolts of blue and orange fabric, with large paper flowers fastening the ends in each corner. "It's a little . . . colorful."

"No, it isn't. It's perfect."

Perfectly gaudy. But Gray wasn't looking for a fight.

More paper flowers filled large urns sitting in corners and dotted throughout the room.

A long table groaned under the weight of finger sandwiches, tea cookies, fruit in large crystal bowls and a lavish ice sculpture in the form of an elegant swan. Francesca had brought along a staff of servants to help serve.

"It's just as I envisioned it," she exclaimed, her blue velvet skirt billowing as she turned, viewing the room with delight. Seldom had Gray seen her so adamant about a project.

"When the guests arrive, you and I will greet them at the door. Then Samuel will take their coats, and Suzanne will serve them. The music will have begun before anyone arrives. There will be dancing, conversation and very little business talk." She smiled. "I know how you hate business talk."

They moved through the hall, overseeing the frenzied preparations for tonight's events.

"I still think it's too elaborate," Gray told her.

"You worry too much. I *want* it to be special." She tightened her hold on his arm. "I want them to know who I am."

"And who are you?"

"Why, I'm going to be your fiancée once again," Francesca said, her gaze daring him to dispute her.

"You've gone to a great deal of trouble and expense. I hope you won't be disappointed."

"I won't, you'll see. They'll be talking about this party for years to come."

Gray didn't doubt that.

The first guests arrived promptly at seven o'clock.

Gray introduced each one to Francesca, and she gingerly shook hands. Murmuring a greeting, they timidly entered the lavishly decorated room, eyes wide with curiosity.

Beulah and Raymond came in and chatted for a few minutes before moving to the refreshment table.

April arrived with Riley closer to seven-thirty.

"Francesca, April Truitt and Riley Ogden, her grandfather. Riley regularly beats me at checkers."

"I am so pleased to meet you," Francesca said.

"And we're pleased to meet such a lovely friend of Dr. Fuller's. He's been a godsend to our town." Riley took her hand.

"I'm sure he has," Francesca said, "though we do miss him terribly in Dallas."

Gray noticed Henry was absent again. Was the pompous idiot spending his evening with his other woman, leaving April to make excuses for him?

Murmuring a soft greeting, April brushed past him, trailing the scent of lily of the valley as she entered the gaily decorated hall. He had a strong urge to follow her, but refrained from doing so.

Disgusted with himself for what he was thinking, Gray knew he should have never allowed Francesca to hold this party. She didn't understand the citizens of Dignity and would end up insulting the very people whose trust he'd tried so hard to gain.

People were slow to mingle. The four musicians played violin and viola, classical music Francesca favored but few in Dignity enjoyed.

The guests were reluctant to dance. Instead, they stood in small groups, awkwardly holding the china plates Francesca had transported from Dallas, and staring at the strange sandwiches the white-coated hired help kept offering. When an hour had passed, and still no one was dancing, Francesca became more and more frustrated.

"What is wrong with them?" she hissed to Gray. "Why aren't they dancing?"

"Perhaps this isn't their kind of music," he suggested, recalling the livelier tunes played at summer picnics and get-togethers.

"How could that be? Well, never mind. We'll show them how to waltz properly."

Leading him on to the dance floor, she looked around, smiling, her eyes encouraging others to follow.

"Have you ever seen such a flop?" Beulah whispered as she and April stood on the sidelines. Ray Grimes was off getting punch.

"I feel rather sorry for her," April admitted as she enviously watched how gracefully Gray guided Francesca around the floor. "Do you think he'll formally announce their engagement tonight?" She noted the way the Frenchwoman looked up into his face, as if they were the only two people in the room.

April realized he didn't look quite as enthralled. Still, she envied the woman. If Henry ever looked at her that way, she'd be the happiest female on earth.

Or would she? Was it Henry she wanted? Or the handsome doctor who appeared to be enamored with Miss DuBois? Something told April that Gray wasn't as happy and devoted as he wanted everyone to think.

"What is wrong with these ungrateful ninnies?" Francesca huffed. "They stand around in their dowdy dresses and their shiny suits and stare as if they've never seen a waltz before. Have they no manners? These are the people you want to spend the rest of your life with?"

She was working herself up into a frenzy again. Gray saw the signs and hoped to avoid a scene. Had she listened, she would know Dignity was a simple town with simple ways.

"Just because they're not dancing doesn't mean they're not having a good time. Relax, they can see you're upset."

"But they're not even trying to mingle, or to talk, or to enjoy the fine things I've brought for them to enjoy."

"You talk as if they're impoverished children. They don't need to be plied with gifts for you to win their favor."

"Nonsense, gifts can achieve anything one wants. I'd hoped to show them the social niceties that aren't available in this boorish town—"

"Show them, or show me?"

"Honestly, Gray. You're so defensive. After all,

there's precious little here for you, if you'd only admit it. Tell me you don't miss the opera, the symphony, the plays. There's nothing—" her gaze swept the room pitilessly "—of . . . social value here."

Clell Miller picked that time to strip off his coat, unbutton his shirt, cup his hand beneath his armpit and pump his arm, resulting in an obscene noise that sent Missy Parker into peals of mirth.

Francesca looked faint as the room erupted in laughter. Clell's mother swatted him, even though he was full grown.

"Some may be lacking in social graces, but they're warm and giving people," Gray said. "And they need me."

"Hah! Anyone would do. These people aren't discriminating."

"No, they need *me,*" he insisted, knowing that he needed Dignity, and its people, as much as they needed his doctoring skills.

All in all, the party fell far short of Francesca's expectations.

The crowning blow came when Clarence Cole burst into his rendition of a song he had written, "Rooster in the Henhouses, Hidey Ho," while clicking spoons against his leg in a well-meaning, albeit disastrous, attempt to liven up the party.

Francesca's sour look turned rancid when Clarence asked the string quartet to jump in anytime they felt like it.

She pouted the rest of the evening, leaving the social

amenities to Gray. Around nine o'clock the guests started filing out of the hall.

Gray stood at the door, saying good-night. They were gracious but unable to stop sending curious glances at Francesca, who cloistered herself away in a remote corner.

Gray was embarrassed for her—and by her—but he kept his temper in check. What he'd really like to do was walk away from her. All he wanted was to be the best doctor he knew how in order to help the people of Dignity.

The evening ended on a dour note. Decorations were stripped and packed into a carriage, to be transported back to Dallas. Expensive chocolates were put back in boxes and cases to be used at a later time.

All in all, the party was a flop.


"April, could you send the boys more of the elixir? And more pamphlets? They're so busy they don't have time to come get them."

"Of course, Mrs. Pinkham. I'll go right away."

"If you don't mind. I'll have Charlie put the boxes in your carriage."

Within the hour Lydia's son Charlie had loaded the vehicle, and April, making up yet another excuse to Riley why she would be gone for the day, was on her way to Burgess to help them with the new outpost. The sun was shining through the bare branches of maple trees. Her mind traveled back to the DuBois party the night before. It had been a grand affair, and she felt sorry for Francesca that people hadn't responded to her efforts.

"She obviously wanted to prove something to us," Beulah had speculated as they'd got their coats to leave.

"Such as?"

"That she's better than we are."

"I don't think so. I think she's only trying to fit in, and the town isn't helping any."

"You're too nice. She was playing queen to the peasants, and when we didn't drop to kiss her feet she got in a snit. I feel sorry for Dr. Fuller. He was embarrassed."

"He was . . . uncomfortable," April had to admit.

The Fuller–DuBois alliance was puzzling. Gray and Francesca didn't fit together. They were oil and water, sugar and salt, vinegar and sarsaparilla. They just didn't match. Some would say the same of her and Henry. Even she was having second thoughts at times. Henry didn't seem eager to commit himself to a wedding date, and she wasn't so sure she was ready, either. He was beginning to look like the scoundrel others had warned her about.

April delivered the supplies to Dan and Will at their hotel. The building's interior was sad, with dull, faded paper, the hallway poorly lighted. She was disappointed she'd missed Henry, yet strangely relieved. Will said he was out making contacts.

The encounter with Grace refused to leave her. At the oddest times April resented Henry, feeling as if he had betrayed her, when in fact she didn't know that. One day she was going to muster enough courage to come right out and confront him with Grace's strange accusation—let him assure her it was laughable. Perhaps then she could regain her former trust and affection for him.

"Do you need to get back right away?" Will asked.

"No, just as long as I return before dark. Why?"

"Could you take a few of these bottles to the Brown Pharmacy?"

Agreeing to make the delivery, April left the hotel shortly before noon. For the next hour, she window-shopped. Finally purchasing new gloves and a soft cotton camisole, she left the store feeling good. There was nothing like a shopping trip to take a girl's mind off men.

When she realized it was noon, she went inside the Green Palm to have lunch. As she was being seated, it occurred to her that she was near Clara's, the café where she had encountered Grace Pruitt three weeks earlier.

Glancing around the room, she was relieved to see she hadn't been followed.

*This is silly. The woman made a mistake.* Somewhere in the area there was a conniving man by the name of Henry who was toying with two women's affections. That man was not her Henry. *Her* Henry Trampas Long was at this moment walking the streets, intent on building a secure future for her.

No sooner had the thought occurred to her than she

sensed someone approaching her table. With a feeling of dread, she looked up, to see Grace Pruitt coming toward her with a full head of steam.

"*You!*" the woman practically shouted.

Closing her eyes, April sank back in her chair. This was too much. What *was* it with her? Did she lurk around Burgess's eating establishments, waiting to see April pull into town? How did Grace know when she conducted business here? Uncanny luck?

"Please," April murmured, praying she wouldn't make a scene. Dressed the way the girl was, and with Emogene's Pleasure Palace a block down the street, it didn't take a clairvoyant to guess her occupation. "You have me confused with someone else. Would you please just move on?"

April opened the large menu to hide behind as Grace stopped at her table, pointing a bejeweled finger at her. "You conniving hussy!"

All sounds in the room ceased, and everyone turned to look in their direction.

"Will you please lower your voice—"

"No! I told you to leave Henry alone, but you didn't listen. You continue to see him—and don't try to tell me you haven't because I have contacts—*reliable* contacts—who tell me different."

April stood up and reached for her cloak. She would not sit here and be subject to such humiliation. The young woman was clearly deranged.

"No, you don't, sister!"

Before April realized what was coming, Grace reached out and grabbed a handful of her hair.

Unable to move, April ordered through clenched teeth, "Let go of my hair!" Trying to hold on to her cloak and bag, she reached for Grace's arm to break her hold.

"Henry is mine!" Grace yanked her hair hard, then whacked her, bringing tears to her eyes and knocking the bag to the floor, spilling brown bottles of Pinkham compound.

"You have *obviously* made a mistake! My Henry is Henry Trampas Long!" April grunted, trying to jerk free.

Grace tightened her grip, dislodging April's hat. It fell to the floor, pulling loose strands of hair with it.

"Henry Trampas Long is *my* Henry!" Grace muttered through clenched teeth. "And I want *you* to keep your lily-white hands off him!"

Tears spurted in April's eyes, and she saw stars as Grace continued to pull her hair out by the roots.

"Ladies! Ladies!" the proprietor shouted. His handlebar mustache stood straight out as he waded in to separate the two.

"She's no lady!" Grace gasped, pinning April to the floor in a bruising headlock.

"Please . . ." the man begged, trying to pry them apart.

"Someone call a constable," April choked out, trying to break her assailant's painful hold.

"Ladies, I insist you stop this!"

A couple of men on the sidelines stepped in to help.

Shaking them off, Grace stood like a spitting panther, glaring at April, who was trying to pick herself off the floor.

"That woman is seeing my fiancé!"

"I am not! I don't know who your fiancé is!"

"Liar!"

"Idiot!"

Grandpa would *die* if he could see her now, but April wasn't about to let this . . . this beast scratch her eyes out!

Straightening, Grace struck her across the cheek with a white glove.

April glared back at her.

"I challenge you to a duel."

"A what?"

"A duel."

The men in the crowd shrank back with muffled oohs.

"A *what?*" April repeated, certain she'd misunderstood. Women didn't fight duels. Men did.

"You heard me right. A duel. Saturday. Miller's Glen. Sunrise."

Grace's words refused to register. A *duel?* April stood paralyzed in shock while everyone around her babbled with a mixture of consternation and humor.

Two women, dueling!

Who'd ever heard of such a thing?

Someone took April by the arm as the constable arrived. Grace lunged again, making another attempt to get at her.

"Stop it! Right now!" the officer insisted.

Order was quickly restored. Overturned tables were set back in place as a couple of stout men led a still-spitting Grace out the front door. "Miller's Glen, Saturday morning! You'd better be there or I'll come after you!"

"Ha," April muttered, trying to pin mussed strands of hair back into place. "You don't know where I live."

"I heard that! You live in Dignity!"

April hated Henry at that moment. Hated him with every fiber of her being. Wanted to tear his limbs off piece by agonizing piece. The awful truth came tumbling down on her. Henry *had* deceived her. Grace's Henry *was* her Henry. The same Henry Rotten Trampas Long who'd made her believe there was no other woman in the world but her.

With an apologetic glance at the café owner, the constable marched Grace out the front door. April could see him escort the woman back down the street to Emogene's Pleasure Palace.

"Are you all right, miss?"

Other than a few missing hairs and shattered composure, April wasn't hurt.

First for Burgess. Two Women to Duel Over the Affections of a Lydia Pinkham Pitchman.

April clipped the article out of the newspaper, then quickly refolded the paper and laid it beside Riley's breakfast plate. There was no way she could prevent him from knowing about the duel, but she hoped to buy time—time to wring Henry's neck. Oh, she'd already let him have it, but according to Henry he was a "victim of circumstances." Grace had pursued him mercilessly even though he'd thwarted her advances.

April had spun on her heel and walked off. She wasn't that big of a fool. Now she had to do everything possible to ward off a possible heart attack should her grandpa discover what she was about to do. Grace Pruitt was mentally unhinged. If she challenged April to a duel, April had best be prepared to fight. But she couldn't fight—publicly brawl like a common hooligan. She had to bide her time until this thing cooled down—and make sure Grandpa didn't hear a word about it. He'd not only be furious with her for seeing Henry, he'd be livid at her for causing such a scandal. And Beulah couldn't know, either. This was April's problem.

Riley entered the dining room, yawning. Rays of mellow sunshine dappled the freshly polished floor. Scents of lemon oil and baking bread permeated the room as he took his seat at the head of the table.

Snapping open the paper, he started reading, then frowned.

April busied herself sprinkling brown sugar on her bowl of steaming oatmeal, careful not to look up.

"Who's been tampering with my newspaper?"

Feigning innocence, she murmured, "What's wrong?"

Shuffling the pages, Riley impatiently searched through the rest of the paper. "Somebody's cut a hole in the front page!"

"No!" April was on her feet, peering over his shoulder indignantly. "Who would do such a thing?"

"I don't know, but when I find out I'll give them a piece of my mind! Datha!"

The girl instantly appeared in the doorway. "Yes, sir?"

"What happened to the front page of my newspaper?"

She frowned. "It's in your hand, sir."

"Someone's cut a hole in it!"

"Cut a hole?" Datha hurried around the table, her dark eyes wide with concern. "Why, sir, I can't imagine how that happened."

"Did Davy bring it to the door as usual?"

"As usual, Mr. Ogden. Said he picked it up shortly after it was delivered to the emporium."

"Kids!" Snapping the paper open, Riley grumbled under his breath as he tried to read around the gaping hole. "You tell Davy to be more careful in the future."

"Yes, sir, I'll do that."

Datha hurried back to the kitchen as April dropped back into her chair. One crisis averted.

There weren't many folks in Dignity who subscribed to the Burgess periodical. She only hoped Grandpa would be satisfied he hadn't missed anything important, and drop the subject.

April spent the rest of the day in fear that another sub-
scriber had seen the article about her and Grace and
would tell Riley.

Once her head cleared, she had sent a note to Grace
in an attempt to settle their dispute peacefully.

By the time she had gotten back to Dignity, she was
feeling rational again. She'd hoped the duel would be
canceled once they both calmed down, but the note
she received Monday from Grace informed her it was
still scheduled for Saturday at sunrise.

There was going to be a duel. If April didn't appear
at the appointed hour, Grace would come here to Dignity to confront her.

The embarrassment would kill Riley. How could
April face the people she'd known all her life if
Grace arrived in Dignity and announced to the town
that she was challenging April to a duel, over a
man?

Over Henry Long?

She had lain awake nights, worrying that Riley would
find out what she was doing. The fact that she'd been
involved in a public row in a Burgess restaurant would
put him in a dither, and the thought of a duel . . . well,
it was unthinkable.

Henry. She'd broken off their relationship immediately.

An ache squeezed her heart when she thought of his
betrayal. How could she have fallen so deeply for a
man without morals? Grandpa had warned her about

Henry's philandering ways, but she hadn't listened. Now look where she was.

After considerable thought, she knew the man she wanted to have help her out.

Gray Fuller.

Gray would not want to get involved in the sticky situation, but he was the only man she knew who had a stake in the outcome. As Riley's physician he wouldn't want to see her grandfather shaken. She had no one else to confide in.

A duel? She was heartsick at the thought. *Father, forgive me. I never meant to get involved in such a disgraceful thing. I can't fight a duel. It would be wrong, nothing for a child of Yours to take part in, but I don't know how to get out of it.*

She couldn't let Grace come to Dignity, and she most certainly couldn't fire at someone made in the likeness of God, either. What was she going to do?

Throwing a cloak around her shoulders, April called to Datha that she was going out, and started walking toward the town square.

Reaching Gray's office door, she hesitated, then, squaring her shoulders, went in.

The waiting room was empty, and for a moment she feared he might be away on a call, or upstairs in his living quarters.

Hoping that he was working and simply hadn't heard the bell over the waiting room door, she moved quickly to his private office and rapped softly.

"Come in."

She hesitated, then turned the handle.

He was sitting behind a desk littered with papers and open ledgers. His eyes became guarded when he saw her. "Miss Truitt."

"I need to speak to you."

"Do you come in peace or war?" he asked dryly, returning to his paperwork.

He had every right to be leery of her, but not for the usual reason. She needed his help far more than she needed to argue the pros and cons of medicine.

Now that she was here, her confidence plummeted. Standing in Grandpa's library, rationalizing that Gray would help her, was a far cry from actually standing in front of him asking for his help.

Getting to his feet, the doctor stepped around her to the filing cabinet. "What brings you here, Miss Truitt?"

She took a deep breath and began. "I'm in trouble."

His expression didn't change. "What kind of trouble?"

She felt a blush warm her cheeks. "Really big trouble."

Closing the file drawer, he smiled distantly. "Do I need to examine you?"

April's blush deepened, and she realized she shouldn't have come. It was just too embarrassing. She'd insulted his profession, accused him of being thoughtless, uncaring and a pretentious quack. Now she was here wanting his help.

She'd bungled things with Gray from their first

meeting. Why on earth would he be willing to help her now?

"I shouldn't have come," she said, turning away. This was insane. She had no right to involve him in her problems. If she'd been foolish enough to believe in Henry, then she had to suffer the consequences.

Muttering under his breath, Gray reached out and caught her hand. "I'm assuming this isn't a physical problem. Are you here to talk about a personal problem?"

"It's just that . . ."

Motioning toward the chair, he said softly, "Sit down, April. Tell me what you came here for."

He flashed her a smile, and she obediently sank into the chair. Walking around the desk, he sat down in turn, leaning back and eyeing her speculatively. "What's troubling you?"

Swallowing, April studied her hands as she twisted the strings of her purse.

"Come now. April Truitt speechless?" He lifted his eyes, silently mouthing a grateful thank-you.

"I've been challenged to a duel Saturday morning. Henry's been seeing another woman in Burgess, and she's challenged me to a duel."

Gray simply stared at her. At least she knew she had his complete attention for once.

When he continued to stare, she shifted in her seat uneasily. "Don't look at me that way. I know it's insane, but it's true, and I need your help to stop this."

The legs of his chair hit the floor with a loud smack. "You cannot be serious."

"I assure you, I am. Quite serious." Deadly serious. She twisted her purse strings again. "The problem is, I don't know . . . exactly . . . what all this means."

Gray exploded, jumping to his feet to pace. *"What have you done now?"*

"I'm not sure. It certainly wasn't something I did intentionally. This . . . this Grace person accosted me while I was having lunch in Burgess two days ago. There I am, enjoying my treat, having passed out Lydia's pamphlets and delivered Pinkham's compound, and out of the blue, Grace marches over to me and challenges me to a duel."

Gray stood in the middle of the room running a hand through his hair.

April averted her eyes, willing to give him time to adjust. Clearly, the ramifications hadn't completely sunk in yet.

"You can't fight a *duel*—I've never heard of two women fighting a duel!"

He was blustering, but blustering was good. Once a man blustered his system thoroughly clean, he thought more clearly.

"You have now," she said.

Striding back and forth, he mumbled to himself. She could tell he was thinking. Thinking was good.

"Who is this woman in Burgess?"

"Her name is Grace Pruitt . . . I remember that because her name is so like mine. Grace Pruitt, April Truitt?"

He glared at her.

"Other than that, I don't remember much about that day, other than the fact that she said we were to meet in Miller's Glen at sunrise Saturday."

He ceased pacing. "*This* Saturday?"

"This Saturday."

"Does Lydia know about this?"

April sat up straighter. "Lydia had nothing to do with it. I was simply sitting there minding my own business—"

"When a woman comes over and challenges you to a duel."

"No, a woman came over, announced her name was—*is*—Grace Pruitt, said she was Henry's intended and that she knew I was seeing Henry. Then she takes off her gloves and—"

"Slaps you across the left cheek."

April nodded. "She claims to be Henry's fiancée."

"What does Henry claim?"

"He denies everything—but I realize that I have been played for the biggest fool on earth. Henry Long is a cad." The thought made her ill. To think she'd once trusted him, given her heart to him.

"This 'Grace' demanded I stop seeing Henry immediately. When I told her she had no right to demand anything of me, she, well . . . hit me."

"Hit you?"

"Yes, and I hit her back." Her hand absently touched the slight discoloration on her left cheek. "And pulled her hair. Actually, the whole scene is muddled. I may have whacked her first, then Grace whacked me back, or vice versa. . . . Anyway, the confrontation quickly got out of hand and it was awful—just awful!"

Gray leaned forward slightly to examine the dark bruise on her arm. "This is ludicrous, you know that."

"I know." What was more ludicrous was the way goose bumps suddenly appeared when he bent close to her.

Why, she was no better than Grace!

Here she was, getting gooseflesh over a man engaged to another woman. It was disgraceful, and she should be ashamed of herself.

"I'm not sorry for what I did," April said.

"Well, you should be." Gray stood up.

"I'm afraid we got into a brawl. A constable was called, and we had to be separated." She covered her face with both hands. "It was humiliating."

He sank into his chair, jaw tight. "What about Riley?"

"He'll hear about it. There's no way he can't, but for now he isn't aware of the situation."

Leaning back in his chair, Gray stared at the ceiling. He had warned Henry that he was playing a dangerous game. Now it seemed Henry Long had sold both women short.

If there was anything Gray had learned about women in his nearly thirty years it was that they never fit a pattern. Just when you were certain they would do something, they did something entirely different.

Witness the situation now before him with April.

Somehow "Grace" had discovered April and decided to take out the competition. It would be thoroughly amusing if it wasn't a matter of life and death. April had no idea what this meant. It was easy to see she was nervous and confused, and he knew how naive she was when it came to men. He'd pegged Henry as a gutless slime when he'd come in whining about his toe, and bragging about stringing two women along.

Gray sighed. Only April could get herself in such a fix. She was stubborn. He'd seen it all too often, and he knew that, with him or without him, she'd meet the challenge. She had no choice, but he did.

Bringing the legs of his chair back to the floor, Gray raised his brows. "All right, what do you want me to do?"

April's heart fluttered when she realized he was offering to help her without her having to beg. She felt something very close to warmth—and closer to love—seep through her.

"I'll have to do it. Henry says Grace is a little—well, you know—off. He said she will come after me regardless, so I'd best be prepared to defend myself." April sprang out of the chair and began to pace. "What will I do? I can't shoot anyone—not ever! The Lord says 'Thou shalt not kill.'"

"You'd more likely wound . . ." Gray paused. "No, with your luck you'd kill."

"I don't know what's involved, how that sort of thing works."

"Surely you *aren't* seriously thinking about going through with it?"

April blinked. "I don't have a choice."

"Of course you do!"

"You mean back out? Just not show up? Let that woman shoot—maybe kill me?"

"Back out, don't show up, run . . . You're a woman, not a man."

Stubbornness glinted in her eyes. "I can't do that."

"Why not?"

"It would be a disgrace."

"It would be *insane!*"

April winced at his tone. He was angry with her, as he should be. At the moment, she was angry at herself. "It isn't as if she challenged *you*. She challenged me."

"You've lost your mind! You can't participate in a duel! You'll get yourself killed, Miss Truitt. Shot. Dead." He ran both hands through his hair. "Even the compound won't bring you back."

"Very funny."

"I'm serious. You'd better listen to me."

"Well, at the moment, I can't accept the challenge even if I wanted to. I don't know how to shoot a gun. That's why I'm here. I'd hoped you'd teach me." She looked up, swallowed, then glanced away. "Before Saturday."

Shock registered on his handsome features. "You don't know how to shoot a gun?"

She nodded miserably. "I don't. Don't have an inkling. Never had an occasion to use one, never wanted to use one." She leaned closer. "I'm sorry, I know I shouldn't involve you in my problems, but you're the only one I can trust with this . . . rather weighty matter."

"April—we're Christians, God's representatives. You can't engage in a duel with another woman!"

"I know. I don't want to, but I don't think Grace has the same convictions." In fact, she was fairly certain Grace didn't have any convictions.

Circling the desk, Gray frowned. April could see he was sorting through his options: throw her out on her ear, refuse to help, go straight to Riley and inform him of his granddaughter's lunacy, shoot her, shoot himself or agree to help.

In the end, he did what any red-blooded man would do. He told her he had to think about it.

Getting to her feet, she prepared to leave. She could see there was no use appealing to his protective nature. He had none when it came to her. She could only hope his friendship with Riley would tip the scales in her favor.

"You will let me know as soon as your decision's made?" Wincing, she added, "Saturday's only a few days away."

Walking to the window, he stared broodingly outside.

She took his silence to mean he was thinking.

For a man, it was a good sign.

"One more thing," April said, her hand on the door. "I'm afraid if I don't show up at Miller's Glen, Grace will come to Dignity and hunt me down. If she can't get me, she'll go after Grandpa." April flashed a weak smile. "She's mean."

## Chapter Fourteen

By noon the following day, Gray had searched her out. She was embarrassed he'd found her in yet another peculiar situation.

Her predicament this morning could be explained quite simply, were he to ask, which she was reasonably sure he wouldn't.

She'd been crawling around on the floor in the sanctuary, brushing stray daisy petals into a dustpan from around the base of Jefferson Teal's casket. The florist had been careless when he'd delivered the elaborate floral display, and she was left to tidy up.

As she'd maneuvered around the wooden coffin, she'd suddenly stood up, inadvertently snagging the sleeve of her dress on a corner of the coffin.

Yanking lightly at the fabric, she'd gasped when the sudden, jerking motion sent the lid slamming down over poor deceased Jefferson's face.

Sinking to her knees, she'd tried to loosen the sleeve caught inside the casket without tearing it. But the lid had her pinned to the floor like a wrestler.

She was behind the coffin, partially hidden by a

large bouquet of yellow mums, when Gray appeared in the parlor doorway looking for her.

As his gaze searched the parlor, she'd stooped lower, hoping he wouldn't see her.

"April?"

Crouching lower still, she listened to the sound of her own breathing.

"Datha, she isn't in the parlor," Gray said. "Do you know where she is?"

"She was there a moment ago," Datha called from the kitchen. "Maybe she went outside. She'll be back. Just sit down and keep Jefferson company."

April could hear Datha's good-natured laugh as she went out the back door.

Gray took a seat in the front row of chairs, crossing his hands in his lap as he waited, his eyes casually scanning the room.

The moments ticked by and April realized he wasn't going to leave. Not soon, anyway, and her leg was starting to cramp from the position she was in. She was going to have to speak up and be embarrassed that he'd caught her in yet another foolish circumstance.

Taking a deep breath, she gritted her teeth and said in a small voice, "Help me?"

Gray's eyes snapped to the casket.

When he didn't immediately get up, she repeated more loudly, "Don't just sit there, help me!"

The way she was pinned, it was impossible for her to move without toppling the casket—something she was sure he wouldn't want her to do.

When the silence stretched, she wondered if he had possibly mistook her voice for Jefferson's.

The idea made her giggle. With a little thought, she could have some fun with the stuffy doctor.

"Hey, Doc, open the lid!" she parroted in a gruff voice. Then, in her best grumpy "Jefferson" voice, she muttered, "It's hot in here—oh, wait! Maybe I'm not in here! Maybe I'm oh . . . no!!"

Suddenly aware of censuring eyes on her, she glanced up. Gray was leaning over the casket, peering at her.

"Hi." She grinned, pointing at her sleeve. "Snagged it."

He stared at her.

"Can you . . . open the lid?"

"I suppose I'm capable of that."

When he didn't do so, she looked up again, irritated. "Today?"

Unlatching the lid, he lifted it. Hurriedly releasing her sleeve, she slipped around the casket, jerking off the scarf she'd worn to protect her hair. The freed locks tumbled down her back, reaching nearly to her waist. Quickly pinching color into her cheeks, she turned around. "What brings you here?" When he looked as if he was about to ask her how she'd gotten herself in that position, she rushed on. "I hope you've come to . . ."

Her voice trailed off as she heard Riley coming in the back way. Moving quickly to the parlor doors, she drew them shut. Turning, she whispered, "I hope this means you've decided to help me."

"I've thought about it."

"And?" She held her breath. If he refused to, she didn't know what she would do.

"If you insist on going through with this, I'll help you."

She closed her eyes, light-headed with relief. "What do you want me to do?"

"Nothing. A duel requires two identical weapons, so each opponent has an equal chance. Since Grace challenged you, you have your choice of weapons. In this case, guns. You'll need a second."

"Second?" The term was new to her.

Gray drew a deep breath and stared at the ceiling for a long moment, as if he couldn't believe they were doing this.

"In a duel, it is customary for the two principals to have 'seconds.' Someone they trust, who is willing to stand in for them in case something should happen. If the opponent doesn't show up, the second must step in."

"As long as I show up, the second is in no danger?"

Gray sobered. "There will be no danger. Both guns will have blanks."

"Blanks?"

"No bullets. Grace won't know, so she'll assume she missed. You will miss, too."

"Won't she fire until she hits me?"

"I plan to step in and call it a draw."

"Okay—that sounds good."

"You'll need to look as if you know how to shoot

262

to be convincing. We'll begin lessons immediately."

"Excellent! When?"

"Before dawn tomorrow morning, behind the livery stable. Joe will let us practice on the back side of his land. We shouldn't draw attention there."

"And you'll bring the gun?"

"I'll bring the gun. You just show up."

She turned to reopen the parlor doors, then suddenly turned back. "Thank you. I don't know what I would have done if you had refused to help me. . . ."

A flicker of annoyance hovered in his eyes. "Riley would never forgive me if I let something happen to you."

Riley. Of course. That was the only reason Gray was willing to help her.

She reached for the handle on the door.

"April?"

"Yes?"

"What about Henry?"

She didn't turn around. "What *about* Henry?"

"Apparently this woman in Burgess believes she's engaged to him. What does he say about this sticky matter?"

"Henry and I are through."

"I'm sorry—"

"Don't be. I was a blind fool. I see that clearly now."

"Well, not everything in life is candy. Sometimes we find out the hard way."

Turning around, she leaned against the door, meeting his gaze. "Henry and I grew up together. I didn't really care for him that much in school. We played tag, swung on swings behind the school, shared our dinner pails, but never once did I look at Henry romantically.

"Beulah never liked him, but I thought he was different." April smiled. "How could I not? He read poems to me. He was always careful about how he spoke in my presence, how he dressed. He made trips to Dallas, but I thought it was . . ." She shrugged, wishing she'd listened to Beulah and Grandpa. "I believed him. Work, buying books, that's what he told me his life consisted of."

Gray pulled her gently to him and held her for a moment. Resting her cheek against his chest, she thought how nice it was to be in his arms. He felt good, warm and strong, exactly what she needed. She hoped Francesca appreciated him.

"You're not the first woman to be deceived by a man."

"It's the first time for me."

His hand tenderly moved up and down her back in a comforting motion, while tears rolled unchecked down her cheeks. Gray made her feel safe and secure, as if he would always protect her and make everything all right. His heart beat against her ear, and she relished the warmth of his embrace.

She left his arms only when she heard Riley approaching the parlor.

"I'll see you in the morning," Gray said.

"I'll certainly be there."

April was up before five o'clock. Dressing warmly, she slipped out the back door and hurried through town. The duel was now a ruse—a ruse to make Grace think that she had the upper hand. The guns would shoot blanks—*blanks,* April reminded herself. Nobody would be hurt, and Grace's misplaced sense of outrage would be assuaged. April refused to let herself think otherwise.

The sun wasn't up yet. The community of Dignity was still asleep. A lone wagon rattled across the square on its way out of town.

She reached the livery and walked to the back of the property. Gray was already there, positioning bottles in a long, straight row on an old log.

"Good morning," she called.

She'd lain awake half the night, worrying about the duel, afraid Riley would hear about it and discover she was one of the two "fools" involved.

Gray's gaze rested on her for several moments. How glorious his eyes were, so compelling, so penetrating, as if he could see to the bottom of her soul.

"I see you're still intent on going through with this."

She nodded. "I believe I have to face Grace Saturday morning or she will come looking for me—or worse, Grandpa." The woman surely wouldn't shoot an unarmed, elderly, sick man! But then, Grace had not shown any compassion so far. April couldn't take the chance the woman would cause a scene and Grandpa's heart would give out.

"Then permit me to explain what you've gotten yourself into."

"But . . . you said the guns would contain blanks."

"Yes. Let's just hope that Miss Pruitt's second does not catch on to the ruse."

April swallowed. "What would happen if he did?"

"In that unfortunate event, the bullets would be real."

She swallowed again dryly, then settled herself on a log and adjusted her bonnet. "I'm listening."

"In the first place, dueling is against the law. It has been since 1839. Anyone found dueling, and surviving, can be tried for murder or manslaughter. Do you understand that? You could be imprisoned for murder or executed."

"I understand," she whispered. "Go on."

"A duel is generally meant to draw blood. I can't speak for Grace's intent. The French used to be satisfied with a wound to end a duel, but Americans tend to duel to the death."

"But there will be no real bullets."

"That's the best-case scenario."

"And . . . if they catch on . . . ?"

"You either run as fast and hard as you can, or you faint—you know, the way you did the day we first met?"

She drew a deep breath. This was insane. What if the reverend heard about it? How would she explain to her pastor that she was dueling like a common heathen? What must God think of her behavior?

"Men have it easier," she pointed out. "When they're challenged to a duel, you don't see them making a big fuss over it. They just do it. That's how I intend to handle this situation. Just do it . . . as long as you promise there will be no bullets in the guns."

Impatient green eyes pierced the distance between them. "I have two pistols. They're identical—that will help. I have a feeling that Grace is high-spirited and spoke—or challenged—before she realized what she was doing. We can hope that she has limited knowledge of firearms, so her suspicions shouldn't be raised unless her second is a shrewd gunman. When you meet Grace, she'll have first choice of weapon. Her second will examine the pistol to make sure it's loaded and hasn't been tampered with."

April pressed her lips together, listening.

"You and your opponent will hold your pistols, stand back-to-back, then march a specified number of paces. The seconds drop a handkerchief, the two of you turn quickly and fire at one another. To seize the advantage, you must be calm and steady, don't flinch, hold your pistol evenly and squeeze the trigger, don't jerk it. Understand?"

She nodded.

"These are breech-loading pistols. Safer than most. Smith and Wesson developed a brass cartridge a few years ago that makes firing them safer. Now, this is the barrel, this is the chamber that holds the bullets. When you fire, hold the pistol at arm's length—" he demonstrated "—but don't lock your elbow. Keep it slightly bent to absorb the shock. That way you'll appear more capable of hitting your target. Close one eye and aim down the barrel. See that nib at the end? That's how you sight in your target."

Sight in? Nib?

"I warn you, when you're dueling, you don't have time to think about doing all that. It has to be second nature for you. Like breathing. Now, let's see how you handle the gun, then we'll work on making you look like you're actually firing the weapon. The blanks have sound and smoke, so if you play this right it will look like the real thing. Timing is the key. You must turn and fire exactly at the same time as Grace in order to pull this off. Understand?"

April nodded yet again.

She stood and he handed the gun to her. She almost dropped it.

"Careful!"

"It's heavier than I thought."

"Get used to the feel of it. Rule one, never point a gun at anyone, never assume a gun is unloaded and never walk with your finger on the trigger. Now, lift it, keeping your arm straight."

Gray stepped behind her. She could feel the warmth of his body pressed against her as she lifted the gun, keeping her arm straight.

"Don't lock your elbow. Keep it slightly bent."

She did.

"Sight down the barrel. Move it around, keeping

your right eye on the nib. Forget this is a metal object. Make the gun an extension of your arm."

His warm breath caressed her cheek, and she struggled to concentrate. She hadn't counted on body contact, or his scent, which made her head swim.

"A part of your arm," he reminded her. "Point at the bottom limb on the tree. See it?"

"Yes."

"See the knothole to the right of it?"

"Yes."

"Now, point at one of those bottles on the log over there."

"All right."

"Got it?"

Gray sighted down her arm, his chin nearly resting on her shoulder. He stood very close, his body fitted tightly against her, his arm stretched along hers until his hand folded over her fingers gripping the pistol.

"Ready?"

She nodded. "Won't someone hear the shots, and wonder what's going on?"

"I left word at the livery that I would be target shooting."

His hand was large and warm as it enveloped hers.

"Squeeze the trigger, slowly."

April pulled the trigger.

The morning stillness shattered with a resounding crack that made her jump, the kick against her hand throwing her arm straight up. She would have fallen back a step if Gray wasn't there to catch her.

She dropped the weapon and threw her hands to her ears. "That was a blank!"

"That was live ammunition." He stood back, eyes solemn. "Now you know what you could be facing. If Grace is unethical, she could be carrying a concealed weapon."

"Let's hope she's not," April murmured, knowing without a doubt the woman was capable of anything.

For the next two hours Gray made her fire the gun over and over and over, until April's head rang with the sound of pistol shots.

Again and again he taught her how to stay limber, keeping her arm straight but not tense, how to squeeze the trigger and not jerk it.

"I've had enough," she finally declared, sinking onto a log. Her arm ached, her hand hurt, she was half-deaf and her nose burned from the stench of sulfur.

"We'll stop for today soon, but we'll meet here every morning this week."

She mentally groaned, aware of her aching arm.

"By Saturday you have to look and respond like a pro."

"But if the guns are shooting blanks . . ."

He picked up the spent cartridges. "That's what we're hoping for."

She swallowed. *Hoping—not certain.*

Tilting her chin up with the tip of his finger, he said quietly, "It's not too late to back out."

April refused to look at him, afraid she'd melt and

lose what self-restraint she had left. "I want to, I honestly do, but I can't."

Something perversely headstrong deep inside told her if she didn't go through with it, she would regret it.

She lifted her eyes, meeting his. A deep understanding passed between them, and she hoped her trust in him was not misplaced.

Her confidence wavered again. "What . . . what if I can't do it?"

"You can," he whispered gently, gazing deep into her eyes.

Then he bent slightly, and his lips brushed hers. Her knees buckled at the sweetness of it.

Ever so slowly, he ended the kiss and straightened.

As her eyes slowly drifted open, she saw he'd been as affected by the moment as she.

Clearing his throat, he stepped back. "Let's work on your aim again."

"Yes," she managed to croak.

Try as she might, April couldn't hit the target bottles, and it wasn't because she kept forgetting to compensate for the gun's kick. Gray's presence was distracting. The ground around her was littered with shell casings; the stench of powder hung heavy in the air. Even when he spoke directly into her ear, she could barely hear him.

For the following three mornings, they worked on theatrics. She must not only aim straight, but must be an

271

accomplished actress to carry off the ruse. April practiced timing, turning in a split second, firing, arm straight and gaze unwavering. She eventually hit four out of five bottles—a good sign if this were to be a real duel. But they'd be using blanks, she kept reminding herself. She—and more importantly, her opponent—would be firing blanks. The whole scene would be a performance, one Grace wouldn't know wasn't real.

April's back ached with tension, her arm with the weight of the gun. Her hand stung from its kick, and her ears had a constant ring from the sound of gunfire.

While Gray still stood close behind her to support her or to direct her aim, they were careful to keep their touches brief and impersonal—though she found herself hoping there would be more, then was angry with herself for hoping.

Why was her thinking so irrational? Gray was her friend, a good, steady friend, one who was helping her meet the biggest challenge of her life.

He was seeing another woman. It was frivolous of April to wish for more. At times she longed for the days when she hadn't liked him.

On the fourth morning, when she'd managed to hit five bottles in a row, Gray looked at his pocket watch and said regretfully, "I think I've done all I can." He took the gun out of her limp hand.

He commented on her accuracy, but there wasn't the sense of celebration she'd expected. She felt disappointed.

"I'm sorry, I realize how much time you're taking away from your patients. Is there anything I can do to help you catch up?"

"No, but thank you for the offer. I was due a few hours off. I've been seeing patients afternoons and evenings."

She recalled seeing the light on in his office late Tuesday night when she and Beulah had walked home from choir practice. Because of her, he had to work long hours to compensate for his absence during the morning.

He picked up the spent shells, and she helped. "I don't know how to thank you, Gray. If I make it through this . . . well, we both know it will be a wonder, but I wouldn't have a chance if it weren't for you."

"I wish you would reconsider, April."

"I can't, but thank you for caring."

Their gazes met, and she felt a sense of peace wash over her. No matter what happened, it would be worth it for the hours she'd had with him.

"I'll walk you home."

Silence fell between them. Talk wasn't necessary. They'd said a lot in the four days, nothing earth-shaking or substantial, just nice, easy conversation. So much different than her stilted, superficial discussions with Henry.

When they reached Main Street, she suddenly paused, staring at the black surrey with the matching team of black horses coming down the street.

Francesca. She was back.

Steeling herself against the spurt of jealousy she didn't want to feel, April casually turned to him.

"I have to go. Grandpa will be wondering where I am."

"Tell Riley I'll stop by the mortuary later," Gray murmured.

April followed his gaze to the vehicle, which had drawn to a stop in front of his office. Francesca, wrapped in a dark cloak, stepped delicately down with the help of her driver.

"Gray . . . Francesca is your fiancée, isn't she?"

"No."

"People say she is."

He looked down at her, squeezing her hand. "You can't believe everything you hear."

## Chapter Fifteen

Datha stared out the kitchen window, biting her knuckles until she tasted blood. A cold rain pelted the windowpane, but she was oblivious to the weather change.

What had gone wrong?

She was two weeks late. *Two* weeks late with her monthlies. Every morning she woke up with dread in her heart, praying—praying so hard!—for that telltale ache in her belly, but it wouldn't come. Thinking she might be mistaken, she'd hurry to the necessary and clean herself over and over, hoping to find her monthly.

But this morning she had given up hoping. The awful truth was the awful truth. She didn't know much about babies, but she knew the symptoms, and she sure enough had them. She was pregnant.

A rap sounded at the door, and she jumped. Angrily swiping at hot tears, she went to answer. Her face crumpled when she saw Jacel, all smiles, as if his world wasn't about to come crashing in on him.

Grinning broadly, he handed her a basket filled with potatoes from his cellar. "Hello, Datha, darling."

He frowned when she wiped her eyes.

"What's the matter?"

"Jace . . ." A lump the size of a hedge apple clogged her throat. How was she ever going to tell him? As careful as he'd been, the worst had happened. She couldn't be pregnant! Not when he was about to go off to college and become somebody!

All his dreams, all his hopes of being a fine lawyer someday would be gone—erased in the blink of an eye. Because of her, he'd be forced to abandon his plans for Harvard, disappointing Mr. Ogden, who had so much faith in him. The knowledge broke her heart.

She was having his baby, and he'd think he'd have to stay here and take care of her. He'd insist on owning up to his responsibility, and she was proud he was such a good man, but it was unfair.

So unfair!

And Flora Lee? What would her grandmother say when she found out Datha was carrying his baby? Fear constricted her throat, nearly suffocating her. She caught back a sob. Her life was hopeless, over. *It's not fair, Lord—our love is special—You know that. We ain't ever been with anybody else and we won't ever be. How could You let something like this happen? We want babies, but not now—not until Jacel has his schoolin'.* She couldn't understand it. They were in love, and now this would make their love look dirty.

Extending the basket to her, Jacel searched her face anxiously. "I thought Miss April would like these this morning. What's wrong, Datha? Are you feeling poorly?"

Oh, if only she were! What she wouldn't give for the agonizing monthlies that hurt so bad sometimes she had to crawl into bed with a hot cloth wrapped around her middle to ease the pain.

Accepting the basket, Datha held it, not knowing what to do with it. She didn't trust her voice to speak.

"Put it on the table and come with me," Jacel said.

Now she'd done it. He realized that something more than Flora Lee was bothering her.

When she just stood there, staring at the doorstep, he took the basket from her and set it on the kitchen table. Grasping her hand, he led her out to the woodshed.

Closing and latching the door, he took her into his arms and held her tightly while her tears dampened the front of his work shirt. "What is it, baby?" he whispered against her hair, gently massaging her back. "Have you and your grandmother been fussing again?"

"Oh, Jace," she said, weeping softly.

"Shh, now, it's all right. Whatever it is, I'll take care of it."

She knew he would if he could, but there were some things he couldn't fix.

"You can't," she whimpered, clinging tighter to the front of his shirt. The coarse fabric felt smooth against her roughened fingertips.

"Tell me about it. . . . It can't be that bad. It's Flora Lee, isn't it? Has she been after you about us again?"

"No," Datha sobbed.

He set her back from him so he could look at her. Biting her lip, she gazed up at him. He was so strong, so *good*. He could take care of most anything—most anything but this. For as long as she could remember, she'd run to him with all her problems and he had fixed them.

"Then what? Tell me what it is that has my Datha upset."

"I'm late."

He frowned, not understanding. "For what?"

She suddenly couldn't look at him. "My monthly . . . hasn't come."

"Monthly—" Suddenly comprehension clouded his face. His demeanor changed, turned sober. "How long?"

"T-two weeks."

"Two weeks?" Alarm flicked briefly in his eyes. She reached out, touching him. No sacrifice was too large. Whatever she had to do, she'd do it. For him.

"Are you sure, Datha, girl?"

Nodding, she brought her handkerchief up to her nose to stem the tide. "I keep hoping, but . . ."

Gently pulling her back into his arms, he kissed the top of her head, holding her tighter as she broke into a fresh round of tears. For a long time they held each other, trying to make sense of it.

"Two weeks," he whispered. "That isn't so much. Anything could have happened. It doesn't mean—"

"I've never been two *hours* late with my monthlies, Jace, let alone two weeks," she said in a muffled voice, her face buried against his chest.

"I was careful—you *can't* be pregnant." Easing her gently away from him, he gazed into her tearstained face. "Don't worry. This is all a mistake. Tomorrow, or next day for sure, we'll both have a good laugh about it." He tipped her chin up and kissed her full on the lips. "You'll see. Now, dry your tears and give me one of those special smiles that'll carry me through the long day."

Feeling somewhat mollified—because he'd said it was a mistake, and because she never doubted him, not ever—she complied.

"I guess . . . guess I am being pretty silly. I love you, Jace," she said. "With all my heart."

"I love you, too, Datha girl." They kissed. When their lips parted, Jacel held her for a moment. Just held her, letting his love completely inundate her.

"Datha."

"Yes?"

"You know . . . even if it were to be true, I'd stand

by you. I'd never let you go through this alone. I'd marry you in a minute, and I'd stay right here in Dignity and saw lumber for old man Jordan till the day I died, and never look back."

Tears choked Datha's throat. "I know you would, Jace."

All his dreams, his hopes, his future, he would give up for her if she asked. Trouble was, she'd never ask. She loved him too much to make him give up his future for her.

"Then why you still crying, baby?"

"Because I love you so much, Jace. That's why. I know you love me more than anything, and it doesn't seem fair."

Squeezing her tightly, he grinned. "I'd die for you, Datha. I'd lie right down in front of a train and let its wheels run right over me if you were ever to ask. I'd stand in front of a firing squad and let them blow a big old hole clean through my chest if that's what'd make you happy."

Giggling, she tried to stem the tears for his sake. "That wouldn't make me happy, silly."

She got the weeps sometimes, and she knew it troubled him. Flora Lee said weeps were just part of being a woman, and men would never understand it, so she tried not to get them too often around him.

"Well, I don't think anyone's going to be giving up any dreams," he told her. Patting her on the cheek, he turned her to face the shed door. "Now, you get on back inside and wash that pretty face and stop worrying. If there's any worrying to be done, I'll do it."

Smiling, she stole another kiss, then waited while he silently slipped from the woodshed and disappeared beyond the tall hedge marking the back boundary of the Ogden yard.

Wiping her face with the hem of her apron, she told herself that everything was all right. There was nothing to worry about. God loved her and Jacel. He wouldn't let this happen.

She went inside the kitchen and carried the vegetables to the pantry. Jacel was a good man. A kind and loving man. A man who would someday be very important.

Leaning against a shelf, Datha closed her eyes.
*Oh God, we didn't mean to do anything wrong.*
*Don't let my mistake ruin his life.*


April had dinner with Beulah and her father Thursday night. Nadine Ludwig was staying with an ill sister and wasn't expected back for months.

April realized she wasn't doing a very good job of holding up her end of the conversation. As Mr. Ludwig left the table, she helped Beulah put food away and clear the plates.

"Okay, what's bothering you?" her friend demanded as she stored a cherry pie in the pantry.

"Nothing," April said. She carried dishes to the kitchen.

"Might as well tell me now. I won't let up. You've been distracted all evening."

Beulah gathered the silverware as April poured hot water into the dishpan.

"Did I see you with Gray this morning?"

"Mmm." April scrubbed a dinner plate. "His lady friend is in town again."

He hadn't looked pleased to see Francesca. Hadn't looked the way April would have expected him to when his fiancée came to visit.

"You have to wonder if a man really wants a woman like her running his life."

April silently conceded she'd wondered that, too. Gray never spoke about her.

"You think he'll actually marry her?"

April wondered about the grim expression on Gray's face when he'd spotted the buggy rolling into town. He'd said they were not engaged . . . but why did the French woman continue to visit almost every month, throw silly parties, decorate his office, act as though she owned the man? It was a strange alliance, one April would love to know more about.

"I don't know. Somehow, I can't see those two together." Beulah carefully dried glasses.

April shrugged.

"You two have spent a lot of time together lately."

"He says they're not engaged—"

Beulah turned abruptly and grinned. "You've talked about her!"

"Not talked about her in particular. He mentioned something and I asked if the rumors were true, and he said, 'You can't believe everything you hear.'"

"Then they *could* be engaged?"

"He said they weren't."

"You get this funny, wistful note in your voice when you talk about him."

"For goodness' sake. You're going to have to do something about your imagination."

"Answer the question."

"I forgot what it was."

"I've seen how you look at him, April. Gray is a handsome man."

April rinsed a dish and set it aside. "Not really." Beulah didn't know about the duel and April hoped to keep it that way. By Saturday afternoon the whole thing would be over, and Beulah and Grandpa would never be the wiser. Still, it was odd not to share her dilemma with her friend; they'd told each other everything since they were old enough to share secrets.

But Beulah couldn't know about the duel; she would certainly tell Grandpa, and he would put a stop to it. April couldn't risk it, couldn't ignore Grace's threat as if it had never happened. April had to bluff her way through, and if Gray's plan worked, no harm would come of it. She would salvage her pride, and Grace's anger would be appeased. And April would be rid of Henry. Well rid of Henry.

"How's Raymond?" she asked, changing the subject.

Beulah's cheeks pinked to a high color. "Who?"

"Raymond Grimes. Haven't I seen him coming out of the pharmacy quite a few times in the last several weeks? He isn't ill, is he?"

"No . . ." Beulah began, then stopped. "He . . . just stops by to say hello. You know. Just being polite. We've had supper together once or twice."

"Uh-huh," April said, glad to have finally distracted her friend. The last thing she wanted to discuss was her feelings about Gray. They were difficult enough for her to understand without trying to explain them to Beulah.

"Raymond is a nice man. Quiet, but nice."

Beulah's cheeks grew even pinker. "My, will you look at the time. It's getting late!"

They finished the dishes. Then April walked the short distance to the mortuary, her mind not so much on Beulah and what seemed to be a blossoming love between her and Raymond Grimes, as on Gray and Francesca.

April had no right to resent Gray for entertaining the woman, though it wasn't socially acceptable the way she kept showing up. Apparently she wasn't worried about propriety.

Where were her mother and father? Did they approve of her lack of decorum? Grandpa said the world was in bad shape, but had it gone so far that well-bred young women now shamelessly pursued eligible men?

April slipped in the back way, not wanting to wake Riley, who had been sleeping poorly lately. Datha had her hands full recently, what with Flora Lee complaining more and more about her aching bones.

The door squeaked as April shut it and stepped into the small kitchen. The smells of Riley's supper still hung in the air, meatloaf, potatoes, string beans from Jacel's garden that Datha had canned.

April was so familiar with the household that she didn't bother lighting the lamp. She was halfway across the kitchen when she heard a sound that stopped her in midstep. Her heart thumped, then raced like a windmill.

What was it?

A mouse?

Oh, she hoped not! She'd told Datha to set traps at night!

There it was again.

Where was it coming from? The pantry?

Not anxious to brave a mouse, she crept closer to the cupboard.

The sound was barely distinguishable, but something was in there. She could hear a faint rustling.

Lighting the lamp, she left it on the table, then eased the pantry door open, hoping to catch the rodent unawares. Lamplight spilled into the space, reaching the corners of the narrow room. A piece of gray cloth on the floor caught her attention; then she saw it was part of a skirt.

"Datha?"

The girl was huddled in a corner, her hands over her face. Her thin shoulders quivered as she choked back sobs.

Kneeling quickly in front of her, April frowned. "Datha? What's the matter?"

When she didn't answer, April very gently drew her

hands away from her face. Her eyes were swollen from crying and her cheeks wet with tears.

"Whatever on earth is the matter?" April whispered, trying not to frighten her more. "Datha, talk to me. I want to help you."

"Nobody can help me," she sobbed brokenly.

"Is it Jacel?" April prodded, certain that something must have happened to the young man. "Has he been hurt? Is that it? Please . . ."

April moved closer, her foot knocking over something that, when she turned to look, appeared to be a bottle of Pinkham's Vegetable Compound. A spoon lay beside it.

"What is this?" April picked up the bottle and discovered it empty. "Are you ill? Do you have a stomach ailment? Cramps? Datha, you have to talk to me!"

This brought on a fresh spate of sobs, and April realized the girl was too upset to tell her anything.

"Here, let me help you up. We'll have some tea and . . ."

She began pulling her to her feet, but even as she made the attempt she saw the widening pool of blood on the floor.

"Oh, dear God!" she prayed. So much *blood*. She'd never *seen* so much blood.

"Datha, what have you done?" Taking the girl by her thin shoulders, she gently shook her. "Have you *done* something to yourself? You must tell me!"

"I can't have a baby," Datha sobbed. "I can't, Miss April . . . I just can't."

*Baby?* April frowned. "You're with child? Does Jacel know?"

"No! He *can't* know what I've done. Please—I'll tell him I was mistaken, that I started my monthlies just as he said I would—"

"We've got to get you to a doctor," April murmured. Gray. Where was Gray? "You stay right there. Don't move. I'll go get help."

Running faster than she'd ever run in her life, April raced headlong out the back door and down the steps. Her breath came in painful gasps as she ran through the darkened streets.

All she could think about was the blood.

The deep, crimson pool of Datha's lifeblood.

She was so winded by the time she'd reached Gray's office, she had to stop and catch her breath. Bent double, she stood holding the rail of the outside staircase, panting, trying to think. *Dear God, don't let Datha die before I can get help!* she repeated over and over in a ragged litany.

When she could, she raced up the staircase and pounded on the door.

"Gray! Gray!"

What if Francesca was with him?

"Gray!"

The door flew open and a disheveled Gray looked out. "What is it? Riley?"

"No, Datha. I—I think she's tried to abort a baby. You've got to come!"

"I'll get my bag."

286

April turned, bolting back down the stairway. Gray followed a moment later, pulling on suspenders with one hand, carrying his medical bag in the other.

Side by side they silently ran toward Fallow and Main Streets, saving their breath for the race against death.

Datha was lying huddled in the corner of the pantry, only half-conscious now. She gave no indication she knew they were there.

"I'll get Flora Lee," April whispered as Gray set to work.

"Not yet. She'd only be in the way."

"But if Datha—"

"I'll tell you when to go after her."

"I don't want Grandpa to know." April spoke in hushed tones, hoping that Riley was sleeping soundly on the second floor. "He thinks so much of her. . . ."

Gray unsnapped his bag and removed his stethoscope. "Get some light in here."

April lit two more lamps and carried them into the pantry. Standing back to allow him room, she watched him work for over ten minutes before he impatiently tossed his instruments aside.

"I can't do anything here. I've got to get her to my office."

"What can I do?"

"I'll carry her. You take my bag."

Lifting Datha's slight weight into his arms, he carried her out of the pantry, her blood soaking the sleeves of his white shirt.

He cradled her to his chest, running to his office, with April following behind, taking two steps to his one.

Did Jacel know? April wondered. Had he instigated Datha's decision?

No. April was positive he didn't know. Jacel would be the last person to risk Datha's life.

April reached into Gray's pocket and got the key to the office. Unlocking the door, she lit a lamp as he carried the unconscious girl straight through to the examining room.

"Help me get her undressed."

Grabbing a pair of scissors, April began cutting away Datha's dress. The girl had lost so much blood, April couldn't believe she was still breathing.

"Who would have done this?" Gray cursed under his breath as he laid out surgical instruments that, by the mere sight, made April's skin crawl. Looking at the shiny steel implements brought back painful memories of her mother's death.

"There's a . . . midwife. Mrs. Waterman. She's been . . . helping young women solve their problems for as long as I can remember. She must be nearly as old as Grandpa."

"Where does she live?"

"Up on the hill, at the west end of town. She has a small house up there. She doesn't go out much."

April shivered. She didn't need to see the grim look on his face to know Datha was slowly losing the battle.

Standing at the foot of the table, April gently smoothed a lock of coal-black hair away from the young woman's face. Datha was a good girl. Her only weakness was Jacel, because she loved him too much.

April worked beside Gray, handing him instruments, bandages, towels, wiping the sweat dripping periodically from his brow.

"Butchers!" he muttered, trying to stay the ceaseless flow of blood. "If you and Lydia Pinkham are so intent on crusading, this is what your efforts should be about!"

"It is," April said. "This is exactly what we're trying to change. Because women can't find answers, they're forced to do idiotic things like this."

"No doctor worth his salt would do this to a woman."

"I didn't mean women are looking for abortions. They're looking for help, Gray, for answers when they're scared and don't know where to turn. Doctors should be there to give them answers, not just vague reassurances."

When he'd done all he knew to do, he stepped back, wiping his bloody hands on a towel. Datha lay on the table, as still as death.

Moving closer, April whispered. "Is she . . . ?"

"No, but she's lost a lot of blood. I don't know, April. . . . You should go for Flora Lee now."

Reaching for Datha's hand, April held it tightly, trying to will strength into her nearly lifeless body. She could feel a weak, weak pulse along the inner index finger on her right hand. It wasn't much, but she knew Datha was strong. She could make it through this if she truly wanted to.

If she didn't, the shock would kill Flora Lee.

"Could we wait until Datha regains consciousness?"

Gray's features were stern. "I can't promise that will happen."

A moment later, he parted Datha's lips and forced a few drops of laudanum down her throat.

April looked at him, puzzled.

"I don't want her moving around and starting the hemorrhaging again."

Nodding, April scooted a chair next to the table, continuing to hold Datha's hand. "You'll tell me if . . . when there's a change."

Gray nodded gravely. "I'll tell you."

Sometime during the next few hours, April realized that not all doctors were the enemy.

Gray was a doctor. A physician, a healer with true dedication to saving lives. This wasn't the kind of man who had butchered her mother. This was not the kind of man April had vowed to fight with every breath in her. This was a man who fought to save life, not destroy it.

"I'm glad you were here," she said, closing her eyes wearily.

He was sitting at his desk, cradling his head in his hands. His shoulders didn't look as wide or as imposing tonight. They just looked very tired.

Lifting his head, he offered her an extended smile. "I'm glad you came to me. I hope that means you and I are making progress."

"I misjudged you, Gray. Please forgive me . . . and thank you for saving her life."

"I didn't save it. If she makes it, the credit will belong to a higher source."

"You really believe that, don't you?"

He nodded. "Each time I treat a patient, I know God is working through me. He gave me the gift of healing, and I try my best to use it for Him. Sometimes there isn't anything I can do, but I do what I can, and trust Him for the unseen."

She studied Gray in the dim light. She'd been wrong to assume he was like some other doctors. He wasn't. He was unlike anyone she'd ever known, man or woman. He was uniquely his own person.

"You aren't like most doctors."

"I'm honored by the thought, but I am exactly like most doctors. There are more physicians who want to save lives than those who use the simplest, and often most cruel, method of solving a problem. I'm sorry about your mother. Sometimes even our best efforts fail. I wish I could tell you why, but I'm not God. I don't have all the answers."

Resting her head on the cold wooden table, she watched the lantern burn lower. It was running out of kerosene and needed refilling.

"Thank you."

Yawning, he leaned back in his chair, dragging a

hand through his thick hair. The little-boy gesture touched her. "I told you, she's not out of the woods."

"I know, but thank you. At first I didn't like you, and I judged you harshly. I was wrong. You care . . . you honestly care about your patients."

Staring at the ceiling, he said softly, "Look, April, I'm willing to concede that women do have problems that physicians tend to ignore. I find myself saying, 'Go home, rest, and it will be better in the morning.' I do so not out of indifference, but out of frustration. We do what we can, but medicine is a science. I think of the body as a large, complex map. We follow the recommended routes, but they don't always take us where we want to go. We do what we can, and we guess the rest of the time."

They sat in silence, listening to the ticking of the clock on the wall. Sometime during the night, a shower came by, pelting the windowpane, then moved on. The moon came out, illuming the rain-wet streets.

The two of them moved in and out of sleep, listening to the sound of Datha's barely perceptible breathing. If it were to change, even a fraction, April was prepared to run and get Flora Lee. She prayed unceasingly. She knew Gray was doing the same.

He stirred at last, lifting his head to look at her.

"Who's her second?"

Half-asleep, April tried to open her eyes. "Who's her second what?"

"Grace. Who's her second?"

It dawned on her he was thinking about the duel.

"I don't know. . . . I didn't think to ask."

The admission was so absurd, it broke the tension. They both laughed, temporarily easing the strain.

"I guess I could write and ask," she offered.

Getting out of his chair, he came to stand beside her. Cradling her head, he held her, stroking her hair. His hands smelled of camphor and soap. He didn't say anything; words weren't necessary. He was there, beside her. That, for the moment, was all the support she needed.

Closing her eyes, she rested her head against his broad chest, overcome by her feelings. Henry had never once made her feel this way, comforted, protected.

At the moment, nothing was pertinent but Datha. Not April's feelings toward Gray or Francesca, or silly pistol duels over a man unworthy of such theatrical acrimony.

In the overall scheme of things, that all seemed petty and self-serving when a young woman lay close to death because she'd thought she had no other choice.

"Who's mine?" she whispered.

"Your what?"

"My second?" She realized they'd never discussed it.

"Me," he said.

She nodded. Him. *Thank You, Lord.* Her life was in capable hands.

## Chapter Sixteen

The hands on the clock slowly moved to five. Datha was still unconscious. It would be dawn soon, and April knew she had to let Flora Lee know what had happened. When she woke and found her grand-daughter gone, she would be beside herself with worry.

Gray lay back in his chair, dozing, his feet propped on the desk.

Getting up, April stretched, then moved to the window to look out on the deserted streets. In another hour people would be going about their business, unaware of the drama taking place inside the building with Dr. Gray Fuller painted on the window. Many, like her, took his skills for granted. After tonight she would never take anything about him for granted.

She thought he was sleeping until he spoke quietly from the corner, where his head rested heavily against the wall.

"Let me ask you something. What did you see in Henry?"

April kept her gaze trained on the deserted square. "Does it matter?"

"A little. As a man, I can't see the attraction."

"You know, I don't care about Henry anymore. I just want it over and Henry out of my life." Drawing a ragged breath, she let the curtain drop back into place. "Do you have any coffee?"

He motioned toward a battered-looking white metal cabinet. "In there."

He got the water, and she slid a pot of coffee onto the wood stove.

"Beulah says it's like Henry's too big for his britches. More dream than talent to achieve it."

"Henry wouldn't like hearing that. He fancies himself an entrepreneur."

"I know, but it's true. When we were in school, he always had all these grand ideas about life. Which is fine, but they weren't doable. Working with the Pinkhams gave him the opportunity to think big. And, it seems, it gave him the opportunity to play me for a fool with Grace. To think he could see two women at the same time, even if they lived in different towns, is a little absurd, don't you think?"

"Personally, I think he's the fool."

"And he got away with it for a while, didn't he?" She returned to the window, angry now. "He isn't what I thought he was. I believed he loved me, wanted a life with me. Marriage, children, a home."

"Maybe he does. Men can do some foolish things sometimes."

The tone in his voice puzzled her. He sounded as if he was talking about himself now.

"I was hurt at first, but I soon realized only my pride was wounded. Had I married him, he would have wanted to move, and I couldn't live in Dallas, or Austin or San Antonio. I like Dignity. It's my home."

Silence fell between them. After a while, April

cleared her throat. "He betrayed me for a woman who works in a brothel, for goodness' sake!"

When he didn't say anything, she realized she was being much too forward.

"I'm sorry. I shouldn't be telling you these things. I'm just . . . angry. At Henry. Rotten Henry."

They were both quiet for several minutes.

"Don't worry, I'll be there Saturday morning."

Gratitude flooded her. She was *terrified* of what might happen Saturday, but if he was there beside her . . . well. Having him beside her meant a lot.

"Thank you," she whispered.

He rose and poured them each a cup of the brewed coffee. His gaze met hers over the rim of his cup. "You want me there?"

"It gives me a great deal of comfort to know you'll be there, yes."

As the sun came up, Datha's color improved slightly. Gray bent over her, listening to her heart, gently lifting one eyelid to check that she was not too deeply under with the laudanum.

"How is she?"

"I can't say for certain that she's past the crisis, but there is some improvement. You can go get Flora Lee now."

"Thank you . . . I didn't want to bring her here to watch her granddaughter die."

Gray smiled, absently rubbing the back of his neck. "You know, Miss Truitt, in spite of your prickly nature, you've got a soft heart."

She grinned. "You're not so tough yourself, Doctor."

April hurried to the mortuary, wondering how she was going to tell Flora Lee what had happened to her granddaughter, and why, and that Datha wasn't out of the woods yet.

The quarters behind the mortuary were quiet, but when she knocked gently at Flora Lee's door, the response was immediate.

"Come in."

April gently pushed open the door. Flora Lee sat on the edge of her bed, dressed and obviously surprised to see her instead of Datha.

"Miss April? It's scarcely dawn. What you doin' up at this hour?"

"I've got some disturbing news, Flora Lee."

She crossed to the bed and knelt down beside the aged black woman who had practically raised her, taking a wrinkled dry hand in her own.

Flora Lee looked scared. "Bad news?"

"Datha—"

"Datha? What that girl up to! She run off with that no-account Jacel?"

"No, she hasn't. I'm afraid she's ill. Very ill."

"Sick? What's wrong with her? She was fine last night."

"She . . . I think she went to see old Mrs. Waterman—"

The woman frowned, then her eyes widened with

comprehension. "That girl went to get rid of a baby? Is that what you're tellin' me?"

"I'm afraid so."

"And something went wrong," Flora Lee guessed.

"Yes."

Flora Lee drew a deep breath of resignation, her face seeming to age before April's eyes.

"Is she gone?"

"Gone?" Now it was April's turn to be slow to comprehend. "No, she's alive. But she's gravely ill. She's at Dr. Fuller's. He's been with her all night."

"God bless that man." Flora Lee closed her eyes a moment in prayer. "I know you don't think much of doctors—"

"I've changed my mind, Flora Lee. I know I blamed all doctors for Mother's death, and I know now how wrong that was. Gray worked all night to save Datha. No one could have done more for her. It's because of him that she's still alive."

"I want to go to her."

"I'll tell Grandpa what's happened, then come back for you."

"Go, go. I'll get my cane and start ahead. It takes me a while."

"I'll hurry."

April told Riley what had happened. Still in bed, he shook his head in disbelief.

"Don't know what these young girls think they're doing. God's a loving God, but he sets rules and there's always a consequence to broken rules. If folks would believe that it'd make life so much simpler. You don't worry about me. Take Flora Lee to see about Datha. Do you need some help?"

"No, it's not very far. If we walk, she can get herself under control. Right now she's very shaken."

"I can imagine. I'll come down soon as I get dressed and see if I can help. If I come now, she might think my professional services are needed."

April managed to smile. "I love you." She kissed his round cheek fondly. "I love you a lot, Grandpa."

"And I love you, missy."

April walked Flora Lee slowly down the street, holding the woman's thin arm, talking to her all the while. She told her about how she'd found Datha, how she'd run to get Gray.

The old woman hobbled along stubbornly, leaning on her gnarled cane, listening and nodding. When they arrived at the doctor's office, Flora Lee hesitated at the door as if gathering her courage before going in.

Gray met them in the doorway of the examining room.

"Good morning, Flora Lee."

"Doctor." Flora Lee nodded. "I understand I have you to thank for savin' my girl. I appreciate that."

"She's doing better," he said, glancing over the woman's head at April. "But she has a way to go, Flora Lee."

*She's all right,* April mouthed to him, knowing he was concerned about Flora Lee's fragile state.

April guided the older woman toward the wooden table. "Here's a chair so you can sit beside her. She's still unconscious, but touch her, talk to her. I'm convinced that she can hear you. It will comfort her to know you're here."

"I don't know about that," Flora Lee said staunchly. "I don't agree with what she's done. And it's that no-good Jacel Evans's fault she got herself with child and tried to get rid of it. It's his fault my girl nearly died."

"Please, just tell her you're here. Comfort her as best you can, even if you don't agree with the choices she's made. Deal with those after we have her well. Can you do that?"

"I won't lie, but I won't tell her what I think—not yet, leastwise. Let me sit here and look at her."

"You sit with her and I'll be right outside with Gray—Dr. Fuller."

Flora Lee fastened her eyes on her granddaughter's face and sank heavily into the chair. Gray nodded to April, indicating he wanted to see her in the waiting room.

"Who is Jacel?"

"Jacel Evans. He works for the Jordans. He's a fine young man, Gray. My grandfather plans to help him go to law school."

"You'd better get him over here and find out what he knows about this."

"I doubt he knows what she's done. Datha said she

didn't want him to know about the baby because it would ruin his plans for law school."

Gray looked thoughtful. "So she did it for love."

April nodded.

"Still, you'd better go get him."

"Flora Lee won't like it."

"He deserves to know the woman he loves is in trouble."

She thought about that for a moment. "Yes, of course he does. I didn't think of it that way." She held Gray's gaze for a long moment. "I'll go get him."

April found Jacel at work, unloading logs from a wagon at the sawmill.

"Miss April! You're up early this morning. How can I help you?"

She hurried to his side. "Jacel, now, I don't want you to react without listening first. I have some disturbing news. . . ."

Jacel frowned. "What's wrong?"

"It's Datha. She's done something very foolish—"

"Datha . . . where is she?"

"Jacel, did you encourage her to go to Mrs. Waterman?"

"Waterman? No—where is she?" he demanded.

"She had an abortion. . . . Something went wrong. I found her in the pantry, bleeding to death."

"No, oh, no." Jacel brought both hands up to cover his face, turning in a circle. "Datha! Oh . . . no."

"Did you encourage her to do this?" It seemed so

unlikely, but surely Datha wouldn't do this on her own. She was bright, smart! She would never risk her life this way.

"No! Miss April, I didn't know for certain she was in the family way! I told her not to worry. I—I have to go to college, to be a lawyer, to support the family, but I told her I would stand by her—she's not going to die, is she?"

"She's alive, Jacel, but only because of God . . . and Gray. She's unconscious, but, for the moment, she's still with us."

"Thank You, God! Does Flora Lee know?"

"Flora Lee is with Datha."

Burying his face in his hands again, he started to sob. "She won't want me there."

"I hope the two of you can put animosity aside, because of Datha."

Stiffening, Jacel wiped tears from the corners of his eyes. "I won't stay away because of Flora Lee. Datha needs me—I'm going to her, Miss April."

"I'm asking that you won't let tempers get in the way of your concern for her."

"Take me to my Datha."


Jacel followed April into the doctor's office ten minutes later. Flora Lee glanced at him through the examining room door as he walked in, then turned away. Gray came out to the waiting room and greeted them.

"Gray, this is Jacel Evans."

The two men shook hands.

"How is my Datha?"

"Still unconscious, but I have hope that she'll recover."

"Thank you, Doctor," Jacel said softly, his gratitude evident as he once again shook Gray's hand. "May I see her?"

"Yes."

Jacel followed Gray to where Datha lay, her grandmother seated beside her. April came, too, bracing for the explosion.

Upon seeing Datha so still, so pale, Jacel dropped to his knees beside the table, bursting into tears. When he'd regained his composure, he stood up and, careful not to disturb her, clasped her hand tenderly.

The scene brought tears to April's eyes, and she welcomed Gray's embrace when he drew her close to his side.

"Ain't you done enough harm to my girl?" Flora Lee asked quietly.

Jacel didn't move for a moment, then he slowly turned.

"I didn't know she was thinking of doing this, Flora Lee. I hope you believe me."

"Didn't know you was puttin' my girl in danger? Didn't know she was in th' family way? Didn't know she'd go to that old woman who'd nearly kill her? You a smart boy. Why didn't you *know?*"

Jacel gazed at her, pain evident in his anguished face. "I love this woman. I wouldn't put her in harm's way. I know you don't like me, but that doesn't change how I feel about her. I *love* her, Flora Lee. We both love her. Can't we set our differences aside for the time being?"

The old woman studied the young man's face for several minutes. "Sin has its price. You should know that."

"Yes, ma'am, I do. And it's too high." Tears rolled down his cheeks. "I'll be remembering that from now on."

Flora Lee was silent, then murmured, "Don't mean I changed my mind. I still think you're uppity."

Regaining his spunk, Jacel countered, "That's fine with me, 'cause I think *you're* uppity. But for Datha's sake, let's keep it to ourselves."

Eyeing him sourly, she shrank back as he moved to the head of the table, cradling Datha's face in his hands.

"She's my girl," she reminded him.

"She's my woman."

"Humph." Flora Lee glanced away.

"It's all right, baby, Jacel's here. Nothing's going to hurt my Datha. You'll see, it'll all be just fine." Softly crooning a lullaby, he stroked her cheeks with his thumbs, tears running down his cheeks. "No, sir, Jacel's not going to let anything happen to you, Datha girl. You just rest and get well now, baby. I love you."

Looking up, he locked eyes with Flora Lee.

She stared back, then turned away.

April shrugged. It was a start.

## Chapter Seventeen

Hours before dawn on Saturday morning, Gray arrived at the mortuary. Parking his buggy in the shadows, he trimmed the wick on the lantern, then walked briskly to the back of the house, where April was waiting for him.

Shivering in the predawn chill, she whispered, "Well, I guess this is it."

"I'd hoped that sometime during the night you'd come to your senses."

"No. I'm going through with it. How's Datha?"

"Some improvement. Jacel will come for me if there's any change." Glancing up at Riley's second-story bedroom window, he said softly, "Does he suspect anything?"

"No, he thinks I'm going to be with Beulah all day."

"Then we'd better go. We'll barely make it as it is."

They walked to the side of the house, and he lifted her into the buggy. He was about to climb aboard when he stopped, gazing at her in the dim lantern light, his expression grave. "I don't want you to do this."

Looking straight ahead, she repeated what she'd rehearsed in her head during the short night. "Thank you for your concern, but I'm feeling a little incompetent right now. I need your support instead of condemnation."

"That's hard to give at this moment."

"Don't worry. I've left Grandpa a note on my armoire to be opened in case of my death. In it, I explained that you were adamantly against this. He'll find the note only if I don't return. He never goes in my room."

Gray's eyes blazed with a sudden anger. "You think my only concern is Riley?"

"No . . . but I know he's your friend—"

"*I* don't want you to do this, April." Cupping her face in his hand, he made her look at him. "*You,* April. My concerns are for you, not Riley."

Not for the first time, she envied Francesca, envied her from the very depths of her soul.

Drawing a warm woolen shawl around her shoulders, she said, "I'm ready if you are."

After climbing into the buggy, Gray slapped the reins across the horse's rump. He was silent now. She could see by the tight set of his jaw that he would like to turn her over his knee and paddle her like an unruly child. But she wasn't a child. She was a young woman with a mission, albeit an unpleasant one. How had her life come to this? This gray, damp morning could prove to be her last. What if the ruse failed? What if Grace's second was wise to ammunition and spotted the trick immediately? The blanks would be replaced with live ammunition and April would be . . . She couldn't bear to think of Grandpa laying her out in her casket . . . weeping. Beulah would be so mad she'd never speak to her again—but then, April wouldn't be able to speak. She would be with God. . . .

*Oh, dear Father, please don't turn me away.*

Flora Lee's words crowded her mind: *Sin is never without consequence.* Datha lay fighting for her life because of the wrong choice. Would April be next?

Her hands shook as she straightened the lace on the collar of her pale blue dress. She'd purposely not worn jewelry, but she suddenly wished she had the locket her mother had left her.

The horse's hooves clopped loudly along the deserted streets. Two hours, and she would be . . . What would she be?

Would she be coming back today? Would she ever see Grandpa again? He was unaware that she'd slipped in early this morning and kissed him goodbye.

"Don't think," Gray said quietly, as if he'd read her thoughts. "Remember what we've practiced. If you think, you'll waver."

"Don't think, don't waver," she repeated, going over in her mind the endless hours of practice. The proper way to hold the gun: use both hands, sight carefully, squeeze the trigger slowly—*don't jerk!* Make the pretense look real.

Half an hour before dawn, Burgess loomed before them. April took in the sight with her heart hammering against her ribs.

A small glen just outside of town awaited the dueling parties. By the time they approached, the sun, not yet risen, had begun to pinken the sky. One other carriage sat beneath the trees when Gray pulled the team to a halt.

"Who's that?" April whispered.

"My guess is the doctor."

April swallowed, her mouth as dry as cotton. "I think I'm going to be sick."

"Take deep breaths."

Gray lifted April from the carriage. They walked toward the glen, his arm strongly supporting her.

"If I kissed you right now, would you read anything into it?" he asked.

She knew he was trying to distract her. "Probably."

"Then I won't."

A tall, thin man in a black suit stood in the center of the glen.

Their feet crushed the dry, frozen grass; the man turned at the sound of their approach.

"Miss Truitt?"

"Yes."

He extended a bony hand. "Dr. Reginald Smith. I am here to render my services."

"Th-thank you. This is Dr. Gray Fuller, my second."

The man tipped his hat. "A fellow physician. Pleased to make your acquaintances."

The two men chatted in muted tones as April turned in a circle, memorizing the site. A place where she might soon lose her life. What folly had brought her to this point? Had she completely lost her mind? Henry was not worth one minute of her life. Why, the cad had not even called on her to apologize for his deplorable behavior. She'd seen nothing of him since she'd broken the relationship.

The sound of an arriving conveyance caught April's attention, and the knot in her stomach tightened. Grace Pruitt's carriage, with Henry at the reins, bowled into the glen.

Seeing him with his "intended" made April realize how very real this was. Real and terrifying. Tears filled her eyes and blinded her. Somehow, she'd been hoping, praying, that Grace wouldn't go through with it. She'd hoped—prayed—implored it was a hoax, a humorless farce. But it wasn't. She felt Gray's hand on her shoulder.

Grace was here. April was here. It was real.

Climbing out of the carriage, Henry spoke briefly with Grace, then turned and walked in her direction.

As he approached, his eyes were guarded. "April— I'd like a moment with you."

"I don't believe we have anything to say to one another, Henry."

"Dearest, if you only knew how sick, absolutely sick, I am about this. I assure you, I can explain—"

"Henry," she interrupted.

He paused. "Yes?"

"Were you seeing Grace at the same time you were seeing me?"

"Well . . . yes, but I can expla—"

April walked away. She'd heard all she needed to hear.

Gray turned as she came to stand by him. His gaze searched hers inquisitively.

"He wants to apologize."

"Did you accept?"

"Pffft."

"I need to speak to the rodent for a moment. Anything you want to tell him?"

"Nothing that Grandpa would let me say."

Gray nodded, then left.

Miller's Glen, in another time, was a lovely site. A place where lovers met to tryst, where promises were given and feelings exchanged. Hundred-year-old oaks bent to form a splendid canopy during summer months.

A light breeze sprang up, fragrant with the smells of winter: faint hints of wood smoke, of the pungent dry leaves underfoot. The sky was dawning a magnificent blue.

Would she ever embrace this kind of day again? Would she ever sit in her favorite chair on the back porch and watch the sun set, walk in the falling rain, eat one of Datha's wonderful dinners? She prayed so. That would mean that both she and Datha had survived—that God had extended them yet more grace.

Tears clouded April's vision, and she blinked them back. Gray wasn't going to see her cry and neither was the enemy. She'd had every opportunity to call this off, and she hadn't, or couldn't.

A stream rippled nearby, a haunting accompaniment to the drama about to take place. As the sun began to peek over the treetops, a mist rose from the glen, shrouding it in privacy.

In a few minutes it would be over.

April watched the sun rise, feeling surreal. This might be the last dawn she would ever see. Not that she'd seen that many. She was usually asleep.

If she lived, she'd do better. She'd watch every sunrise for the rest of her life, no matter how early.

"April?"

She turned at the sound of Gray's voice. "Yes?"

"It's time," he said. She focused on the box in his hands. The pistols.

Nodding, she willed her feet to move. They were heavy with dread. "I'm coming."

She avoided Henry's eyes and steadfastly refused to look at Grace. She kept her eyes toward the ground, allowing Gray to steer her into place in the middle of the glen.

"Ladies, are you ready?" The attending doctor's voice seemed unusually loud in the silence.

"Seconds? Prepare yourselves."

April looked up into Gray's eyes. His hand was steady as he reached out and grasped her shoulder tightly. "God be with you."

Everything moved in slow motion, and April felt such despair that she was shaken to the very core of her being.

She glanced at Gray, who now stood off to the side, expressionless.

The doctor's hands moved to her shoulders, aligning her against someone's back—Grace, it must be Grace's back. He gave them both a nod.

"Present the weapons."

Gray presented the pistols, letting Henry and the doctor examine both to make sure they were alike, properly loaded and in suitable condition. They gave no indication that anything was amiss.

"Miss Pruitt, make your choice." There was a rustling of cloth. "Miss Truitt . . ." The doctor paused, glancing up, as if he'd made a blunder. "That is your name? Truitt?"

Swallowing, April nodded.

He glanced at Grace. "And yours is Pruitt?"

April was relieved to learn that even Grace was quaking. Her voice sounded uncertain and faraway.

"Yes, sir."

He looked at Henry, Grace's second, his eyes sizing him up. "Truitt and Pruitt. Interesting. Ladies, take your pistols."

The gun felt much heavier than when she'd practiced with it, but April grasped it with both hands, holding it upright. The doctor began to count off the paces.

Gray's words echoed in her head: *Turn quickly on the count of ten and fire.* How she wished she was still shooting at bottles and cans!

She felt her knees weaken. Quickly, on the count of ten . . .

"One."

*Keep the gun up, squeeze the trigger. . . .*

"Two."

*Slowly. Squeeze it slowly. . . .*

"Three."

*Don't jerk. Whatever you do, don't jerk.*

"Four."

*Why didn't you accept Gray's kiss? So* what *if you read something into it?*

"Five."

"Six."

What had he meant by that? What was she *supposed* to read into it?

"Seven."

*Back out. Right now. Throw the gun down and run.* So what if Grace came to Dignity? She'd fight her there.

"Eight."

"Nine."

*If you're going to do it, do it now!*

"Ten!"

Whirling, April fired. Two shots rang out, then smoke mingled with the gray mist, engulfing her, muffling Gray's shout of agony.

Closing her eyes, April sank slowly to the ground, waiting for the pain to take her.

The fear that Grace would be unethical and bring her own weapon had come true.

April lay rigid on the ground, afraid to move, afraid to die, certain blood was pouring from a gaping wound. *Please, God, let me go quickly and mercifully.* She wasn't any good at dying; she was reasonably sure of that. If she went quickly, Gray would be spared the humiliation of watching her wither in agony, blubbering a coward's lament as the life oozed out of her.

"Miss Truitt?"

The attending doctor knelt beside her. At least she wouldn't die alone. "Tell Grandpa I'm sorry. . . ."

"Miss Truitt!"

"Don't prolong my suffering, please."

"Get up. You're not shot."

"But the bullet . . . it . . ."

"Doctor!" Henry's voice rang out. "Over here!"

"He's hit," she heard someone say.

April rose slowly to her feet, slightly light-headed. Numb. She was numb. She couldn't feel anything. No pain. Lifting her head, she looked around. Grace was still standing, but Henry was kneeling over a figure on the ground.

"Gray!" Shock seized her. Gray was lying prone on the earth, holding his calf while the doctor leaned over him.

Apparently, Grace's shot had hit . . . Gray? Racing to where he lay, April fell to her knees. "What happened?"

"Miss Pruitt shot him," the doctor said gruffly. "Said that all along—women should *not* duel. Someone's bound to get hurt."

"Oh, my goodness . . ." April bent down, patting his cheek. "What have I done?"

"Help me get up," Gray choked out.

"Oh, dear!"

"Miss Truitt fired at the same time Miss Pruitt turned," the doctor explained, tearing Gray's pant leg and clapping a pad of cloth against the bleeding hole in his calf. "Fortunately, Miss Pruitt is an even worse shot."

Henry was on the sidelines, comforting an obviously distraught Grace. April watched as the man she'd once thought was the love of her life walked away with his arm around another woman.

"Gray, I'm so sorry! I'm so sorry—"

"Just get me to the carriage." He reached for her hand, struggling to climb to his feet.

Laughing and crying at the same time, she leaned toward him, intending to give him a hug, but knocking him to the ground.

As he fell to his back, she landed on top of him, giggling.

"I don't see what's so funny—watch the leg!"

"Me." She giggled, her laughter subsiding as she lay on his chest, his big, broad, wonderful chest, gazing at him in wonder. "I'm alive. I'm alive!"

His gentle camaraderie and subtle wit managed to come through in spite of his pain. "I'm bleeding, and you're laughing."

Getting to her feet, she held out her hand. "Come on, we need to get that wound taken care of."

"What? No vegetable compound?"

She leaned closer and kissed him—a very thorough kiss that Francesca would resent. But at the moment gratitude—and something deeper—made the opportunity irresistible.

A faint light twinkled in the depths of Gray's eyes when their lips parted. "That was nice—almost worth taking a bullet for."

## Chapter Eighteen

The doctor loaded Gray into the carriage. April climbed aboard and picked up the reins.

"Can you drive a buggy?" he asked, grimacing as he maneuvered his injured leg inside.

"Fortunately, I drive better than I shoot," April assured him.

"Ah, thank God for small favors," Gray said.

"I'll go straight to the doctor's office—"

"No, you'll go directly to Dignity."

"But your leg—"

"Will heal better there. Besides, I've got patients to see. Datha needs attention."

"All right." April grinned, relieved. At the moment all she wanted to do was go home, give Grandpa a grateful hug and kiss the ground.

Being alive was indeed beautiful!

Flora Lee was sitting beside Datha's cot when April helped Gray into the office.

Seeing the doctor's predicament, she immediately got to her feet. "What happened to you?"

"A little accident," he grumbled, sitting down. "Think you can help me with this?" he asked April.

"If you'll tell me what to do."

"How is Datha?"

"Quiet," Flora Lee said, sitting again. "She woke up a couple of times, but I'm not sure she knew who I was or what's happened. I tell her she's all right, just like you told me to do, and I talk to her. That uppity boy's been here, doin' the same. But she don't seem to know where she is."

Frowning, April went to kneel beside her chair. Rarely would she argue with an elder, but Flora Lee's animosity toward Jacel had to stop—for her granddaughter's sake. "Flora Lee, I know you don't approve of Jacel, but is it necessary to refer to him as 'uppity'?" Jacel deserved her respect. "Datha loves him very much, and when she's better she'll resent your sarcasm."

Turning her troubled gaze on April, Flora Lee said, "But he *is* an uppity man. I don't like him."

"I know you feel that way now, but in time you'll have to learn to get along with Jacel or you'll lose Datha. You don't want that, do you?"

"I'll cross that bridge when I come to it. . . ." Her tired eyes rested on Datha, lying so deathly still. "If I come to it."

"She's young and strong, Flora Lee. She's going to pull through this," Gray told her.

"Yes, my girl's strong," the woman murmured. Turning back to her granddaughter, she softly hummed the same lullaby Jacel had hummed earlier, a haunting melody April had heard since she was a child. A tune, Flora Lee had told her, she'd sung in the fields as a young girl.

Gray oversaw April's efforts as she cut his trouser leg off at the knee, cleaned and dressed his wound.

She clenched her teeth when he flinched at the sting of antiseptic. Somehow Grace had managed to shoot him in his left calf, but the bullet had gone completely through, which was good, he told her.

"Wrap it snugly," Gray instructed, holding one end of the gauze as she maneuvered the other.

When she was through, she saw that his face was pale and sweat glistened on his brow. "I think you need to lie down."

"I need to check Datha first."

"You said yourself that there's nothing more you can do but wait, try to keep her fever down and rouse her enough to take nourishment. Flora Lee and I can do that. But if something happens to you," she said, taking his arm and urging him out of the chair, "we're all in trouble."

Gray tried to protest, but she could see he didn't have the strength.

"You go on up and rest a spell," Flora Lee said agreeably. "Me and the uppity boy can see to Datha."

Sighing, April realized her efforts to change the older woman's attitude had fallen on deaf ears.

Helping Gray up the outside staircase, she unlocked the door to his living quarters with the key he gave her. Her eyes swept the out-of-character furnishing.

She helped him across the room, and he sank down onto the bed, then attempted to remove his boots.

"Well, when you're married, you'll have to convince your wife to let you have some say in decorating," April said as she helped him with the task. Tossing a boot in a corner, then another, she watched as he fell back across the bed.

By the time she returned from the stove with a cup of steaming tea, Gray was lying beneath the sheet.

"Drink this. I put some honey in it."

He managed to push himself upright and take a couple of sips of the hot liquid before lying back. "I'm sorry, I'm suddenly very tired."

"Then rest," she said softly. "If you're needed, I'll wake you."

She stood holding the cup, watching him drift off to sleep. Over the weeks his hair had grown longer until it now nearly covered his ears; his strong jaw was marked by a day-old beard. He was pale, too pale. He'd lost more blood than he wanted to admit.

Lifting the sheet, she checked the bloody bandage. Guilt ripped through her. Gray was in this condition because of her stupidity. She'd made a grave mistake putting her trust in Henry, against the advice of Grandpa and Beulah. Yes, she'd be more sensible in the future.

She owed Gray more than a simple "thanks." Until he was fully recovered she would see to his every need and do whatever she could to keep his practice running smoothly. It was the least she could do.

Gently settling the sheet around his leg, she slipped out of the room, closing the door softly behind her.

The following week, April split her time between taking care of Gray and watching over Datha.

When Riley heard the doctor had been wounded, he was upset until April explained it was purely accidental and wasn't thought to be serious.

"A hunting accident?" Riley scratched his head. "Didn't know he hunted. When does he find the time?"

"Oh, I don't know," April said without bothering to correct him. "You know men—I guess he makes the time."

Riley walked off grumbling. "Wish Datha would get back. Flora Lee's making gravy, and I'm not supposed to have it."

By the third day, infection set into Gray's wound. A fever kept him rambling, half out of his head, leaving him weak and incapable of arguing with her.

April saw to his care and even doled out advice to patients who needed it. By now Grandpa had come to see how Gray was feeling. When he found April there, she was forced to be inventive, telling him she was working as a volunteer nurse. Gray was her first patient.

Grandpa went away mumbling under his breath.

When Mary Rader came to the office demanding her tonic, April was stymied.

Mary, almost hysterical when she found out Gray was indisposed, insisted that April wake him.

Running upstairs, she roused Gray out of a deep sleep to ask him what he gave her.

Staring at her wide-eyed, he muttered something that resembled "pinkhamsgoofycompound."

April mulled the garbled words over in her mind. Mmm. Pinkhamsgoofycompound? A light suddenly clicked on in her head. Pinkham's Goofy Compound! He had been doling out Lydia's tonic to his women patients!

Picking up a pillow, she whacked him soundly over the head.

Grunting, he fell back to the mattress, succumbing to a laudanum-induced sleep.

A fourth day passed, and April decided the doctor was not a good patient. He complained incessantly, found fault with every morsel of food she brought him, and when confronted with the news that she knew he'd been giving Lydia's compound to his patients, he turned downright surly.

Still, she owed him much.

He'd taught her to shoot, had supported her, stood beside her, solved the problem of Grace and what had she done for him? Called him a quack, criticized him and got him shot.

She'd just settled him for a nap Thursday afternoon when a knock came at the door. Blowing a strand of hair off her forehead, she ran lightly across the room to answer it so Gray wouldn't be disturbed. Patients came at all hours of the night and day, depriving him of much-needed rest. She'd made up her mind she was going to get firm with the incessant disturbances. They had to stop if Gray was to recover his strength.

"Yes?"

Francesca stood on the small landing, her mouth open in surprise. "Oh . . . you're the . . . mortician's daughter. I've seen you downstairs." A frown creased her perfectly made-up face. "You are here . . . for what reason?"

"Shh, Gray's sleeping." April stepped onto the landing and closed the door behind her. This wasn't the ideal person to take a firm stance with, but she had to start somewhere.

"Gray's what?"

"Sleeping."

Francesca's eyes narrowed. "I think you'd better explain."

Lowering her voice, April did so. "Gray's been injured—not seriously," she added at the stricken look on Francesca's face. "But nonetheless, enough that he hasn't been able to work. I've been seeing to his needs."

Her eyebrows lifted. "Seeing to his needs? In what way? Oh. You're cleaning for him. He is very bad at housekeeping. I have asked him to—"

"I'm not his cleaning lady," April said, recalling the woman's autocratic attitude the first time they'd met.

"Then why *are* you here?"

"Gray is ill, and I'm caring for him."

It seemed to April that the woman didn't care one whit for Gray, or anyone else, for that matter. Why else would she insist upon staying in Dallas while he was here? She was constantly showing up unannounced, demanding his attention when he had an office full of sick patients!

What kind of love was that?

Francesca's eyes widened. "How hurt is he? Oh, I must see him—"

"No, you don't want to. He's . . . caught something. It might be contagious."

*Shame on you, April Truitt!* Lying was getting to be second nature to her!

"Contagious?" Francesca drew back.

April was ashamed of herself, but her nurturing side was stronger at the moment than her conscience. Besides, Francesca deserved it.

"All kinds of ugly blotches. Really ugly."

Cocking her head, Miss DuBois glared at her. "Then why are you here?"

"I've already had . . . it."

"It? What, may I ask, *is* it?"


Disturbed by the commotion outside the door, Gray stirred, opening his eyes. When he recognized Francesca's voice, he groaned.

When the women's talking grew louder, he struggled to the side of his bed, sitting up. Clasping the bedpost, he pulled himself to his feet, then slowly inched across the room on rubbery legs.

By the time he'd reached the door, the loud voices had turned to shouts that half the town was surely able to hear.

Yanking the door open, he looked out. April and Francesca were face-to-face on the small landing.

"You will move away from the door!" Francesca

told April in a tone colder than a Minnesota January.

She stubbornly held her ground. "The doctor is *resting*. I won't have him disturbed."

Francesca took a threatening step toward her. "Why, how dare you—"

"That's enough, both of you."

April turned at the sound of his voice, her bravado slipping. "Gray—you shouldn't be out of bed."

"What is all the racket out here?"

"She said you were contagious!" Francesca accused, shooting poisonous looks at April. "She won't let me in to see you."

"I didn't say never," April protested mildly.

"You might as well have!" Francesca was worked up now, and getting louder. She stared at Gray. "You don't have any hideous blotches on your face!"

He frowned. "What blotches? What are you talking about?"

"She said you had something terrible!"

"I did not—not exactly."

"Francesca, lower your voice." Motioning for the two warring women to come inside, Gray limped back into the room.

"I will not enter that room with *her* in it."

The ultimatum in Francesca's voice was hard to miss. Gray was being asked—no, ordered—to choose. The mortician's granddaughter or her.

His choice.

And he'd better make it snappy, her tone implied.

Throwing up his arms in exasperation, he limped

back to bed. "Do whatever you want, Francesca."

She stamped her foot. "Gray Fuller!" she yelled. "You come back here! How dare you walk away from me like that!"

Pushing April aside, she stormed into the apartment, slamming the door behind her.

The curtains covering the door gyrated crazily.

Leaning against the railing, April suddenly felt weak-kneed. Why had she done that? Francesca was entitled to see the doctor.

What right did April have to stand between a man and the woman he was courting? She had made a vow to behave better, but the audacity of that woman made her forget her promise.

From inside she could hear Francesca giving Gray a piece of her mind in a strident voice. An occasional rumble came from Gray, but for the most part the French woman was doing all the talking—or rather shouting.

"And you'd better be back on your feet for the party in three weeks!"

Slamming the door of Gray's apartment behind her, Francesca shot April a withering look and marched down the staircase.

Leaning over the railing, April called, "You should be ashamed of yourself! You don't care about his illness!"

What kind of love was that?

She barely heard Francesca's cold and impertinent response.

## Chapter Nineteen

Datha was slowly regaining strength. Flora Lee insisted upon helping April with housework in her absence. She offered to cook, too, insisting that it kept her young—and besides, the Ogdens were family, and what was family for if they couldn't do something nice for one another?

Flora Lee was slowly coming to terms with Jacel and Datha's relationship, although she openly and frequently expressed her anger at Datha for the road she had chosen . . . one that had almost taken her life.

While Datha had been recovering at the doctor's office, Jacel's attentiveness had shown Flora Lee a new side of the young man. His love for Datha, and his constant devotion to her, gradually persuaded Flora Lee to be less judgmental and more tolerant, although she still called him uppity from time to time.

April looked forward to spring. The season held new meaning for her. She'd survived the duel, and she had close friends and family. She had much to be thankful for.

As for Henry, she hoped she'd never see the man again.

"Honest. You've never seen anything like it," she told Beulah. "Gray was powerful—so heroic in the way he handled the ruse."

"But he was shot."

"Only because Grace—as he predicted—brought her own weapon loaded with live ammunition."

"Wasn't Grace furious about the blank ammunition?"

"She didn't *know* it was blank—or if she did she was so embarrassed by her cowardly act she didn't say anything. She left soon after, with Henry in tow. Of course, Gray couldn't confront her about the loaded gun without revealing the ruse, so nothing was said by either side."

Beulah turned from the sink, her face suffused with heat. The Odgens and Ludwigs were sharing Sunday dinner today. "I am *so* angry with you!"

"I know. . . ." April tried to catch her hand in an attempt to mollify her. "I wanted to tell you, but I knew you would only worry, and the more people who knew about the duel the bigger the risk that Grandpa would find out—"

"You think I would have told him!"

"No, of course not. But it's over now, and other than Gray's wound, it turned out all right. Henry's out of my life, and God saved me from marrying a man who would only bring heartache to a marriage."

Sinking down in a kitchen chair, Beulah fiddled with a napkin. April knew that she had hurt her best friend's feelings, but she'd had no choice. Other than a brief mention in the *Burgess Courier*—with no names mentioned—the duel incident had remained quiet.

God indeed had been merciful to April, and she had

learned a valuable lesson: the next man she fell in love with would indeed be a man of honor, a man steeped in his faith.

"I know I'm forgetting something," she muttered, trying to divert Beulah's attention. She wiped her hands on her apron, trying to organize her thoughts.

"I can't imagine what it would be," her friend said. "There's enough food here to feed Europe."

Beulah had arrived early to help. With Datha still recovering and Flora Lee busy in the kitchen, April was running around like a chicken with its head cut off.

In the smoking room, Eldon Ludwig and Riley visited by the fire. There was a huge stuffed turkey in the oven, sweet potatoes boiling on the stove to be mashed with brown sugar and butter, jars of pickles and relish ready to be put into dishes. Pies were cooling on the kitchen table. April already had the dining room table set, and it wasn't ten o'clock yet.

"Sit down and relax a minute," Beulah urged, taking her by the shoulders and lowering her into a chair. "You've worn yourself to a frazzle."

"I can't sit, Beulah! Eight people will be eating at my table in two hours!"

"There's nothing left to be done," her friend insisted. "Flora Lee's run us out of the kitchen twice. Besides, I've got something to tell you."

"Can't it wait until later?"

"No, I'm bursting to tell you right now."

"What's so important that you have to tell me immediately?"

Beulah drew a deep breath. She leaned back, closing
her eyes, grinning from ear to ear. "See what I'm
doing?"

"Savoring the moment."

She chuckled mysteriously.

Now April's curiosity was piqued. Not only by
Beulah's strange behavior, but by the smile curving
her generous mouth.

"Come on, what? Don't keep me in suspense."

"I've been seeing Raymond."

April stared at her. "I know that."

"But I mean, really *seeing* him."

April absently rearranged a place setting, jumping
when her friend swatted her hand.

"I *mean,* he's coming by every week now."

"I thought his work brought him to Dignity every
two to three weeks?"

"It does, but he's been altering his route so he can
come through Dignity more often . . . to see me."

A smile crept across April's face. "To see you."

"Yes. To see me."

"And?"

"And Papa likes him, and he's brought me little
gifts, like this locket." She held out the enameled heart
on a delicate chain around her neck. "I think—oh,
dash it all! I'm almost afraid to think. What . . . what
do you think?"

"I think he sounds like a man who's seriously infatuated with you, if not in love," April said, laughing when the pink in her friend's cheeks deepened.

"Do you think so?" Beulah whispered.

"I think," April whispered back, "that we'd better start thinking about wedding dresses."

"Oh!" Beulah wailed, her hands coming up to cover her mouth. "I'm afraid to think of it, but I do like him. So much." She giggled. "So very, very, very much. He . . . he says I'm perfect, just the way I am. He actually said that. I even . . . well, I asked him if he minded me being, well, fat, but he seemed surprised that I'd even ask. And it wasn't an act, he was completely sincere. Do you think . . . do you honestly think he means it?"

April patted her hand. "I honestly think he means it."

Beulah bit her lower lip. "I know I shouldn't be so happy—I mean, nothing is official yet, and I don't want to make you feel bad."

"Why should it make me feel bad?"

"Well, because of Henry."

"Henry who?"

After a momentary hesitation, Beulah laughed, and April joined her. "Indeed, Henry who?"

Gray arrived promptly at eleven-thirty. He brought a large pan of onion pudding and admitted that Frances Marlow and her daughter had brought it by his office the day before.

He looked so striking in his dark blue suit and tie, with his hair slicked back and slightly damp. And he smelled so good she wanted to get closer, as Beulah would say, to savor the moment.

She glanced at his wounded leg. "Is everything okay?"

"Excellent. I'm seeing a good doctor." He grinned.

"I'm glad you could come."

"Thank you for inviting me." He still favored his left leg, but she could see that he was getting back to normal. Stuffing his gloves into a pocket, he handed her the pudding and his hat and muffler.

"Grandpa has the checkerboard set up—"

"Just waiting for somebody to beat," Riley called from the parlor. "Come join us by the fire."

Gray laughed. "He sounds in rare form today."

Grinning, April drank in the sight of the doctor. She hadn't seen him in over a week, and she missed him.

"You coming or not?" Riley called. "Eldon and I haven't got all day."

"Anxious to get beat?"

"First time for everything," Riley taunted.

April left the men to their game and went to the kitchen to get on Flora Lee's nerves, asking whether the turkey was going to be ready on time and when to mash the potatoes.

Around one o'clock they sat down to eat. Holding hands, they bowed their heads and listened as Riley said the blessing.

Jacel and Datha sat across from April—with Flora Lee. The woman was bad to carry a grudge, but like Grandpa had predicted, she'd come around eventually.

After the blessing, Datha picked up the bowl of potatoes and started it around the table.

"I have some news, Jacel's been accepted for the fall."

The old woman looked surprised. "He has?"

"Yes. And he's already got a place to live in the city. He'll go a couple of weeks early to find a job near the school to help pay for his books."

"How'd all that get done?"

"Mr. Ogden wrote him a letter of recommendation, and so did Dr. Fuller and Mrs. Langston, his teacher. She's even offered to tutor him."

"Dr. Fuller found him some law books to read the last time he was in Dallas," Beulah added.

*The last time he was in Dallas seeing Francesca,* April thought.

"Pestering me all the time, wanting to know about medicine." Mr. Ludwig laughed. "Him and that Grimes boy."

"Raymond?" April asked, glancing at Beulah. Seeing the flush rise in her friend's cheeks, she grinned. "Does Raymond know a lot about medicines?"

"Nearly as much as any doctor." Eldon Ludwig nodded. "Except for Dr. Fuller."

"Thank you," Gray declared. "You've been a great help to me, getting settled here and all."

April brought them back to the subject. "Tell me what you know about Mr. Grimes."

Beulah kicked her under the table, and she kicked back.

Mr. Ludwig paused with his fork suspended in midair. "What is there to tell? He's twenty-eight, his parents are gone, only has an aunt he visits from time to time, has a good education, likes selling, doesn't like the traveling. A good boy. Asks a lot of questions."

"Oh? What kinds of questions?" Riley asked.

"He asks many questions about my Beulah. I tell him, ask her yourself."

"Papa!"

April's eyes danced as Beulah became even more dedicated to the food on her plate.

"He does seem the perfect mate for a woman," April said, ignoring Beulah's silent plea to let the subject drop. "No doubt he'll be settling down soon."

"He told me he would be coming through town every three weeks or so," Gray said, "but I've noticed he's making his rounds almost every week. I thought it was my stimulating conversation—" he winked at April "—but I see I was wrong."

Beulah's face was red as a beet from all the teasing. "Really, people, can't you find anything more interesting to discuss?"

"More interesting than Raymond?" April asked.

Everyone burst into laughter, and Beulah turned crimson.

"This is a special day," Riley began. "A day like any other day, but one when we should pause and give thanks for the good things sent our way. I'd like for each of us to share one thing that we're thankful for. I'll start." Lifting his glass, he studied the contents. "I'm thankful for my granddaughter. She brings me much joy. And for friends, old and new."

He saluted Gray.

Gray lifted his glass in return. "I am thankful for new friends and for the acceptance I've found here in Dignity."

"For a good year, and hopes for another good year," Mr. Ludwig intoned, adding his salute.

"For my sweet Datha being returned to me," Flora Lee said. "Thank You, God, and Dr. Fuller."

"Part of the thanks goes to April," Gray said. Turning to her, he met her gaze as he lifted his glass in another toast. "Thank you for showing me that modern medicine can sometimes learn something from old-time ways."

April raised her own glass. "And my thanks goes to your skill and compassion and devotion in helping my grandfather, and Datha . . . and being a good teacher," she exclaimed softly.

They saluted one another, their eyes sharing their secret.

"I'm thankful that the good Lord saw fit to . . . forgive my mistakes, and let me keep my Datha," Jacel said.

"Hear, hear," Riley added softly.

Very slowly, Flora Lee lifted her glass to Jacel, who grinned at her in response.

"And I'm thankful the Lord saw fit to spare me in

my foolishness," Datha whispered as tears filled her eyes. "And for my grandmother, and the good Lord, who loves me no matter what."

Jacel drew her against him, and Flora Lee patted Datha's hand.

"And I'm thankful . . . for warm fires, good food and family to share it with. I love you, Papa," Beulah said, laughing when her father ducked his head. "And—"

"Traveling salesmen?" April said.

"I was going to say I was thankful for good friends!"

Everyone laughed, then lifted their glasses in another salute to one another.

Later, after stuffing themselves with pie, they retreated to the parlor to sit before the fire and recover.

When she felt able to get up again, April went to the kitchen to clear the table and put away the food.

"Let me help," Gray said as he entered the kitchen, taking a platter from her hands.

"Nonsense, you're a guest."

His eyes softened. "Come on. It'll take less time if I help. Besides," he whispered, "Flora Lee told me to."

April laughed and surrendered. "But you don't really need to help," she told him as she tied an apron around his waist. "Beulah will be glad to."

"Actually, I'm selfish. I wanted a few minutes alone with you."

She felt a flush warm her cheeks as she picked up the teakettle and poured hot water into the dishpan. If Gray Fuller wanted her undivided attention, he had it. "Is something special on your mind?"

"No," he admitted. "Where's a dishtowel?"

Tossing him one, she added soap to the pan. "Gray, what did you say to Henry the day of the duel?" She'd wondered, but was always reluctant to ask. Whatever it was, Henry deserved it.

"Just that if anything happened to you, I'd shoot him."

Grinning, she looked up. "Really?"

"Really." Picking up the towel, he dried a glass. "What did you say to Francesca the day she popped in?"

"Which day was that?"

"I forgot. There're so many of them they're hard to pin down. The day she came and discovered I'd been shot."

"I don't remember, exactly. Something about you being contagious. I wasn't very nice."

He grinned this time. "Oh?"

"Well, I think she 'pops in' far too often, but then who am I to say?"

"Just the woman who nursed me back to health." For a moment the kitchen was very quiet. The murmur of voices drifted to them from the parlor, but it felt as if they were alone. "I didn't see Francesca going out of her way to care for me," he said.

"It wasn't her fault. I wouldn't let her come in," April admitted.

"I don't know if I've been remiss in telling you how much I appreciate what you did. I could say I hope to return the favor, but considering the circumstances . . ."

336

"There's no need to thank me," she murmured. "I wouldn't let anyone else come near you."

Laying the dishtowel aside, Gray approached her. There was an intriguing look in his eyes, and April thought he might be going to kiss her. She wished with all her heart that he would.

Taking her into his arms, he said softly, "You spoil me, April Truitt."

"Would that be so bad?"

His eyes softened. "If I kiss you, we'll both read something into it, won't we."

"Most assuredly," she whispered.

Pulling her closer, he lightly pressed his lips to hers. She yielded to his overpowering mastery, knowing nothing would ever be the same between them. This man could not love Francesca DuBois. He was a man of honor; he respected God's laws. He was not a fool.

If only she knew the real reason why he continued to let the French woman remain in his life.

"April?" Grandpa called from the parlor, shattering the brief intimacy. "Coffee's getting cold. Can you bring more?"

Breaking away, she drew a deep breath, trying to still her trembling.

"April," Gray said as she moved to the stove for the coffeepot.

"Yes?"

"Thank you for letting me come today."

"My pleasure, Gray."

• • •

Two days later, April answered a knock at the door to find Henry standing on the step.

Her temper instantly flared. "What are you doing here?"

Holding a hand playfully in front of his face, he said in a cajoling voice, "I need to talk to you. May I come in?"

"You said everything I need to know the morning of the duel."

"It's cold out here—let me in, April. I can explain my unseemly actions. . . ."

Her voice was colder than the weather. "If you want to talk to someone, talk to Grace."

"April, you owe me—"

"Nothing, Henry. I owe you nothing. Now please leave."

He rubbed his hands together as he shifted from one foot to another. It was cold outside, the wind whipping around the corner of the house, but she wasn't about to invite him in.

"I was a fool."

She folded her arms, hugging warmth to her body, wondering why he no longer meant anything to her. It was nice to see him groveling, but not as nice as she'd pictured it. She felt nothing, actually. Just cold.

"You're being stubborn, April."

"I'm being realistic, Henry. You made a fool of me."

"I don't love her! It was just a small dalliance—you know how men are. We're like that. . . ." His voice became persuasive. "The important thing is that I love *you,* not Grace, and I'm here to make amends. I know you're angry with me, but if you'll only be reasonable, we can work this out."

She stared at him.

"Could I come in? Please?"

Expelling a sigh, she shook her head.

"I wanted to . . . *had* to tell you . . . how foolish I've been."

"And how foolish is that?"

He looked at her as if he didn't recognize her. She hardly recognized herself. She'd thought she loved this man, and now she just felt pity for him.

"I'm trying to say, April, that I made a mistake."

She recognized frustration in his voice. She knew the sentiment. He should have heard her the morning Gray was driving her to the duel.

"I—I got carried away with—"

"The thrill of having two women in love with you?"

"Well, yes. It was childish, foolish, and I realize that now. I know how shallow Grace is. She's only interested in controlling me. You aren't like that—"

"I don't think I like being compared with Grace, Henry."

"I know that." He waved a hand apologetically. "I'm sorry. There is no comparison. You made me believe I could be a success. She was only interested in dominating me." He looked stricken. "You have to forgive me, April. All I think about is you, and what a fool I've been. Please forgive me."

She stared at him.

"Please say you'll give me another chance."

She remained silent, hoping he'd take the hint and leave.

"It doesn't have to be this way. You can be sensible about this. Can't a man make a mistake?"

Still staring, she shifted position.

"I can make you love me again. . . ." Henry was beginning to look baffled. April could see that he'd fully expected her to take him back. The old April would have. The new one wouldn't dream of it.

"We'll be working together, and the situation has to be cleared up."

"No, as much as I believe in the compound, I've told Lydia that I can't work with it any longer."

"Because of me?"

April almost laughed. "Don't flatter yourself, Henry. Because of Grandpa. I don't want to jeopardize his health by my actions."

"You're deserting Pinkham's Compound?"

"No, I'll always believe in it, but I've come to realize doctors are invaluable, too. The compound is good, as a supplement to a doctor's skills. Even Gray recognizes the value of herbal treatment in tandem with medical intervention."

Henry turned petulant. "Gray?"

"Dr. Fuller," April amended, finding it increasingly hard to think of him as just a doctor. He meant so much more to her.

"You've told Lydia your feelings?"

"Yes, and she understands."

"Well, I don't."

"No, a man like you wouldn't understand."

He left reluctantly, and she watched him meander slowly down the walk toward the town square. There was a sadness inside her, not for the death of a love, but for Henry. She had a feeling his life would include an endless succession of Graces.

Throwing on her heavy cloak, she left the mortuary, struggling against the blustery wind as she made her way to the pharmacy.

Beulah looked up as she entered the store. "April! What are you doing here on a day like this?"

"I needed some air," she said, slipping off her hood and stamping water from her shoes.

"Well, you should have a bushel basket of it by now. Want some tea?"

"I'd love it," she said, following her back to the stove to warm her hands.

As her friend set water on to boil, April told her about Henry's visit.

"The cad."

"The rodent."

"Have you gotten your invitation?"

April frowned. "To the spring social? Yes. What are you planning to wear?"

Beulah added tea leaves to the pot, avoiding April's gaze. "Raymond Grimes."

April smiled. "What?"

"I'm going to wear Raymond on my arm."

She laughed. "He's invited you to the spring social?"

"Just this morning!"

"I'm thrilled!"

"I am, too."

"You're really serious about him, aren't you?"

Beulah's cheeks warmed. "I really am. He's shy, rather quiet, but I do like him . . . no, I love him, April." Laying the spoon aside, she turned weepy. "I love him so much it hurts."

"Well, then maybe I ought to be thinking about a maid of honor's dress?"

"Oh." She blushed. "I wouldn't be in any hurry, but, well . . ." She shrugged. "We'll see."

April clasped her hand, squeezing it. "So why the sad face? You're in love with a wonderful man, and for what it's worth, I like Raymond, too."

"But what if he doesn't love me?" The words hung between them like a millstone.

"Why wouldn't he?"

"Well . . . you know."

April quirked an eyebrow questioningly. "I *don't* know. What's not to love?" Her friend was waiting for her to mention her weight, but April wouldn't. No matter how many times she told Beulah that her weight didn't matter, she wouldn't believe it. It would take years of being adored by a man like Raymond to convince her.

"Oh, I guess I'm just being silly. He probably won't ask me to marry him, anyway, but I can dream, can't I?"

"You sure can. Now, where's that tea?"

For the next half hour the girls huddled in the back room, discussing the advantages of a wedding dress with a long train versus one without a train, a long or short veil, satin or taffeta, an Empire waist or princess style. By the time April started for home, she felt happier than she had in weeks. Her own hopes and dreams of marriage were gone, but Beulah's were alive and well, whether her friend believed it or not.

## Chapter Twenty

"Don't you love winter?" April asked.

"Yes, ma'am." Datha opened the door, letting in flurries. "Good thing we don't get snow here often."

"That's why it's so wonderful when we do!"

Adding a heavy muffler over her cloak, she set out again at a brisk pace toward the square. A cold wind whipped the hem of her cloak. Pewter-colored clouds threatened to add more snow to the inch already on the ground. Laughing, she kicked at the flakes, hoping it would snow a foot.

"I love winter!" she shouted, then quickly ducked her head and walked faster when people turned to stare.

Preparing to cross the square, she saw Gray coming toward her. Her heart hammered against her ribs as she stood for a moment, looking at him. He hadn't dropped by the mortuary in over a week. It was almost as if he was avoiding her, and she didn't know why.

He hadn't spotted her yet. Reaching down, she scooped up a handful of snow and formed a ball.

Obviously deep in thought, with his head bent, he didn't see her.

He was too serious. She needed to do something about that.

With a youthful glee she hadn't felt in a long time, she fired the snowball at him, catching him squarely on the side of the head. He staggered, stopped, then whipped around to look in the direction the missile had come from.

Grinning, she crouched behind a small spruce.

Leaning down, he scooped snow off a bench, quickly formed a ball and arced it toward her.

"Missed," she called, taking aim again.

"On purpose," he replied, pelting her soundly with the next snowball.

Bolder now, she packed more snow and started toward him. Dancing to one side, he returned fire, and before long they were pelting one another with snow at a steady rate until they were within feet of one another.

As she scooped up a handful with the intent of dumping it down his collar, Gray leaped forward and grabbed her around the waist, swinging her in a circle.

"Oh, no, you don't," he warned, stuffing a handful of snow down her neck.

April screeched. "Not fair!" she cried. "You're bigger than I am."

"Didn't stop you from throwing that first snowball."

"Truce?"

"Too late," he said, pushing more snow down her collar.

They were hidden from view of the stores by a clump of shrubs in the square.

"Gray!"

"Beg."

"Never."

His breath was warm against her cheek. "Beg," he whispered, pulling her closer until her body molded tightly to his.

"I never beg."

"Then surrender, or I'll kiss you, Miss Truitt."

"Never!"

Turning her in his arms, he looked into her eyes for what seemed an eternity before his lips descended on hers.

His skin was cool from the wintry air, then warm. She forgot the fact that they were kissing in a public place.

"Surrender now?"

"Never." She shoved her handful of snow down his neck.

He jumped, and she ran laughing across the square.

Not looking where she was going, April ran straight into Willa Madden, bowling her off her feet. Packages flew every which way as Willa spilled to the ground in a tangle of wildly flailing arms and legs.

Grinning, Gray dug snow out of his collar and watched April make apologies, then help the woman to her feet while trying to gather the scattered bundles.

He laughed to himself. April's mishaps warmed his heart. She wasn't prim and proper, constantly worried about the way society viewed her. She was refreshing. Exactly what he wanted in a woman. A wife.

A second later April sprinted off, her bright red cap bobbing like a cork in a white lake.

April spent the rest of the day warring with her emotions. At suppertime, she was still mulling over her earlier encounter with Gray.

But she had to forget what had happened. One experience with a fickle man was enough. The last thing she wanted was for Francesca to single her out for a duel. Of course, April was experienced now, but she doubted Gray would survive another assault. She smiled at the thought.

"What is the matter with you?" Riley demanded when April spent the first twenty minutes of supper moving her food about her plate.

"Just tired."

"Uh-huh. Pass the creamed corn."

April listlessly handed him the bowl.

"Have you seen Gray lately?"

She glanced up, wondering if he could read her mind.

"I . . . love him," she whispered.

Her grandfather set the corn down with a loud thump. "What?"

She hadn't realized she'd spoken the words out loud. Now that she had, why try to pretend any longer? "I love him."

"Does he know this?"

"No."

Riley took a bite of chicken, keeping his eyes on his plate. "You and Gray been seeing each other?"

"No," she admitted.

"But you're in love with him."

"Yes." She sighed again.

"Pretty foolish of you, isn't it? Falling in love with a man who's reportedly courting another woman."

"Yes."

"Then I'd suggest you two stop kissing in the public square." He took another bite of chicken.

Her head snapped up. "You know about that?"

"I've known about it *all,* April."

It didn't surprise her. She knew her luck would run out someday. "Was it Gray who told you I was working with Mrs. Pinkham?"

"No, Midge Shoeman told me."

"*Midge* told you?"

"Yes, why?"

"No reason." Wrong again. April went back to stirring her peas.

"Gray told me about the duel."

"Oh, for goodness' sake!" She dropped her fork on the table.

"Now, that was stupid." He reached for a biscuit. "If you ever get it in your mind to do something that foolish again, you just get it right out again. Do you hear me, April Delane?"

"I wasn't shot!"

"The doctor was almost killed!"

"Not by me. That was Grace."

"From now on, I don't want to hear of you packing a gun. You hear me?"

"Yes, sir."

"And what's this rot going around about Pinkham's tonic? I've never heard such drivel—you aren't responsible for that, are you? Charley Black is down-right scary lately!"

"No," she said honestly. "I'm not responsible for that."

Beulah was.

"Selling Pinkham's hogwash, fighting a *pistol* duel over Henry Long," he muttered, slathering the biscuit with butter he shouldn't have. "What next? Set your hair on fire and run cross-eyed through the town square?"

A rapid-fire staccato knocking drew April from the kitchen at a run the next morning. Expecting to find a messenger with a dire emergency, she was relieved to see Beulah, who rushed in before April could get the door all the way open.

"Where's the fire?"

"Raymond asked me!"

"Asked you what?"

Beulah was dancing in place as if she didn't know what to do with herself. "Asked me to marry him!"

"To marry him!" She grabbed her friend's arms, and they danced around the kitchen together, laughing and crying at the same time.

"When?" April asked when they were finally able to talk.

"May."

April's mind was racing. She was deliriously happy for Beulah, but it was obvious she had to take control of the situation. Beulah was so excited, she wouldn't be a bit of help.

"You need a dress."

"Yes, and I don't have much time to have one made! What will I do?"

"Let's not panic." April paced the foyer, trying to formulate plans. "Datha can help. She's very good with a needle, and since she's not able to do much around the house, she'd be happy to sew your dress. Now, we've got to talk to Reverend Brown, reserve the church, see about flowers, bridesmaids . . ."

"You'll be my maid of honor. You can wear the green dress you wore at Thanksgiving."

"But I've worn it!"

"Only once. It'll be perfect. Raymond is going to ask Gray to be his best man."

"He is?"

"Uh-huh. Oh, my goodness!" Grabbing April's waist, Beulah swung her around the room again. "*I'm getting married!*"

• • •

The following weeks were a flurry of activity as Datha cut and sewed an ivory silk dress with an Empire waist and lace insets. April busied herself in wedding plans and preparations, purposely filling every minute so she wouldn't think.

She was happy for Beulah—deliriously happy. But, oh, why couldn't Gray look at her the way Raymond looked at Beulah? She knew—she *knew*—he did not love Francesca. He never spoke of her, and her frequent visits appeared to annoy more than please him. Did April dare ask his feelings for the spoiled, worldly debutante from Dallas?

"I'm going to Burgess," she told Riley that evening. "I want a new dress for Beulah's wedding."

"Thought she said you could wear the green one."

"She did, but I want something new. After all, I'm the maid of honor, and I want everything to be perfect."

"Hogwash. You're buying a new dress to impress Gray Fuller."

"Guilty," she admitted, "for what good it will do me."

"Don't count yourself out," he advised.

She paused, whirling to confront him. "Why? Do you know something? Has he said anything to you about me? Does he—"

Grandpa threw up his hands. "Hold on! All I meant was before you give up, don't you think you should let

350

the man know how you feel? He's not a mind reader."

April paused, her hand on the stair railing. "No, that wouldn't be proper." She hurried on up the stairs.

Scratching his head, Riley grunted. "Since when did that make any difference?"

The clock downstairs chimed three. April lay awake, thinking. She was happy for Beulah, there was no question of that. It was just that . . . she was jealous. That was it, though she hated to admit it. Jealous.

She wanted Gray. More than anything she'd ever wanted in her life, she wanted the good doctor. She wanted to marry him, be the mother of his children, grow old and die with Gray Fuller.

And a mere dress wasn't going to accomplish her goal.

She could buy a hundred dresses and never catch his eye.

What she needed was a plan, not a dress. A plan to make him see her. April Truitt.

Smiling, she wiggled deeper beneath the covers, suddenly very sleepy.

Life was so much simpler when you figured out the basics.

Morning dawned with sunshine glinting off heavy frost. April hitched up the carriage and added a couple of heavy blankets to keep her warm on the ride to Burgess.

Driving through town, she saw Gray coming out of

his office. She pulled the carriage to a halt and waved at him. "Good morning, Dr. Fuller!"

"Where are you off to this morning?" he asked, coming over to the buggy.

"Burgess. To buy a new dress for Beulah's wedding."

"I was just going to the hotel for coffee. Care to join me?"

"I can't stop for coffee, but I woke up this morning with a raspy throat. Can you look at it?"

He frowned. "Me?"

Unable to meet his eye, she handed him the reins. He tethered the horse, then lifted her down as if she weighed no more than a feather.

Their eyes met, and she noticed he held her a bit longer than necessary. Not that she was complaining.

What was she doing? This was insane. She didn't have a raspy throat. How was she going to explain that?

She wasn't the sort of woman to entice an unsuspecting man. She needed to leave now, while she could, before he saw through her sham.

Opening the door to his office, he allowed her to enter first. She stood in the waiting area, unsure of her next move.

Gray walked straight through to the examining room. "May I take your cloak?"

"My cloak?"

"You can keep it on if you're more comfortable."

Her heart pounded. "Okay."

She lifted the collar closer to her neck.

He gestured toward the table that stood in the middle of the room. "Have a seat."

Her feet felt as if they were made of lead. Buckets of it. Her shoes were new, and slick. She had to be careful on the wooden floor or she would fall and make a bigger fool of herself.

She took tiny steps across the room, watching as Gray's tall frame bent over and picked up a stool.

"You'll need this to reach the table." He positioned the stool.

"Thank you."

"You're welcome."

April was mesmerized by his presence. "Thank you," she repeated, barely above a whisper.

Gray abruptly turned away, and she wondered what had gone through his mind to make him react that way to her. Maybe she wasn't pretty enough for him. She certainly didn't have Francesca's exquisite beauty.

Lifting her skirt, she stepped on the wooden stool and lost her footing. A scream escaped her throat, then darkness momentarily overtook her. She woke in Gray's arms.

Concern filled his eyes. "Are you all right?"

Her sight was blurred slightly. "I must have bumped my head."

"Yes, you did. Can you stand up?"

"I think so." Excruciating pain shot through her when she tried to stand. She leaned against him, grabbing her leg. "My foot!"

The power in his strong arms, as he easily lifted her off the floor, and laid her on the examining table, amazed her.

His gaze never left hers. He was close, so close she could feel the warmth of his breath fan her cheek, detect that heady aroma that belonged only to him.

He backed away. "I'm sorry, did the stool trip you?"

Henry had never affected her this way. "I think it's my shoes. They're new."

Clearing his throat, Gray moved to the end of the table. "Let's take a look at that bump on your head."

"I have a bump on my head?"

"I don't see how you could escape it."

Loosening the hairpins allowed her tresses to fall free. He eased his fingers through her hair in a search for the bump.

She closed her eyes and enjoyed his professional probing.

"Do you feel anything?"

She experienced a myriad of emotions: excitement, fear—guilt. But why? She hadn't done anything. His mere presence brought out feelings she had never experienced.

"April?"

She opened her eyes to find his face only inches from hers. Her gaze lingered on his mouth, then shifted upward. Something elemental showed in his eyes, so intense it reached deep into her soul. A slight whimper of wanting passed her lips as the space between them became shorter and shorter. Her heart skipped a beat. She closed her eyes in anticipation. Then the warmth of his body was suddenly gone.

Before he moved away, she caught a glimpse of the scarlet color his face had acquired. He reached into a cabinet and removed a bandage.

"Yes, well, we'd better take a look at that ankle, then the throat. My advice would be to cancel your trip to Burgess, Miss Truitt. I don't think you're in any shape to go anywhere today."

"I suppose not. . . ."

He chatted as he examined her ankle, then wrapped it.

"You never mention family. Do they live in Dallas?" she asked.

"Mother died when I was eight, and my father brooded a great deal. He never got over losing her. We lived near Dallas. Branch Creek. Ever hear of it?"

"No. Do you have brothers or sisters?"

"No . . . just me."

"Is your father alive?"

"He died while I was in medical school."

Finished, he rolled her stocking back into place with the informality of a man who'd done it before. Many times. "There, it should be healed in plenty of time to wear your pretty new dress."

Taking her hand, he helped her off the table. "Now, if you'll excuse me, I have a patient due in a few minutes."

Her knees were still quivering from the fall.

As she opened the door to leave, Gray said softly, "About that raspy throat."

Turning around slowly, she met his gaze. "Oh . . ."

"Gargle with saltwater twice a day."

"Thank you. I will."

Closing the door, she leaned against it weakly. So much for her ruse. He'd seen right through it.


## Chapter Twenty-One

Beulah Ludwig's wedding day dawned sunny and warm. Wildflowers dotted the shores.

April got to the church two hours early, certain she'd forgotten something. Something so colossal, so enormously important, it would make Beulah's happiest day tantamount to the burning of Atlanta.

She stood in the center aisle, critically studying the altar profusely banked with greenery and two dozen candles waiting to be lit.

Two hours. *In two hours Beulah and Raymond will walk down the aisle and pledge themselves to one another.*

"I wish it were me," she whispered.

Then, feeling as if the selfish wish would rob her friend of some of her glory, she amended, "No, I wish it was me, too."

She wanted Beulah to be happy. She truly did. But she wanted Gray Fuller.

There were men in Dignity looking for a wife. Keith Williams, Zack Myers, Logan Booker . . . oh, who was she trying to fool? She didn't like any of those men, and Christmas would come on the Fourth of July before she would ever marry one of them.

Beulah arrived, a bundle of nerves.

"I can't do this," she said for the tenth time. "Mama is so nervous, she can't help me with anything. She and Papa are pacing in the foyer. My stomach feels like a volcano about to erupt."

"Well, whatever you do, don't let it erupt right now," April murmured around the hairpins in her mouth. "You're going to have to stand still so I can finish your hair and get this veil on."

"Can you believe it? *I'm* getting married. And to a perfectly marvelous man who thinks I'm perfect. Me. Perfect." Her round face filled with hysteria. "Do you think there's something wrong with Raymond—like maybe he's blind and hasn't said anything?"

"No, I don't think Raymond's blind. Now, stand still."

Beulah stared in the looking glass, dismayed. "I look—"

"Perfectly marvelous," April said. "And if you don't quit fidgeting, your veil is going to fall off when you walk down the aisle, trip poor Raymond, and he'll be laid up with a broken leg on the honeymoon."

Beulah stood still long enough for April to finish pinning the last curl, and position the long veil on top.

"There. Now, aren't you pretty?"

"Oh, April," she cried softly, her hands covering the

lower half of her face. "I never thought—I really don't look so awful, do I?"

"Beulah Ludwig, you look ravishing." April hugged her, knowing that after today things would never be quite the same between them. Beulah would have a husband to look after, and she . . . well, she would go on taking care of Grandpa for as long as he needed her. Bittersweet tears stung her eyes as she clung tightly to the bride-to-be, desperately wanting to hold on to the past, but knowing that she was losing a part of her best friend.

"Thank you," Beulah whispered.

"For what? You're the dearest friend a girl ever had."

"Dash it . . . I promised myself I wouldn't cry." But cry she did. Tears rolled down her cheeks, blending with April's.

"I know, I told myself the same thing."

"It won't be so bad. . . ."

"No, of course not. You're not dying, you're just getting married."

"Sure. Not dying, just getting married . . ."

They rocked in each other's arms, reluctant to let go, knowing that when they did, they would never come back to this hour, this precious moment, when they said goodbye to their youth.

"I love you."

"I love you, too, silly. Go, be happy."

The small chapel was overflowing. April waited in the coat closet with Beulah, the only place in the church a bride could dress for her wedding, until the pastor knocked lightly on the door.

"Ready, girls?"

"Girls?" they mouthed, breaking into giggles.

"Someone needs to tell him we're women," Beulah whispered. "He still thinks of us as six-year-olds!"

They giggled again.

"We're ready, Reverend Brown." Opening the door, April gave her friend a look of assurance and slipped out.

Gray was waiting in the chapel doorway for her. His commanding appearance took her breath away. He was dressed in a charcoal-gray suit with a snow-white shirt and black tie. His hair, still a shade too long, was brushed back off his face, with soft curls lying against his shirt collar. She had the absurd urge to smooth them over his ears like a hovering mother.

He offered his arm as she approached.

"You look beautiful."

She couldn't meet his eyes. "Thank you. You look very nice yourself."

"How is the bride holding up?"

"Nervous as a long-tailed cat in a room full of rocking chairs."

He smiled. "The groom paced off half his shoe leather and quoted me the price of every piece of equipment and pharmaceutical product available on the East Coast. That's nothing compared to the Ludwigs. I thought I was going to have to use smelling salts on them."

April managed to laugh, wondering if he really thought she was beautiful or if it was just something to say. Did she look pretty? Did her hair, drawn up into a loose nest of curls atop her head, and fastened with a ribbon that matched her peach-colored dress, look all right? Was the single pearl strung on a delicate gold chain around her neck appropriate?

As she took his arm, she realized she was trembling.

"Don't worry, no one's going to bite—unless he's invited to."

She glanced into his eyes, feeling very fragile. "I think I'm going to be sick."

He patted the hand that wasn't grasping a quivering sprig of greenery.

"Not now, Miss Truitt. Right now we are going to get Beulah and Raymond married."


A smiling Reverend Brown waited at the altar as April walked slowly down the aisle holding tight to Gray's arm. Wedding bells pealed overhead from the steeple as Edna Folsom played the "Wedding March." Edna wasn't very good on the organ, but she was dedicated. The strains of the music, though not perfect, brought tears to the eye.

As they parted at the altar, Gray lightly squeezed April's hand before stepping to Raymond's side.

The guests rose, waiting expectantly as Beulah and her father stood framed in the doorway.

Beulah was radiant and smiling, her eyes focused on Raymond as she started down the aisle. Datha had done a wonderful job in such a short time on the ivory silk wedding dress. It flared and nipped and tucked exactly where it should. A strand of pearls, a gift from the groom, nestled around Beulah's neck. Her dark hair was lifted back and up from her face into a swirl, capped by a crown of lace cascading into a floor-length veil.

She carried a bouquet of flowers Datha had fashioned with bits of lace and ribbon.

Candlelight bathed the altar in golden flickers. As Beulah approached, the glow surrounded her in a golden light that brought tears to April's eyes. It was as if God looked down—and smiled in approval.

When the bride reached the groom's side, April looked at Gray and their gazes joined. With a dazzling leap of imagination, she pictured him slipping a wedding ring on her own finger, then dashing down the aisle with her to begin a life together.

The ceremony was brief but poignant. Vows were made and exchanged in hushed reverence. Beulah and Raymond pledged their love with emotion-filled voices.

Then the moment they'd all been waiting for arrived: Reverend Brown pronounced Beulah and Raymond husband and wife, and a trembling bridegroom lifted the veil of his bride and kissed her.

April closed her eyes and imagined Gray's lips on hers.

Snapping out of her reverie, she saw the newlyweds, flushed and grinning as they turned to face the congregation.

The pastor announced, "Ladies and Gentlemen, I present to you Mr. and Mrs. Raymond Grimes."

Applause accompanied the pair up the aisle, then guests poured from the church to rain rice down upon the happy couple. Raymond hurried his bride into a carriage liberally decorated with ribbons, and everyone followed to the town hall, where the reception would take place.

Menson's Bakery had volunteered the wedding cake, an elaborate, three-tiered confection that caused many an aaah. Addy Menson had insisted on overseeing the reception, and nearly every woman in town had helped with the decorations. The new Mrs. Grimes was well loved by her neighbors, as was evident by the joy that shone in their faces.

Almost as soon as Beulah and Raymond arrived, townsfolk started handing them gifts. The shower of presents and warm wishes continued throughout the festivities, until at last the bridal couple cut the cake. The day was indeed perfect for all in attendance.

"Miss Truitt? A cup of punch?"

April turned at the sound of Gray's husky, liquid voice. She told herself one cup wouldn't hurt.

"I trust you're enjoying the festivities?" They drank the punch, watching the activities.

"I'm having a wonderful time, Dr. Fuller. And you?"

"It's a lovely wedding."

Severn and Mary Rader walked by. "Perfect wedding, eh, Doc?"

Smiling, Gray acknowledged Severn's greeting.

"Gray, I'm sorry Francesca couldn't come," April murmured. "The Ludwigs sent an invitation. I hope she isn't ill."

His eyes turned distant, reserved. "Francesca is fine."

"She sent a lovely gift. It's an elephant . . . something."

Throwing his head back, he laughed. April decided it was the nicest laugh she'd ever heard.

"Ivory tusks, no doubt?"

"Beulah and I couldn't decide." She grinned. "But they're expensive, whatever they are."

Conversation was easy now.

"Perhaps you could help me with a question," he began.

"Of course. What is it, Dr. Fuller?"

"Why is it that all brides are beautiful?"

Gratefulness glowed in April's heart. Immense gratitude that he appreciated her friend, regardless of her physical shortcomings. "That's simple. Because her wedding day is the happiest day of her life."

Their eyes met, and she was caught by the candidness she saw in his, the simple honesty. "A woman's wedding day should be just the beginning of her happiness."

April was stricken by the irony of it all. Francesca had everything she wanted. Money, position, and quite possibly, him.

It was the "him" April envied the most.

"That's a noble sentiment, Dr. Fuller."

"Not so noble, Miss Truitt. If a man loves a woman, he wants to give her everything her heart desires."

April gazed up at him, sensing a hundred unspoken feelings hanging between them. Fool that she was, she wanted him to know—needed him to know—that she loved him. "When all she desires is her husband's heart?"

She could barely breathe now. His gaze confirmed what she knew. They were talking about more, much more, than a silly schoolgirl crush. They were speaking of love—deep and enduring love between a man and a woman.

He said softly, "Perhaps you can help me with the most perplexing problem of all?"

"I'll try."

"How does a man choose between what he wants, and what he feels is his obligation?"

"That's harder," she admitted.

"But you know the answer?"

Yes, she knew. "He follows his heart."

"May I borrow Miss Truitt?"

April glanced up, her spirits sinking when she saw Henry Long. How did he have the nerve to ask to speak with her?

Smiling, Henry bowed mockingly, offering his arm. "Miss Truitt?"

Glancing at Gray, she shrugged. She didn't want to cause a scene. Gray seemed to understand, and reluctantly gave her over to Henry. She felt bereft as she left the doctor's side.

Taking her hand, Henry swept her outside as she continued to look over her shoulder at Gray, who was threading his way toward the front of the reception hall.

"You look ravishing, my love."

April kept her distance from him. When he tried to pull her closer, she resisted, keeping him at arm's length.

Arching his eyebrows, he gazed at her. "April, darling, I thought I had allowed you enough time to pout. Come now, let's settle our misunderstanding and get on with it. Men will be men, my love. You know it."

"I didn't know it, but I do now."

"What have I done so wrong? One tiny little indiscretion, and you're ready to draw and quarter me. Grace means nothing to me. She was a mere diversion to pass the time. I was lonely, love, working long, hard hours to secure our future. Surely you won't deny me?"

"I expected more of you, Henry. I believed you when you said you loved me and we had a future together."

"More?" He seemed puzzled. "What haven't I given *you?*"

"Honor, loyalty—you, Henry. You didn't give me you."

His brow pulled into an affronted frown. "I must say, April, this is a side of you I've never seen—and frankly, I don't like it. You're still angry. What must I do to win back your favor? Tell me—I'll do anything.

You know you're the only woman I truly love."

"Move on with your life, Henry, and let me move on with mine."

He seemed contrite, shocked at her insensibility. "You don't mean that. Have you no idea how much I regret my faux pas? Grace had *no* right to confront you like that—"

"Henry, please. This is Beulah's day. Let's not ruin it by dredging up unpleasant memories."

He was silent for a long moment. "Well, I must say, Porky doesn't look as fat as usual today."

"What?"

"Porky. She actually looks very nice—" he grinned "—for a hog."

Disgusted, April walked away leaving him red-faced, trying to look as if the parting was mutual.


It was late when April swept the last grain of rice out of the town hall. After storing the broom in the closet, she blew out each candle and lamp.

Closing the door behind her, she locked it, then walked slowly home in the dark.

The sky was clear, a full moon glistened off freshly plowed fields, and thoughts of Gray were vivid in her mind. Though it was late, the lights were still on in Flora Lee's place when April arrived. Worried that she might have eaten too much wedding cake, April made her way down the path to the cabin and knocked softly on the door. Datha opened it, grinning when she saw who it was.

"Miss April?"

"I was just wondering if you were all right. I saw the light on in the window. . . ."

Datha smiled widely. "Nothing's wrong. Come in."

April stepped inside. "I thought Flora Lee might have eaten too much wedding cake."

"Flora Lee's just fine," the old woman cackled from the fireside.

Surprised, April saw Jacel sitting next to Flora Lee. "Oh . . . I'm sorry I've intruded—"

"You could never do that," Datha said, closing the door.

"Come, sit a spell," Flora Lee invited.

"Grandmother and Jace and I have been talking."

"Thank goodness," April breathed. "I've been afraid . . ."

"I'd take a broom to Jacel?" Flora Lee laughed, waving a hand good-naturedly.

Seeing the grins on each of their faces, April started to smile. "What is going on here?"

Datha rested a hand on Jacel's shoulder, smiling at him lovingly. "She's found out that Jacel isn't the most evil man in the world."

"Never thought he was," Flora Lee muttered.

"And," Datha said, "we've come to an agreement."

"Oh?" The news was almost too good to be true, but April was glad they had apparently settled their differences. It was good to know that some things worked out for the best.

Holding Jacel's hand tightly, Datha said, "We, Jacel

and me, made a mistake. One that almost cost me my life."

Jacel took Datha's other hand in his large one, and the adoration in his eyes was nearly blinding.

"We're not going to talk about that," Flora Lee said. "That's all in the past, and you've learned from your mistake. The good Lord don't hold grudges."

"What Datha's trying to say," Jacel said, "is that we're going to wait until I'm out of school before we get married, but we're not going to, well—"

"I understand," April said softly. "You're not going to take the chance of ruining your future again."

"That's right," Datha said. "What we did was foolish—what I did was wrong. I'll never forgive myself for . . ."

"It was my fault," Jacel said.

"It's past," Flora Lee repeated. "God's going to give us a better day tomorrow."

"Yes," Datha whispered. "A brand-new day."

Still gripping Datha's hands, Jacel said softly, "What we have will last a lifetime. Once we're married, we're going to have babies, lots of babies, and we're going to thank God every night that he forgives mistakes."

"Everyone makes mistakes, Jacel." Somewhere in her mind April heard her mother's voice saying, *"How can we appreciate the good, if we don't know the bad?"*

"Yes, ma'am."

When April saw Flora Lee was getting tired, she

quietly excused herself. "It's late. I'll go and let you get to bed."

"You want me to walk you back to the house?" Jacel asked.

"No, I'm fine. It's just a few steps."

"You take care, Miss April."

This was a night of celebration, of victory for everyone but her. It only made her feelings for Gray more intense, and the fact that God didn't intend Gray Fuller for her more regretful.

Riley had already gone to bed. The house was quiet when she let herself in the back way. Only the snap of dying embers in the kitchen stove disturbed the silence.

Removing her hat, she tossed it onto the chair in front of her vanity. The image of her reflection caught her, and she stopped to look. Her hair was coming loose from its pins, and she took them out to let it fall over her shoulders. Her reflection gazed back at her with . . . what? Sadness? No. She was happy for Beulah—and for Datha.

Then what? April wasn't sure why she felt she was staring at a stranger.


## Chapter Twenty-Two

The DuBois house was lit up like a Christmas tree. Light spilled from every window as Gray rode up. A footman took charge of his horse, and he climbed the steps to the front door.

Louis DuBois and his daughter were in the middle of another spring celebration, he realized. These people would celebrate anything—even a rainstorm. Music and loud laughter filtered from behind the closed doors.

"Good evening, Dr. Fuller," the butler said as he took Gray's overcoat and hat. "I'll inform Miss DuBois you have arrived."

Gowns of red and blue and gold formed a colorful pattern on the ballroom floor as couples waltzed beneath elaborate crystal chandeliers. A large ensemble of musicians played from the alcove.

Glass clinked against glass as guests took refreshments from four long tables heavily laden with food and drink. As usual, the room was too warm. Gray's gaze moved over the crowd, searching for Francesca.

He was able to single her out from among the swirling array of lavish female finery. She was dancing with a tall, older man wearing a black suit and a red cape. Her clear, tinkling laughter came to Gray as he stood in the doorway, watching.

Spotting Louis chatting with a group of men, he moved in that direction, threading his way across the crowded room.

When Louis spotted him, he paused in midconversation, smiling. "Gray! I wasn't expecting you! Francesca thought you wouldn't be attending this evening."

No, he wouldn't be expecting him. Gray had sent apologies by messenger earlier this week, saying he would be unable to attend tonight's gathering. Louis had no reason to believe he'd changed his mind.

"Good evening, Louis. May I have a word in private?"

The older doctor glanced at the group of men standing around him. "Now?"

"Now."

Making his apologies, Louis quietly excused himself from his associates.

The two of them crossed the room to Louis' study. As he closed the heavy double doors, Louis turned, smiling. "Should I ask Francesca to join us?"

"That isn't necessary."

"Ah, well, she is dancing with a dear friend of mine—Count Evelyn, from England. Have you met?"

"No, I don't believe we have."

"No matter." Louis crossed the room to his desk. "You know, Gray, at one time I thought Count Evelyn would be a perfect match for Francesca, but she set her cap for a very promising young doctor." He smiled. "You. I have to say, my daughter is very astute. The greatest compliment you could give her is to tell her you've decided to join me in my clinics." Gray's expression turned solemn; Louis' smiled faded. "No, that would not be why you're here this evening."

"It isn't."

Walking to the fire, Louis stared into the burning embers. The silence in the room was suddenly deafening.

"So, what brings you to Dallas? Francesca isn't expecting you."

Removing an envelope from the inside pocket of his jacket, Gray laid it on the table.

Turning, Louis spared the missive a fleeting glance. "What is it?"

"The final payment on the financial debt I owe you."

Louis looked at the envelope as if he wouldn't take it. "I've told you before, this isn't necessary," he began.

"Louis, I want you to know how much I appreciate your faith and confidence in me. Without you, I would not have been able to achieve my dream of becoming a doctor."

"Nonsense, you're a brilliant man. I can assure you, if I hadn't taken you under my wing, someone else would have. You give me far too much credit."

"You will always have my gratitude. The kind of faith you've shown in me can never be repaid."

"I don't expect it to be repaid. When you marry my daughter—"

"Please." Gray stopped him. "Hear me out, Louis."

"Of course." He circled the large mahogany desk and sat down.

"It is precisely my gratitude that makes what I have to say so difficult."

Louis studied him, a frown forming on his distinguished features.

"I don't love you daughter."

The words were like a shotgun blast, reverberating off the richly paneled walls.

Louis didn't flinch, but his eyes mirrored his great disappointment.

"I'm sorry. You have my deepest respect, but I don't love Francesca. I would only hurt her if I were to marry her."

Leaning back in his chair, Louis closed his eyes, his fingers gently massaging his temples. He looked old, weary.

"I can't say that I saw this coming."

"Francesca deserves someone who will love her, Louis. I don't. I've tried. Good Lord knows I have, but I don't."

A deep sigh escaped the older man as he straightened and poured himself a drink. "This seems rather sudden—are you certain you've given this proper thought, son?"

"It isn't sudden, Louis." Moving to the study window, Gray looked out. His decision wasn't sudden. He'd thought of nothing else since the day he'd moved to Dignity. "I've thought about it for months."

"Does Francesca know?"

Gray was silent for a moment. He'd tried to tell her in a hundred—a thousand different ways, but she wouldn't accept what he knew to be true. Whatever attraction she'd once held for him was gone. "She knows, but won't accept."

"Ah . . . yes. She wouldn't. I'm afraid that I've never said no to her."

Life was a precious commodity. Who knew that better than he and Louis, men who dealt with life and death every day? Gray didn't plan on wasting his in a meaningless marriage to a woman he didn't love. "By the time I leave here tonight, she will understand. And accept."

Kneading his temples, Louis said softly, "Of course, I'll see to it you'll never practice in Dallas again."

"Would you do that for me, Louis? I'd deeply appreciate it." Threats didn't faze him, although Gray had expected more from the man. But Francesca was his daughter, and she would be embarrassed and hurt by his decision.

"I see my power and prestige hold no meaning for you."

"On the contrary, I respect you, Louis. You're my mentor, a man whose talents I admire immensely. That won't change. But my admiration does not extend to marrying your daughter."

The check lay on the desk in front of Louis. He nodded. "I ask that you be gentle with her."

"I don't want to hurt her, but I'll hurt her more by marrying her. Dignity is where I belong, not in Dallas, where Francesca wants me to be."

Gray knew now what he had only suspected until recently. He had changed. He had gone to Dignity in search of a practice; instead, he'd found a family, a real home. A woman he wanted to spend his life with.

"Surely there is a way you and my daughter can reach a compromise," Louis said softly.

Gray studied the painting of Francesca hanging over the imported mantel. "Look at her, Louis. She's young, beautiful, spoiled. She's known nothing but the finest things in life. She would wither away in Dignity."

Louis was silent for a long time, then murmured, "She is a difficult young woman. I indulged her, as my only child, far too much. Perhaps if I had been less lenient . . ."

Gray's relief was almost tangible. He hadn't dared hope Louis would understand, and in his own way, support his decision.

"Thank you."

"Don't thank me." Louis reached for the glass decanter again. "My parents chose a woman for me back in France, but she was not the girl of my own choosing. I refused to marry her, and they never forgave me." Pausing, he looked thoughtful. "Like you, I could not bear to marry someone I did not love."

Louis sipped from his glass. "Is there another woman?"

"Yes," Gray admitted. "But she doesn't know it. I only knew for certain recently."

"I was afraid of that." Getting up slowly, he extended his hand to Gray. "Of course, you now become the no-good heel who deserted my daughter." He flashed a tired grin.

Smiling, Gray accepted his hand.

"You are a good man, Gray Fuller. An honorable man. You have my best wishes for your future."

"Thank you, sir."

Louis grew sober. "Be assured, should you ever need my help, my advice or my service, I will be available. Now, let us join the celebration. You and Francesca can talk at the end of the evening. It will be . . . simpler, yes?"

"Yes," Gray said. "It will be simpler."


Picking up a Lalique vase, Francesca hurled it against the study wall. "You cad! You despicable woman-izer!"

Gray was indifferent to her wrath. "It's over, Francesca. Let it go."

Striding across the room, she drew her hand back to strike him, but he thwarted her efforts. Their eyes locked in a silent duel.

"You have a right to be angry, but if I married you it would be the worst mistake of our lives."

"You insensitive infidel!"

"Francesca. Only dogs can hear you now." Letting go of her hands, he turned away. "You need to learn humility, Francesca. The world isn't your bowl of cherries."

"It's April Truitt, isn't it? The mortician's little granddaughter. She's been after you from the first day she laid eyes on you—"

Turning, Gray pinned her with a hard look. "Leave April out of this."

Francesca resorted to tears. "Can't you see what she wants? She smells money, Gray. Power. She's using

376

her grandfather's ill health as a ploy to entrap you. She can never love you the way I do. Don't be swayed by sweet innocence!"

"April is a woman of integrity."

Her brows lifted with resentment. "And I'm not?"

Gray smiled with the calm strength of knowledge.

"Consider what I've done for you, Gray. The things I bought—the things *father's* done for you. How can you think of throwing it all away on that little—"

"Enough!" His tone took on a dangerous edge. "Not another word about April."

Francesca stared at him. "You actually *love* her."

"Yes, I actually love her."

"Well," she said in biting desperation. "Why should I care?" Her eyes assumed a look of superiority. "You fool. I never loved you. You were merely a diversion, couldn't you see that? Do you honestly think I would marry a picayune doctor like you?"

"No," Gray admitted. And at the moment, nothing was more clear.


It was raining again; Dignity was experiencing a cold spell.

April stared out the window of the mortuary, wondering if it would ever stop. Mud piled high along the sides of the road. Only a few lone travelers braved the inclement weather.

Shivering, she let the curtain drop into place and moved to the fire. She missed Beulah. There was no one to pour her heart out to, no one to share her melancholy, no one who understood her love for a man she couldn't have, like Beulah did.

Suddenly the walls seemed to be closing in on her. Grabbing her cloak, she ran down the stairs, calling to Riley as she passed the smoking room, "I'm going for a walk, Grandpa!"

"At this hour?"

"I won't be gone long."

"Can I eat the last piece of sweet potato pie?"

"Sure, enjoy yourself." He had been so good about his diet and walking, she didn't have the heart to tell him he couldn't.

Besides, there was only half a piece left; she'd eaten the other half earlier.

The wind was moaning through the trees as she stepped out of the house, wrapping her cloak tightly around her. It was a horrible night for a walk, but she was getting used to adversity.

If Beulah were here, she'd tell her to buck up and stop feeling sorry for herself.

No, she wouldn't. She'd say, "Dash it all, April, if you love Gray Fuller, stop mooning around and do something about it!"

Well, she loved Gray Fuller, but she didn't know what to do about it. Her one attempt to capture his full attention hadn't worked. She'd limped out of his office that day feeling as though he'd seen right through her foolish ploy.

She had to back away gracefully, prove that she was mature enough to know when she was beaten.

The damp night air enveloped her. Blowing rain nearly obscured the gaslights lining the square. A few were dark, unable to withstand the onslaught of Fickle Spring. She circled the square twice, hoping to make herself so tired that she'd fall into bed, exhausted. Her breath came in thick, vaporous puffs as she started on her third round.

Thunder rolled overhead; rain whipped through the trees and saturated her cloak.

Where was Gray? In Dallas. Grandpa had let the information slip during supper tonight. He'd left three days ago. In the past his visits had been brief, but had Beulah's wedding reminded him that it was time that he and Francesca set a date? He wasn't getting any younger, and men wanted—needed—a wife and children, didn't they? Pain, as swift and sharp as a razor cut, took her breath. What if this very moment Gray and Francesca were making plans . . .

Maybe not.

She wouldn't think about it.

She couldn't. She would dissolve in tears, in a crumpled heap, and die of longing.

Her footsteps slowed as she realized she was standing in front of his office. Wouldn't you know it? She wasn't going to let it rest. She started to cry. Foolish, wasted tears that would result in nothing more than a miserable chapped face.

Silent weeping turned into deep, heartrending sobs as she realized that Gray would never be hers. Never. And it hurt. Worse than her mother's death, and the long hours she'd spent holding Datha's hand, praying she would live.

Leaning against the building, April tried to hold it in, but that only made it worse. *Why, God? Why would You allow this man to come into my life and yet deny him to me? Why did he ever have to come to Dignity in the first place? How dare he come here and steal my heart, then run back to Dallas and Frances—*

From out of nowhere, a handkerchief appeared. A nice, snowy-white handkerchief.

Unconsciously accepting it, she blew her nose, trying to stem the salty tide of weeping.

Suddenly she looked up. Where had the handkerchief come from?

Trying to focus on the blurry apparition blocking her path, she whispered, "Gray?"

Taking her in his arms, he started waltzing with her. Right there in the middle of the sidewalk in a blowing rainstorm. He danced with her as if it were as natural as breathing. Moving her gracefully about the puddled sidewalk, he held her closely, his gaze locked with hers. "Now, where were we when Henry so rudely interrupted us?"

"Gray?" she repeated, stunned by his almost ghostly appearance. His overcoat was drenched, as if he'd been out in the weather for some time.

Whirling her lightly, he caught her by the waist and lifted her off the sidewalk, setting her down in the middle of the street.

As their feet moved again, his gaze held hers in the gaslight.

"Did I get around to telling you how beautiful you looked at Beulah's wedding?"

Regaining her composure, April turned angry. How *dare* he dance with her in the rain, hold her indecently close and gaze at her as if they were destined to be man and wife? And how *dare* he make her want him more than anything she'd ever wanted in her life.

When she opened her mouth to berate him, he kissed her. Kissed her so hard, so thoroughly, so completely, he rendered her speechless.

As their lips parted many long moments later, he whispered, "Merry Christmas."

Laughter bubbled up inside her. Kissing him left her giddy, feeling as carefree as a child. "Christmas is seven months away."

He frowned. "Are you certain? I have a gift for you."

"You do?"

He reached into his pocket. "I believe . . . yes, here it is." He opened his hand, revealing a small blue velvet box resting in his palm.

She wouldn't let herself think—no, she wouldn't let herself hope. But strange as he was acting, there was no reason to hope he was here to—

Taking her hand, he closed it around the box. "Aren't you going to open it?"

"No." She looked away, refusing to invite disappointment. What right did he have to be giving her gifts when he was seeing another woman? It was disgraceful. Immoral . . .

"Coward."

"Gray . . ." She was tired of playing games. "Unless that's an engagement ring, I don't want it." There. She'd said it. Let him have a good laugh, then run back to Dallas.

His brows lifted in surprise. "Engagement ring? You want an engagement ring from *me?*"

Well, now she did feel stupid. How could she have blurted that out—an engagement ring. Why hadn't she said a . . . diamond tiara or, better yet, a stupid old Ming vase!

Gray reached out and brushed back a strand of hair the wind had blown from beneath her cloak. "If I gave you an engagement ring, that would mean I would be obliged to marry you."

"Well . . . would that be so bad?" She gazed up at him, willing him to say the words she wanted to hear.

He pretended to think about it.

She didn't find that funny.

He shrugged. "I guess not."

She gasped. "You guess not!"

Pulling her to him, he brushed her lips with his again, exquisitely, then kissed her more deeply. "Perhaps that's why I purchased the ring—the only one I've ever purchased in my life—to give to a woman—the only one I've ever loved enough to spend the rest of my life making happy, and am now asking for her hand in marriage—or trying to."

"Oh, Gray!" Her words issued forth in a rush of disbelief. Joy started to grow inside her. "Do you mean it? I thought you were in love with her?"

"Her who? If by 'her' you mean Miss DuBois, then I must confess that at one time I had thought to marry her." His features sobered and he quietly explained the loan, his obligation to repay Louis. How he'd garnered enough trust in Dignity to obtain a new loan from the bank, and repay Louis. The DuBoises were now out of his life. "If you agree to marry me, darling, we will be poorer than church mice, but I make you this promise."

He drew her closer. "I will love you with every ounce of my being. Till death do us part." He gazed at her with such love, such perfect devotion, that she started to cry again. Opening the box, he displayed a tiny sparkling diamond. "Will you do me the honor of being Mrs. Gray Fuller?"

"But Gray . . . darling . . . we disagree—a lot."

"Never about us."

No, that was true. Over the Pinkham tonic, the duel, her impetuous nature, and they hadn't fought over that in a while. . . . Actually, they hadn't fought about anything lately.

Really, she loved him exactly the way he was.

"And if disagreeing worries you, get over it. We'll do that a lot in the next fifty years."

Suddenly, he lifted her off her feet and kissed her again. When the kiss ended, he gazed down at her, rain coating his long, dark lashes. "Well?"

"Well . . . yes. Yes!" She kissed *him* this time.

*Yes,* she thought—she would be honored to be Mrs. Gray Fuller for at least the next fifty years. And if God ordained, even longer.

**Center Point Publishing**
600 Brooks Road • PO Box 1
Thorndike ME 04986-0001 USA

**(207) 568-3717**

**US & Canada:**
**1 800 929-9108**
www.centerpointlargeprint.com